CANCELLED:
THE AFTERMATH
PART TWO

ALSO BY TD DURHAM

Cancelled: Flight 3236 (Part one)

Cancelled: The Aftermath (Part two)

Coming Soon:

Cancelled: The Trial (Part three)

CANCELLED: THE AFTERMATH

PART TWO

TD DURHAM

ABRIDGE PUBLISHING COMPANY

aBridge Publishing Co.
210 Postage Way #2603
Indian Trail, NC 28079

The characters and events portrayed in this book are fictitious. Any similarity to real persons, living or dead is coincidental and not intended by the author.

ISBN-978-1-7342982-3-9

First Printing: April 2021

Cover design by: Kristy Beausoleil

Printed in the United States of America

DEDICATION

This is dedicated to my friends and family who bought Cancelled: Flight 3236. Thanks for your support. I appreciate each and every one of you.

This is also for anyone who has experienced cancelled flights and/or has been stranded at an airport.

Preface

Dear Reader,

Thank you for your interest in this novel… Part Two. We are grateful you've chosen to continue this story - their story.

We hope you have fallen in love with the characters and stick with their stories to the very end. We promise you an adventure filled with lots of surprises and twists. FYI - I started this novel in 2009. There are some references that may be outdated. For example – Facetime wasn't a "thing" and cars still had CD Players. My cousin, read book 1. In reference to the Kami story she asked, "Why didn't she just Facetime him?" (LOL). Could I rewrite some parts? Absolutely! But it takes away the fun. Besides, technology is constantly changing. Twenty years from now, I want the reader to Google or ask Alexa, "What's a CD player?"

We apologize for any errors, you may find. Although we have read this several times, and corrected numerous errors, there are certain to be some we've missed. It is our hope that this does not distract from the story.

Finally, we would love to hear from you. Please e-mail us at td.durham.author@gmail.com or aBridgepub@gmail.com with any comments you may have – what you loved and what you hated. All comments are welcomed (no matter how brutal).

If you really enjoy the book(s) please rate us favorably on Amazon or Goodreads. Reviews means a lot. It helps others find my books.

Without further ado, we present: CANCELLED: THE AFTERMATH Part Two

TD Durham & aBridge Publishing Company

SUMMARY

Book 1 - CANCELLED – Flight 3236

"May I have your attention, please?" The airline representative, Clarissa, asked. "Ladies and gentlemen of Flight 3236, may I please have your attention?"

Total silence engulfed the waiting area.

"We have just received word from the air flight control tower...."

Dread whipped through the air.

Then she uttered five little words that would change the lives of Kevin Hinderblocker, The Meadows Family, Kami Phillips, Janice Monroe, Erich Coppenhauge, Jade Morales, and The Winthrop Family **FOREVER.**

"Flight 3236 has been cancelled."

Later that Evening

With shattered dreams nestled snuggly inside them, the passengers of cancelled Flight 3236 go their separate ways to prepare for their new journeys.

Let's re-meet the former passengers of Flight 3236:

- **Kami Phillips** – is an event planner married to Dante, an Officer in the Air National Guard. She's in Charlotte organizing an event and he's in Tucson visiting friends. They arrange a romantic weekend in New York. Kami has tried several times to deliver her incredible news to her husband, but circumstances keep preventing her. She's decided the Universe wants her to share the news in person. The cancelled flight has only delayed her plans. The real question is will Dante still be waiting for her when or if she gets to New York?

- **Janice Monroe** – has finally accepted her long time marriage is over. Her husband has moved on so why can't she? The mountain of bills on her kitchen table may be what's holding her back. Jobs for Interior Designers in the Charlotte area are scarce. A fantastic job opportunity presents itself in New York. It's exactly what she needs to keep the bill collectors from repossessing all she owns. When the flight is cancelled, Janice remembers the foreclosure sign tacked to her front door. Getting to New York is a necessity... not an option.

- **Kevin Hinderblocker** – is intent on keeping his promise to his wife despite the difficulties he and his children have experienced throughout the past year. A trip to Puerto Rico via New York seems like the perfect remedy until the cancelled flight hands Kevin more to life than he ever bargained for.

- **The Winthrop Family** – Ian has everything a young boy could want – a successful orthopedic surgeon for a father, an ex-fashion model for a mother and a nanny that adores him. When he is diagnosed with a brain tumor, his parents make arrangements to fly him to the best hospital in New York where a world-renowned surgeon is standing by. Once the flight is cancelled, Ian discovers what the phrase – "God helps those who helps themselves" really means. This time, he's taking control of his young life.

- **Erich Coppenhauge and Miriam Bainbridge** – Erich has it all. He's a young, wealthy, good-looking accountant with a home in prestigious Lake Norman and a beautiful woman by his side. He is close to his family. When he learns his twin sister is sick and he's the only one who can save her life, Miriam, his fiancée, immediately books him a seat on Flight 3236 to New York. When he hears the dreaded words, "Flight 3236 has been cancelled", he jumps into action. He makes other arrangements. As he paces back and forth in the waiting area of the airport, his twin sister tries desperately to hang on to her life.

- **Brett & Marla Meadows** – Brett's a computer wizard and Marla is an attorney. If they can get to New York, Brett's business will survive its devastating setback. Marla is determined to get Brett to New York. When the flight is cancelled they make the only sensible decision. This decision gives Marla a chance to reveal secrets she has kept for years. Confession is good for the soul or is it? One wrong turn changes their lives forever.

- **Jade Morales** - is plagued with a tragedy every five years. Why she agreed to stand as the maid of honor in her youngest sister's wedding in the year she is to turn thirty, she will never understand. San Juan, Puerto Rico is her final destination. Once Flight 3236 is cancelled, the plan to meet her oldest sister in New York is no longer an option. Her new flight arrangements will turn her life upside down... again... but this time, chances of survival are questionable.

The former passengers of Flight 3236 are back and ready to continue their journey. This time they're not waiting for the airline to set their destiny. They are making their own plans. Unfortunately, Mother Nature decides to make an appearance and disrupt their lives once more, making travel across the east coast close to impossible. Everyone is watching the storm from hell wrack havoc.

Will the former passengers of Flight 3236 be able to weather the storm the next days of their journey?

This new journey will take them to places not on their original flight plan or covered in the price of their ticket. This journey will lead to an outrageous discovery. A discovery that can only be made if these passengers can survive ... **the aftermath**.

PROLOGUE

Live life to the fullest today so there's no room for regrets tomorrow.

What is that annoying sound? The patient wondered. The hum of the machines was a continuous slow swishing.

WHY WON'T SOMEONE TURN IT OFF? The patient yelled silently.

The patient tried turning towards the noise, but could not move.

What is going on? What is that horrid smell? Is it disinfectant? Is it death? What is it?

The patient tried calling out but it was difficult with a mouth that couldn't open and a parched tongue.

A flicker of light darted behind eyes that couldn't open under heavy eyelids.

The patient was excited. *Is someone here?*

Maybe the questions swarming inside the patient's head would finally get answered.

The patient felt a touch and smiled inwardly. Finally, someone had arrived.

"Sweetheart, can you hear me? It's Mother."

MOTHER? What in the world? Why is ***she*** *here?*

The patient desperately wished the voice trapped inside a coffin called a body could be heard.

The patient's mother was exhausted. She had been by her child's side since receiving the dreadful call eight months prior.

Everyone was urging her to 'let go'; 'let her child rest in peace'; 'Your child wouldn't want to live as a vegetable'; 'Stop being selfish'; 'Your child is gone'."

Despite the oppositions, she refused to kill her child. She was the one responsible for her child's medical decisions. She would fight for her child's life with every breath in her body. Isn't that what mothers do?

"Dear, if you can hear me, squeeze my hand. Please sweetheart! Give me some sign that you're alive," she pleaded, as she did at each visit. She waited on the sign, the hope that only her child could give.

Maybe everyone was right. Maybe it was time to..."No!" she proclaimed loudly. No matter what anyone said, she was not ready to let go. She knew her child was alive and struggling to get out of the catatonic state that had gripped a defenseless body.

"Honey, the doctors want permission to take you off life support. If you can hear me...WAKE UP... NOW!"

Life Support? Doctors? Ah... the disinfectant smells! I'm in a hospital! But why?

At last, the patient had some answers but it only led to more questions.

The patient's mother laid her cheek against her child's. As strong as she was, she could not stop the tears spilling from her eyes.

What's on my face? Something soft, wet, and hot was pressed against the patient's cheek. It was causing the patient's nose to itch. It badly needed scratching. Unfortunately, the patient's traitorous hands couldn't move.

Mother, my nose is itching. I can't scratch it. The patient screamed silently. *Mother, please, help me. Mother, please! This is irritating.*

The patient's mother jerked up and stared at her child. It couldn't be, yet, she was certain it was.

She ran to the door, flung it opened, and yelled, "Doctor Kincaid! Someone! Anyone! Come quick! Please hurry!"

Mother, just.scratch.my.nose! Why are you calling the doctor?

A nurse ran breathlessly into the room. "What happened? Why are you screaming Mrs....?"

"My child moved!" the patient's mother yelled with excitement. "My child's nose moved. Dear Lord, my child **is** alive."

The nurse saw the joy lighting up eyes that had been dormant for months. She didn't have the heart to douse that joy.

"I'll page the doctor," she said noncommittally, exiting

quickly from the room.

The patient's mother returned to the chair beside her child's bed. Stroking a motionless hand, she said, "I knew you'd come back to us. We've prayed and prayed and finally our prayers have been answered. We've missed you so much. Wait until your father hears. He hasn't been the same since...well, you know..." her voice trailed off as Doctor Kincaid entered the room.

"Good morning. How are you today?" he inquired.

"Just wonderful, Doctor," she replied with a wide grin on her attractively tanned face.

"I see," the doctor replied, returning her smile. "Nurse Gray said you believe your child had some nose movement."

She frowned. Accentuating each word, she spoke slowly, "No, Doctor. I do not BELIEVE anything. I FELT its movement."

"Okay," he said. "Would you mind stepping into the hall while I examine my patient?"

"Certainly, Doctor," she said, refusing to let him extinguish her happiness. She walked into the hall with an extra pep in her step.

Several minutes later, the doctor exited the room wearing a grim expression. He left the door slightly ajar.

"I'm sorry to report there is no change in your child's condition."

"But..." she began.

Doctor Kincaid held up his hand. "Please, let me finish."

She pursed her lips tightly together, adopting a defensive stance.

"Sometimes the body experiences what are called involuntary reactions to outside stimuli," he explained. "This is not controlled by brain activity but the nervous system. Usually, it's in the form of tics or twitches. My examination shows that your child is non-responsive. Simply put... your child... is still in a coma."

Pulling herself up to her full height, she gathered her strength, and squared her shoulders. "Doctor, no disrespect intended. You may have a medical degree, but I am a mother. I know what I felt. It wasn't a tic or twitch or whatever you want to write it off as. My child's nose moved. I don't care what your machines or examinations are telling you. My child is alive. God brought my child through..." Not wanting to have an emotional break down in front of the doctor, she let her sentence fade before continuing. "I'll be damned if I allow you or anyone else to try to convince me otherwise. My child **is** alive."

Without giving Doctor Kincaid a chance to refute, she turned on her heels, sauntering away. She went into the bathroom to collect herself.

The patient overheard the entire conversation.

A steady stream of tears flooded closed eyelids as endless memories besieged the once comatose patient.

The darkness in which the patient had been living for the past eight months began to grow lighter and lighter. Like a sudden bolt of lightning, it all came crashing back; the trip to the airport, the cancelled flight, the decision... everything.

The patient wanted to crawl back into the safety of the coma. As hard as the patient tried, it was impossible. The memories.... *STOP! Oh please stop!*

The patient silently screamed.

THE AIRPORT

Day 1

June 21

Without darkness, you can't appreciate the light!

~1~

THE AIRPORT

"I repeat...Flight 3236 from Charlotte to Kennedy Airport is officially cancelled."

Total chaos erupted.

Clarissa Taylor, the airline representative, couldn't put the microphone down fast enough before the first irate customer started his rant.

Why did I come in today? She wondered, smiling politely at the customer yelling at **her** as if **she** controlled the situation. *How will I feed my children without a job?* Clarissa, a single mother of two toddlers thought, nodding at the shouting customer... smile intact.

This and a part-time job were her only source of income. She didn't receive child support from her children's father.

"Let's see what I can do?" she said, addressing the passenger, wishing she had gone to college instead of getting pregnant, twice, while in high school.

Kami Phillips couldn't believe her ears. Surely this was a sick joke. She dropped into a nearby chair. Nauseous threatened to engulf her. Dante was leaving tomorrow night. She had to see him. What was she going to do?

Pulling out her cell phone, Kami called him. It rang a few times before connecting. *Hello! Hello? I can't hear you.... Hello? Hello? Speak-up! Gotcha!* Kami grinned sadly. She heard the smile in his voice. *You've reached my phone. You know what to do.* Beep.

Putting on a brave voice, she said, "Hey handsome, change of plans – again. I know. I know." She chuckled slightly to keep the misery from her voice. "My flight was...is...was...is can... cancelled. I'm not su..."

Kami was on the verge of a nervous breakdown. She knew nothing about Charlotte, North Carolina or what happened after a flight was cancelled. What should she do? She was clueless.

Pull yourself together. You can do this. Dante has enough on his mind. He shouldn't have to worry about you too. Inhaling, then exhaling deeply, she said in a calm, strong voice, "Well Lover, I'm not sure what I will do. I'll call back once I have a plan. You'll have to keep those bells warm a little longer. Love you, my heart. PS: answer the phone. I miss you."

She quickly disconnected the line.

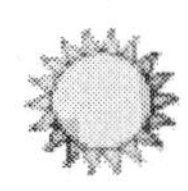

"Hell no," Janice Monroe exclaimed, forgetting she was in the midst of a conversation with the most "beautiful" man she'd ever seen. "Is she shitting us? What am I supposed to do? I HAVE to get to New York. I have to get this job," Janice screamed hysterically.

"Go to the counter. See what they can do," Kevin Hinderblocker suggested.

Half-heartedly she said, "Right... it was nice meeting you."

"Good luck with the job. Maybe you can get a telephone interview. Those are becoming popular. It'll work out the way it's supposed to."

'It'll work out the way it's supposed to?' What kind of crap is that? She thought to herself. *Janice, relax. He's a male. He meant nothing by that dumb statement.*

Aloud, she said, "Hopefully, I can catch another flight. If not, maybe I **can** do a telephone interview as you suggested. Take care of yourself and your beautiful children."

"I will. Take care," Kevin responded, watching the very attractive Janice Monroe disappear into the crowd of furious people surrounding the ticket counters.

It amazed him that the commotion hadn't awakened his sleeping children. He would keep one eye on them and the other on the volatile Ms. Monroe. She appeared desperate to get the job in New York. He really hoped things worked out for her. From the few minutes he spent speaking with her, he could tell she was a walking time bomb, a firecracker. He could read people well. He sensed if things didn't go her way, she would explode.

And God protect whoever gets in her way, Kevin prayed silently. Things at the airport were about to get heated.

~2~

Meredith Winthrop found herself in a lengthy line waiting her turn to speak with an agent. Finally reaching the ticket counter, she spoke politely to Miles, the ticket agent.

"Hello, can you book my husband, son, and me on the next flight leaving for New York?"

"Hmm... let's see. The next flight is at 7:30. May I see your tickets, please?"

"I left them at my seat. Are they absolutely necessary?"

"No, ma'am. It's just helpful to have. Makes changing your information quicker. But no worries..." Miles clicked a few buttons. "Hmm...there are thirty-six vacant seats available on that flight, but they are filling up quickly. May I have your driver's license, please?"

"That's also at my seat?" Meredith admitted sheepishly.

Noticing how fast the lines were growing, she didn't think to grab her handbag in her rush to get in a line.

"Can you pull up my original reservations using my name then transfer that information over?"

"I can," he replied tersely. "It'll take longer. Having either your license or original tickets makes it easier. Like I said," he shrugged, "seats are going fast. We're already down to thirty-two."

"I do apologize, and," Meredith said, reverting to her southern charm. "I really hate to make you go through all this trouble, but I don't want to wait in this very long line again. I won't mention how irritated the other passengers will get if they have to wait while I retrieve my purse from waaayy over there." She pointed to an area farther away from where her family sat.

Miles understood her point. It was easier to re-key her information than to deal with an angrier crowd.

He said, "Your name?"

She grinned while giving him her details.

A few minutes later, Miles said, "Here you are. You're traveling with Brian and Ian Winthrop."

"That's us," Meredith said brightly.

After a few more keystrokes, he handed her three ticket vouchers. "Y'all are now booked on the 7:30 p.m. flight to JFK International Airport in New York City. Unfortunately, the system is not allowing me to issue seat numbers. I think it's because that flight is filling up really fast. My suggestion is to come back forty-five minutes to an hour before the boarding call. We may be able to assign seats then."

Meredith was all smiles. "Thank you, Miles. You're a lifesaver."

He was unaware of how true her words were.

"You're welcome, Mrs. Winthrop. Have a pleasant flight."

Meredith took the newly issued tickets back to her waiting family. Waving them in the air, she said, "There's been a change in plans."

Kami glanced around. Mobs of people were at the counters. It made little sense to join them. She dialed the one person who was always available to her, her best friend, Debra Collins.

Kami and Debra met at *Pepperdine University.* They were both public relations majors, minoring in communications. Their paths crossed so often, they couldn't help but become friends.

"Deb, everything is such a mess. My flight was cancelled. I'm stuck in Charlotte. I don't know what to do. Dante's in New York waiting for me. He still doesn't know I'm pregnant, and he's leaving tomorrow night. Oh, Deb...." Kami burst into tears.

The nearby customers stared at the beautiful woman with concern and compassion.

Debra was trying to follow her friend. *Why is she still in Charlotte? She should have left hours ago. Where is Dante going tomorrow night? I thought he was home for a year. Did Kami tell me this before? I honestly can't remember. I've been so caught up in* An Affair to Remember *and my financial problems, I haven't been there for my friend, yet, she's trapped in Charlotte because of me.*

Guilt consumed Debra. If she hadn't sent Kami to Charlotte to help Jessica with the *A Total Change* fundraiser event, she'd be with Dante.... in New York?

Being a great friend, Kami wanted Debra's event planning business, *An Affair to Remember*, to succeed. When Debra asked her to go to Charlotte on her behalf, she only hesitated slightly.

"Kam, slow down. Why are you still in Charlotte?"

Kami explained in between sobs. "Because of the incompetence of the car rental people I missed my flight. They booked me on a new one, but it's been cancelled. The airline is saying it's because of engine problems, but I don't buy it. When I checked in, the clerk told me the flight wasn't full. I should have had him change my reservation then. There's a flight leaving for New York at 7:30."

"New York? Why are you going to New York?" Debra asked puzzled, forgetting to ask what happened at the car rental place.

"Dante and I made plans to meet there for a romantic weekend, but since I came to Charlotte, we decided to meet today instead. Then he received orders from his General or some Officer that he was being deployed sooner than later. They gave him permission to leave from New York tomorrow night. He'll meet his unit wherever they're shipping from."

"Okay," Debra drawled, catching up. "So now you're at the Charlotte airport and your flight to New York has been cancelled?"

"EXACTLY!" Kami exclaimed, elated she and Debra were finally on the same page. "AND I don't know what to do."

"Go to the counter. Find out what the airline will do for you. They cancelled your flight. They have to make provisions for you."

"You're right, Deb. I'm happy I called you. I'll call yo..." her phone beeped. Checking the caller ID, she saw Dante's number. "Deb, I'll call you back. Dante's calling."

"O..." was all Debra managed before silence engulfed her. Placing her phone on the hotel's coffee table, she picked up her proposal for her upcoming meeting. She couldn't concentrate. If things didn't work out for her two best friends, she'd never forgive herself.

"Hey, Lover, did you get my message?" Kami asked Dante.

"I did. What happened? Why was your flight cancelled?"

"I don't know. They're saying engine trouble."

"You don't believe that?"

Kami thought for a moment. "Honestly, I don't know what to believe."

"So what happens now? I'm getting lonely. I miss you, Lovely Lady."

Kami wanted to cry again. She missed her husband so much it hurt. Softly she said, "I miss you too. I'm about to wait in a very long line to see what my options are. Stay near your phone. I'll call you back."

"Okay. I love you."

"I love you more."

Kami went to the nearest line.

Once WorldLine Airways Flight 3236 was officially cancelled, Clarissa, the airline representative whom Erich Coppenhauge spoke with, remembered the handsome man's words, "*if Flight 3236 is cancelled, can you make me the first person you place on another flight/airline to New York this evening? I really must get there.*"

In between helping furious customers, she added Erich's name to the 7:30 flight's standby list. Although it was against WorldLine Airway's policy, she also booked him a first-class seat on the 6 a.m. flight. Since she'd still be on duty when the 7:30 flight departed, she would remove his name from the 6 a.m. flight if he was fortunate to get on that evening's flight.

Clarissa paged Erich. When he approached her counter, she handed him the new ticket without boarding passes, informing him of his new flight status as standby passenger number two. He thanked her before returning to his seat to weigh his options.

Twenty-five minutes later, he went to a different customer service desk. Although he was pleased that Clarissa was sticking her neck out for him, a stranger, he was hoping to get a seat on a different airline and be in New York by 7:30 p.m.

Nothing beats a try but a failure, he thought as the agent, Susan Brown, greeted him, not bothering to smile or look up from her computer screen.

"May I help you?" she asked, annoyed.

Following Ms. Brown's cues, he said bluntly, "Flight 3236 was cancelled. What's available on another airline?"

"I'll check," she replied, fingers flying expertly across the keyboard. After several seconds, she said, "I've checked all the surrounding airlines. There's nothing."

"Unbelievable," Erich exclaimed. "I cannot believe there aren't any available seats on any other flight leaving this airport."

Ms. Brown didn't reply. She glanced pointedly at Erich, then at the long, never-ending line of cantankerous customers. It was going to be a long night.

Erich realized she wasn't planning to say anymore, so he asked, "Why was Flight 3236 cancelled?"

Not looking at him, she replied, "I don't know, maybe the engine. Next in line."

Erich threw Ms. Brown a displeased look before abruptly turning and walking away. At least he was standby number two for the 7:30 p.m. flight. People were leaving the airport. If he was lucky, perhaps standby number one would also leave.

"Excuse me? Will you please check the flights leaving for New York tonight?" Brett Meadows begged the airline representative, Clarissa.

"Sir, there is one more flight scheduled to depart at 7:30 and arrive in New York at 9:30 p.m. It is a non-stop flight, but..." Clarissa paused as she checked the computer screen. "...with the recent cancellation of Flight 3236, it is completely booked. I can put you and your wife on standby. You will be numbers six and seven."

"You're kidding? Six people are in front of us?"

"No sir. Five."

Brett cut Clarissa a sharp look. The computer screen held her attention. She didn't notice.

"Then try another airline... please," Brett said, not hiding his aggravation.

"You must go to the information counter where they can further assist you. Once the flight is cancelled, I can only rebook for this airline. Should I put you on the standby list?" Clarissa asked pleasantly.

"That's not what you told me earlier," Brett admonished. "First, you couldn't help me because the flight wasn't cancelled. Now you can't help because it is. This is ridiculous. Are you making up rules as you go?"

"No, sir, just doing my job. Would you like me to place you on standby for the 7:30 flight?" Clarissa asked again, looking at the fuming, growing crowd behind Brett.

"Sure, why not? What happens if I can't get on a flight tonight?" Brett asked.

"The first flight tomorrow is at 6:00 a.m. scheduled to arrive in New York at 8:00 a.m. Shall I check availability on that?"

"Please," Brett said. He heard the collective protest from the people waiting directly behind him.

"Sir, that flight has only three remaining seats."

"Well, sign me up. I only need two," Brett teased, feeling hopeful once more. "That'll work since I must get to New York before 10 in the morning. Thank you."

"No problem," Clarissa said, smiling. "I'll need your driver's license."

Brett pulled it out and handed it to her.

Marla came over as Clarissa was processing the information.

"What's going on?" she asked.

"She's putting us on a 6 a.m. flight," Brett explained.

"Will that give you enough time?"

"Yes, as long as it's on time and not cancelled. It'll get in around 8. That'll give me time to check into our hotel, shower, dress, and get to mid-town by 10."

"Ma'am, I need your ID," Clarissa requested.

Marla complied.

Clarissa typed in Marla's information then pressed several buttons on the computer keyboard. A scowl flickered before quickly disappearing from her face. Marla caught it.

"What's wrong?" Marla questioned.

Clarissa held up a finger to indicate she needed time to work through the dilemma she was facing.

How rude, Marla thought, tempted to bite the agent's finger.

~3~

While Brett Meadows was talking to one agent, Janice Monroe was fussing with another.

"How many times do I have to tell you I NEED TO GET ON A PLANE NOW?" Janice was near hysterics.

"Miss, you NEED to calm down," the ticket agent countered.

"WHAT? DON'T YOU DARE TELL ME WHAT I NEED TO DO," Janice screamed. "The ONLY thing you NEED to tell me is what time the plane to New York is coming."

The agent checked the computer screen. "There is another plane leaving tonight at 7:30. Let's see..."

Janice interrupted. "Excellent! Put me on it."

"...that flight is over-booked. I can put you on standby. You'll be...."

"What the fu..? Stand by? Why can't you bump someone off and give me their seat? Why the hell was Flight 3236 cancelled? No one has given an answer."

"It doesn't work that way, ma'am. Please, calm down. I understand you're upset. You have every right to be, but yelling will not change the situation."

In a measured tone, Janice said, "And I will tell **you** again, not to tell **me** what to do. Just get me on the freaking flight...NOW. Do YOUR DAMN job!"

Losing patience, the agent screamed, "Lady, the sooner you stop yelling at me and give me a chance to do MY JOB, the sooner we'll be rid of each other. You're not the only person here, you know."

"Wait, a goddamn minute. Who the fuck do you think you're talking to..." She read the agent's name tag. "Michael? You better watch your funky attitude. Your JOB is to SATISFY your customers and hello - this customer IS NOT satisfied. NOW, if you insist on being rude, I will have your JOB. Say another disrespectful, fucking word to me, and I WILL speak to your boss and his boss and his boss." Snidely, she asked, "Hmm... where were we? Right... you were getting me on a flight - TONIGHT."

Michael did not believe he disrespected her... at least not at first. He very slowly counted to ten then said tightly, "We can ask people to voluntarily give up their seat but we can't FORCE them to do so. Also, you will be number six on the standby list."

Janice exploded. "Number six? What the fuck? Are you purposely trying to sabotage my chances of getting on the next flight?"

"No ma'am," Michael said, doing his best to control his temper. "...but I respectfully ask that you not use profanity."

"Or what?" Janice challenged.

The agent studied Janice, trying to decide what to do. He needed the job, but at what price? Did it mean he had to deal with abuse? Again, he asked himself, *how badly do I need this job?* The answer was simple – badly. If he lost another job, his mother would go ballistic. She was already threatening to throw him out of the house.

Angrily, Janice screamed, "I'm done dealing with your simple ass. Go get the damn manager."

"With pleasure! I've had it with you, too. They don't pay me enough to deal with crazies like you."

"Crazy, huh? I'll show you fuckin crazy." Janice was removing her earrings, preparing for an altercation, when Kevin walked to her side.

The customers behind her were trying to get a better view of the situation. They were no longer bothered by the wait. Many were chuckling, sneering, and egging her on. They were stuck at the airport. They may as well have some entertainment. Janice was providing plenty.

"What's going on?" Kevin inquired, although he'd witnessed the scene from his seat.

"I'm about to whip the shit out of this country-ass, still wet behind the ear, upstart," Janice replied heatedly.

"Woman, I wish you'd try," said the equally heated Michael.

"Janice, take it easy. Put your earrings back on."

"Ah, man, leave them be," yelled the passenger directly behind her. A few others agreed.

Ignoring them, he addressed the agent. "Son, people like Ms. Monroe book airline flights so they can get to their destination quickly. She has an important appointment in New York in the morning. Her livelihood depends on it. Please understand this is an emotional strain on her and absolutely nothing personal towards you."

If you only knew the truth of your words, Janice thought, mentally rereading the foreclosure notice she'd recently received.

"Sir, I understand she's upset, but that doesn't give her the right to verbally abuse me. If she wants respect, she has to give respect. My mama taught me that." He threw Janice a reproachful look.

"Your Mama should have taught you some manners, young blood," Janice responded.

Sighing, Michael added, "Using obscenities and being rude will not get her the results she wants... at least, not from me. I will not be intimidated into doing something that's beyond my control."

"Oh, you think I was rude?" Janice yelled. "Well, buddy boy, you haven't seen rude."

The passengers in line laughed.

"Janice," Kevin implored. "Please. Let him do his job. He didn't cancel the flight."

Kevin was right. She was afraid. She needed the job. If she didn't get it... she and her children could kiss the life they'd grown accustomed to goodbye. She couldn't let that happened.

Maybe I overreacted... a tad bit.

~4~

After her ex-husband's abandonment, Janice had been forced to stay strong to survive. She found Kevin's take-charge personality admirable. She'd been on her own for so long, she welcomed the change. She let Kevin take over.

"What should I do?" she asked timidly, replacing her earrings.

Michael did a double-take. Who the heck was the woman standing before him? One minute she was challenging him on every level, the next, she was demurely asking for guidance.

She must be related to Sybil, Michael thought, referring to a woman, of whom a book and television movie was made documenting at least 16 personalities. He had already witness three of Janice's.

A few of the waiting customers muttered crossly, knowing the situation had been defused. One even "booed" and called Kevin a name not worth repeating.

"Michael, what can you do for Ms. Monroe?" Kevin asked, ignoring the hecklers.

Get her the help she needs, he thought unkindly. "As I was telling Ms. Monroe before she took off her earrings..." Janice rolled her eyes. "...I can get her on standby for tonight's 7:30 flight." He referred to his computer screen. "She'll be number nine...."

"Nine? You said six a few minutes ago," Janice exploded.

"True, but that was before you wasted so much time acting ghetto," Michael said smugly. "The flights are booking..."

"Ghetto? You little piece of..."

"Janice!!" Kevin stopped her. "Let me handle this."

Reluctantly, she backed off.

"As I was saying..." Michael said. "The flights are booking fast. You are now number ten on the list."

Janice sucked her teeth, inwardly seething. *Ghetto... I'll give you ghetto.* She caught herself. She was a grown woman acting like a child. The ticket agent was young enough to be her son. She was embarrassed by her behavior, but not enough to apologize.

"There's a flight leaving tomorrow morning at 6:00." Michael rechecked his computer screen before continuing. "It has six available seats. Ms. Monroe went off before I could give her the information on that flight."

"Ms. Monroe will listen to all of her options without interrupting you." Kevin addressed Janice, "Isn't that right?"

Janice huffed but remained quiet. She was conflicted. Part of her was furious by the current situation. The other part was excited to have the handsome Kevin Hinderblocker take control. She was getting turned on.

Michael reiterated. "Those are her options. She can be standby number eleven on the last flight out tonight or she can have a seat on the 6 a.m. flight."

"Can you book her on both flights? She must get to New York by tomorrow morning."

"Sir, that is against the rules." He hesitated before whispering conspiratorially. "Since these **are** extenuating circumstances, I'll do it. I'll monitor both flights. If she's able to get on tonight's flight, I'll remove her name from tomorrow's flight."

"That is very kind of you, Michael. We appreciate you. Will you do one more thing for me?" Kevin flashed that beautiful, wet your drawers smile.

"Sure, anything to help, sir?"

Janice's mouth dropped open. Maybe the saying was true – you can catch more flies with honey. *Kevin has this kid eating out of his big, strong, masculine... dear lord... I need to stop right now. I'm getting horny.* Janice smirked.

Bruce had been her first and only lover. She wondered how it would be to make love to someone else.

"I'm number three for standby tonight. Why don't you switch us? Make Ms. Monroe number three and change my tickets to whatever is available."

Sexual thoughts pushed aside, Janice was flabbergasted. "You'd do that for me?"

"Sure. This is important to you. I can catch a later flight. The children and I don't have to be in New York right away. Our flight to Puerto Rico leaves in three days. My sister-in-law will be disappointed. Once I explain the circumstances, she'll understand. I'm sure we'll get on tomorrow's flight. It's doubtful we'll make tonight's."

Tears built up in Janice's eyes. She was not used to people being nice to her unless they wanted.... hey, that must be it... *he wants something.*

Michael asked, "Your name, please?"

"Kevin H.i.n.d.e.r.b.l.o.c.k.e.r."

"Let's see now." After pressing various keys, Michael said, "You and your children are further back on the standby list for tonight's 7:30 flight BUT you have three seats on the 6:00 a.m. flight. Ms. Monroe, you're number three on the standby list for tonight's flight **and** are booked on the 6 a.m. flight to JFK."

"Bless you, Michael," Kevin said. "May I have your full name and the name of your manager? I'm going to write a complimentary letter explaining your outstanding service."

Hot dog! Michael beamed. *Talk about a nasty situation turning around.* He wrote his full name, the name of his manager, and the corporate address. He handed the paper to Kevin. *That's what's up! Guess you won't be kicking me out anytime soon, Mama. Maybe I'll get a raise or a promotion.* Michael grinned. *Mama will be very proud of me.*

"Sir, if you need anything else, anything at all, please, let me know. I hope you both have a wonderful flight."

"Thanks, Michael," Kevin said, folding the paper into his pocket and moving aside for the next passenger. He had every intention of writing a complimentary letter to Michael's supervisor.

"That was incredible," Janice replied, as they walked away from the counter. "How did you do that?"

"Do what?"

"Diffuse the situation like that. You had that guy eating out of your hands." Janice blushed, recalling her previous thoughts.

"It was nothing. I don't have the emotional attachment you have. A good friend once said getting angry is a waste of precious time and energy."

"Preach, brother!" After a moment of silence, Janice asked frankly, "What do you want from me?"

Kevin replied, "Absolutely nothing."

"Absolutely nothing," she mimicked. "Uh-huh, sure. Everyone wants something. Spit it out."

"Why must I want something?" Kevin inquired, eyes crinkling.

"Because... you don't know me."

"Busted. You got me. I do want something," he teased.

"I knew it," Janice exclaimed. "You want to sleep with me, don't you?" She blurted without thinking.

Kevin burst out laughing. "No ma'am, I think that's the other way around."

She blushed. No sense in denying it.

"Truth? I want you to get to New York and get that job. The way you attacked that young brother and your earlier comments tell me that getting this job is important to you."

Kevin was astonished when the strong, sassy Janice Monroe broke down. He led her to a nearby chair close to his sleeping children.

After a few minutes of a good hard cry, she dried her eyes on the proffered tissues, and softly explained. "I'm not use to people doing nice things for me. I've struggled my entire life to get everything I have - which isn't much. If I don't get this job, I will lose everything, except my kids. My ex-husband may take them, but I doubt it. My children and I will be on the streets without even a car to sleep in. I've been unemployed for about four years. That's when my ex-husband, of twenty-one years, decided he needed his freedom. He sold our company, left me a few dollars, and moved to Texas. I've been doing odd jobs here and there to make ends meet. I've just about used up all of my savings. My electric bill is past due, my house is about to go into foreclosure, and my car is on the repo's list. I parked in long-term parking, hoping the repo-man won't find it. I am very desperate. So thank you, Mr. Hinderblocker for your kindness. I mean that."

Whoa, Kevin thought. *This poor woman has endured a lot. I'd be angry too. What kind of man abandons his wife and children? What a punk!* He removed the sympathy from his eyes before looking at Janice. He knew she would not appreciate it. "Don't worry, Janice. Everything will work out. We'll get you on a flight."

"From your lips to God's ears."

"How many children do you have?"

"Three wonderful, over-active boys. They are my life. They are spending a few weeks with their estranged father in Austin. None of us are happy about it, but I couldn't afford to bring them with me. After today's fiasco, I'm glad they're in Texas."

Kevin studied Janice. She was very attractive – smooth chocolate skin, full lips, large soulful eyes, a cute button nose, and short thick medium brown hair. Her 5'2" frame only added to her body… and what a body it was… small waist, wide hips, medium-size breasts, and that ass. Um! The *Commodores* sure had Janice in mind when they sang "*Brick House*". Her ex-husband was a fool… a foolish punk.

They sat in comfortable silence for a few seconds before Janice snapped her fingers. "Shit, that guy never answered my question."

"What guy? What question?"

"The ticket agent, Michael. The reason the flight was cancelled."

"You're right. They never gave us a reason." He watched Michael helping another passenger. "Doubt we'll get an answer now."

"Maybe later," Janice agreed. "Let's get something to eat."

"My treat."

"Oh, no you don't. I don't take handouts, Mr. Hinderblocker."

"And I don't give them, Ms. Monroe. There are three of us and one of you. It's silly to ask for two checks and I won't allow you to pay for me and my children. Besides, when we return to Charlotte, I'll expect you to take me out to eat." Kevin smiled... beautiful white teeth on display.

Janice melted. "It's a date."

Not wanting to give her the wrong impression, he corrected. "It's one friend paying back the other friend." He winked to soften his words.

"Yea, okay." Janice grinned. "You got a deal... **friend**!"

Kevin chuckled. He consulted his watch. "We have a couple of hours before the 7:30 flight. I'll wake the children so we can go eat."

~5~

Jade Morales waited patiently for her turn at the counter. Her sister, Rosario, was going to kill her and it wasn't her fault.

After the flight was cancelled, she called her oldest sister, Viviana, to let her know the original plan to fly to Puerto Rico together was a bust. She didn't want Viviana missing her flight waiting on her.

Please, Lord, let me get on the next flight, she prayed.

"Yes?" the agent asked.

"I need to get on the next flight to New York, please," Jade said politely.

"You and the other 66 people who were on that cancelled flight," snapped the ticket agent.

Madre de Dios, por favor, help me maintain my cool with this jerk. I am begging for patience. I don't want to go off on this pendejo.

"What can you do for me then?" Jade asked, handing him her driver's license.

He checked his computer screen. "I see your final destination is San Juan, Puerto Rico. Let me see if there's a direct flight leaving here tonight." After a few keystrokes, he said, "There isn't. And your original, connecting flight in New York was the last one leaving from Kennedy Airport." Continuing to review the screen, he added, "I **can** get you on a direct flight **tomorrow**. It leaves from here at 9:45 a.m. arriving in San Juan at 2:12 p.m. That's the best I can do."

Excited, Jade exclaimed, "I'll take it," forgiving his rudeness.

Not having to connect was wonderful. She would be in a much better mood to deal with Rosario, who was putting everyone through hell with her upcoming nuptials.

I'll call Rosario to let her know I'm getting in tomorrow afternoon. She'll be upset, but she'll get over it, reasoned Jade. *She has to. She said things will be fine as long as I'm there before the wedding and I will be. I promised.*

The only problem remaining was returning home to deal with Carmen, her father's young, live-in girlfriend, for another night.

As the ticket agent was booking her flight, she asked, "Why was the flight cancelled?"

The agent looked at his screen before replying, "Maintenance problems."

He finished the transaction, handed her the new ticket and boarding pass, and said, "Good luck tomorrow. Have a wonderful evening."

"Thank you. Thank you very much," she gushed, taking the documents. She left the airport.

On her way home, she pulled out her cell phone and texted Viviana: *plane had maintenance problems. Going home. Booked on 9:45 a.m. flight. In SJ at 2:12 p.m. be safe. Luv u. J.*

Returning Brett and Marla's driver's licenses, Clarissa glanced nervously at Brett, "Uh, sir, there's a problem." Her fingers continued to fly across the computer keys.

Marla asked, "What kind of problem?"

Again, addressing Brett, Clarissa explained, "It seems another agent has booked the last remaining seats on the 6:00 a.m. flight to JFK. You are now on standby. The good news is you're numbers 2 and 3."

"How is that possible?" Brett shouted, shocked the seats were gone so quickly.

"There are so many people rebooking their flights, I guess I wasn't fast enough."

"You guess you weren't fast enough?" Brett exploded. "Miss, do you have any idea how bad I need to get to New York?"

As Clarissa turned towards them, the business card Erich Coppenhauge had given her holding Doctor Israel's telephone number fell between the opening where the edge of the desk and podium met. Marla picked it up and placed it in her handbag without looking at it, believing it was the ticket agent's business card.

Marla intended to file a complaint with the airline headquarters. She had nothing against Clarissa, but the more information she could provide, the more the powers that be would take her complaint seriously. Not providing a replacement plane or making provisions for the passengers booked on the cancelled flight when the original plane showed problems was poor business practice. She intended to complain to all who would listen. She would launch a class-action suit against the airline if they forced her hand.

Checking the screen once again, and ignoring the question, Clarissa said brightly, "The next available flight with twenty-five remaining seats is the 7:30 flight tomorrow night. I can definitely get you both on that one."

She looked at them triumphantly, as if she expected them to rub her belly, and give her a milk bone.

Brett was dumbfounded. He swore he explained his need to get to New York before 10:00 a.m. Why was she acting like she'd just performed a miracle?

Marla said, "Clarissa, I'm sure my husband said we need to get to New York BEFORE 10:00 A.M. NOT P.M. so a 7:30 p.m. flight is far from acceptable. Now, do you have anything else that will get us there BEFORE," Marla then spoke very slowly, loudly, and deliberately, "10:00 A.M.?"

Clarissa glared at Marla. *Who in the hell does Miss Siddity think she is speaking to?* She silently questioned, not daring to speak the words aloud. She couldn't risk losing her job.

Plastering a taut smile and ignoring Marla, Clarissa said, "Sir, you're booked on two standby lists. There's nothing more I can do."

Screaming, Brett repeated, "Nothing more you can do? Are you kidding me? Don't you understand? I must get to New York. I need to get there, like yesterday."

Then you should have booked your flight "like yesterday" and maybe you'd be there, thought Clarissa, keeping a professional look on her face.

Marla grabbed Brett's hand into her own. She didn't need to say anything. Holding his hand usually calmed him. Usually!

"Mr. Meadows, I understand you're upset. I wish there was something I could do. Go to the information desk. They may be able to help you. As long as there are passengers on this line, I cannot research other airlines. Good luck, Mr. Meadows," she said dismissively. Then she called, "next".

Before Brett could protest, Marla tugged him away from the counter.

"Come on. Let's go to the information desk."

"Marla what am I going to do? I will not win the bid if I'm not in New York in the morning. We need this job." Brett whispered, trying to control the enormity of his plight.

"Brett, we don't NEED it. It will be great to have, yes, but we're doing just fine."

Quietly Brett replied, "No, we're not, Marla. There's something I need to tell you."

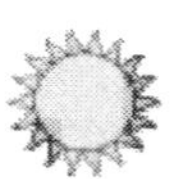

Erich found an area in the waiting room with a scattering of people to call Doctor Israel.

"Hello, Doctor, this is Erich Coppenhauge."

"Hello, Erich. How's it going?" he asked.

"That's why I'm calling. My flight was cancelled and none of the other airlines have flights to New York with available seats."

"Erich, that's unbelievable."

"Those were my exact words. I'm number 2 on standby for a 7:30 flight out this evening, arriving at JFK by 9:30 p.m."

"That's later than we expected. We won't be able to operate tonight. I'll reschedule the surgery for first thing tomorrow morning. Come straight to the hospital when you arrive in New York. I won't be here, but the hospital personnel will be expecting you."

"How's Erika?" Erich asked anxiously.

The doctor hesitated wondering how truthful he should be. Erika's condition was very volatile. He didn't want to alarm Erich. "She's stable. However, the team and I think it's best to perform the transplant within the next 24 hours."

"Twenty-four hours! That doesn't give me much time. If anything else occurs, Doctor Israel, I will leave word with your service. I hope to God I'm on that 7:30 flight."

"So do I, Erich." Doctor Israel mumbled. "So do I."

Not wanting to speculate on the doctor's grave tone, Erich asked, "Did anyone from WorldLine Airways call you?"

"No. Should they have?"

"I gave your number to an airline agent to verify how critical it is that I get there. I thought she might call."

"No one's called. Good luck with the flight and thanks for keeping me abreast of your plight."

"Thank you, Doctor Israel. Goodbye for now."

"Goodbye, Erich."

Erich was punching in Miriam's cell phone number when he stopped. He didn't want to alarm his fiancée while she was driving to Florida with her friends. He decided to call once he boarded the plane.

"Here you go, Mrs. Phillips. Your new boarding passes and seat confirmation for WorldLine Airways Flight 8962 departing at 7:30. We'll see you at Gate five, thirty minutes before the flight boards. Here is a food voucher. Enjoy."

The ticket agent handed Kami the aforementioned items. She accepted them with a smile as wide as the Grand Canyon, thanking him profusely. She was elated. She'd listened to the surrounding conversations while waiting in line. It had not sounded optimistic. The gods were smiling down on her after all. **She** had a seat on the next flight. She called Dante with her new arrival time. After a brief conversation, she hung up, and went searching for food for their growing child.

At exactly 6:45, Meredith Winthrop returned to the counter. Reading the ticket agent's name, she said, "Hello Matt, will you please assign us seats on the 7:30 p.m. flight to New York?"

"Certainly, may I have the tickets please?"

"Absolutely!" She handed them to him, glad she'd brought them with her. As Matt searched for seats, she engaged him in conversation.

"So Matt, why was Flight 3236 cancelled?"

Matt looked up from the computer screen, then quickly around to make sure no one was within hearing range. He motioned for Meredith to move closer. "The airline couldn't get a pilot to fly the plane."

"Is that right?"

"That's what I heard."

A few minutes later he exclaimed, "Uh oh, Mrs. Winthrop, there's a problem."

"I don't like problems, Matt."

"Who does? But that doesn't change the fact that one exists."

Meredith sighed. "Let's hear it."

"It appears the 7:30 flight is overbooked. I cannot get you seats."

"What do you mean?" Meredith asked. "I have tickets."

"True, but there are no available seats. I guess agents were booking so fast double tickets were issued, which is probably why you didn't get seat numbers when you booked the flight."

"You guess? Probably? Appears? Sounds like a lot of speculating to me."

"It is. In the two years I've worked here, I've seen some crazy things. Very little surprises me."

"What do I do? We need to get on the flight?"

"Unfortunately, it won't be tonight. Not only is it overbooked, there are people on standby... a lot of people. You have two options: you can rebook on a different flight on a different day or you can get a refund. We would rather you rebook with us but will issue you a refund at your request."

Meredith looked across the waiting room at a smiling Ian talking to Brian. The painkillers were finally working. "Thank goodness," she muttered.

"Ma'am?" Matt questioned.

"What time is the next flight?"

Matt checked his computer screen. "6 a.m. There's also a standby list for that."

"6 a.m.? Standby? That won't work. We needed to get to New York tonight. It's a matter of life and death." Seeing skepticism sprint across Matt's face, Meredith added, "I swear it's true. My son is having brain surgery in the morning at Sloan Kettering." She swallowed the emotions threatening to boil over. Composure in place, she asked, "Can you book us on another airline?"

Skepticism gone, Matt said, "I'm sorry. I'll check other airlines flying out tonight."

He quickly searched the various airlines. "Mrs. Winthrop, every single airline to New York is booked solid."

"What about Newark or surrounding airports?" A hopeful Meredith asked.

"I'll check." Several minutes later, Matt shook his head. "There is absolutely nothing available, ma'am. Do you want to book another flight for tomorrow?"

"We need to check with the doctors. Thanks for your assistance, Matt."

"Good luck," he called after a retreating Meredith.

Returning to her seat, she informed her family of the latest development.

Brian said, "I'll call the doctors to see when they can reschedule the surgery."

"I'll stay with Ian."

Brian walked to a quiet area to place the calls.

"Mommy, maybe this is a sign," Ian said slowly. He deliberately took his time when speaking so not to slur his words.

"A sign of what?" Meredith snapped. At the crestfallen look on Ian's face, she apologized.

"A sign... from God. Maybe we... shouldn't go to...'o... New York. Maybe I'm 'upposed to kee this brain thing." He slowed down. He could feel the headache trying to make a comeback. That's when it was the most difficult to speak. He steadied his breath. His mother was watching him closely. *Please go away. Please,* he prayed silently.

"Ian?" His mother questioned.

He closed his eyes tightly and controlled his breathing. He was beginning to feel like himself. The old Ian. The healthy Ian.

"Ian?" She questioned again.

1, 2, 3, 4, 5, he slowly opened his eyes. He smiled at her.

"I'm fine, Mommy." He said brightly.

She looked skeptical.

"Maybe I'm supposed to keep this brain tumor and the headaches for the rest of my life." He wasn't slurring. Hooray! Ian was relieved. "Maybe the surgery won't be successful. Maybe I'll... die."

"That's nonsense talk, Ian," She yelled forgetting her recent concern for her son. The stress of the day was reflected in her tone. "This isn't a sign from God. Why would He want you to keep the brain tumor forever? God has big plans for you, Mister. Why else would He have sent Doctor Brunn, all the way from Germany, into our lives? He has performed a lot of surgeries –

many just as complicated as yours. He has a one hundred percent success rate. One hundred percent, Ian. There are no better odds than that."

Stubbornly Ian said, "Then why was the flight cancelled?"

"That has nothing to do with God. Airlines cancel flights all the time."

Brian returned to his family. "I spoke with Doctor Brunn and Doctor Lafayette. Doctor Brunn has surgery scheduled for the rest of this week. He's taking advantage of the use of the facility while he's in the country. They have rescheduled the surgery for one week from today - first thing next Wednesday morning."

"Great!" Meredith exclaimed, face lighting up. "I'll change our flight to next Monday. This way we'll be in New York a couple of days before the surgery and can do some sight-seeing. Isn't that wonderful, Ian?"

"Just great," he muttered, dejectedly. *As if I have a choice.*

Meredith was already on her way back to the counter to change their tickets. Brian excused himself to the restroom. Ian sat alone in the wheelchair, engulfed in sadness. He kicked the wheelchair with his foot. He never wanted to sit in the stupid thing, anyway. He felt helpless.

How am I going to get through another week? The tears he contained while in the presence of his parents started a slow descent down his young, innocent, troubled face.

~6~

At 7:10 p.m., the boarding call for the 7:30 p.m. flight was made. A mob of people bombarded their way to the podium, Kami among them. She handed her boarding pass to the check-in clerk, who scanned it then stepped aside to let her pass. Eyes staring straight ahead, she dashed inside the safety of the plane, placed her luggage in the overhead compartment, her purse under the seat in front of her, and sat down with a sigh of relief. She called and spoke briefly to Dante, informing him she was finally on the plane awaiting departure. They agreed to meet at the airport. With a smile plastered across her beautiful, elated face, and her hand across her flat belly, she nestled deeper in the airplane chair with scenes of a Dante/Kami reunion dancing joyously in her head.

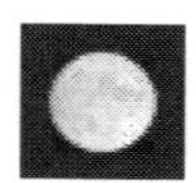

Back in the terminal, an airline agent surveyed the crowd. There were a lot of irritated faces remaining. She quickly ducked behind the safety of the dais before announcing the flight was full.

"Great. There's no chance in Hades I'm getting on the plane," Erich surmised, turning to go to the counter to confirm his seat on the 6 a.m. flight. He stopped when he heard incentives being offered to anyone willing to give up their seats.

A surge of hope cruised through his body. Maybe, just maybe... Erich held his breath and prayed like never before.

Please, someone, anyone, give up your seat. Please! After a minute, he let out his breath... five minutes - his body trembled slightly... ten minutes later it took everything he had not to scream like the insane man trapped inside of him going mad. He watched the gate door close along with his chance of getting to New York that evening.

Weakly, he dropped in a nearby seat, wondering why God was allowing this to happen. He knew how much Erika's life depended on him.

What if she dies? Dear God, please... he stopped. God wasn't listening to him.

"Unfuckingbelievable!" Janice screamed. "How the hell do you overbook a flight by twenty-nine people? I can understand two, maybe three but twenty-nine? AND you have people on standby to boot. What kind of crapola airline is this?"

"Janice, calm down," Kevin said using the same soothing voice that worked earlier.

"Don't fucking tell me to calm down. This is bullshit," Janice ranted.

"Children, let Daddy deal with this situation. Go sit right over there. Don't get up. I need to see you at all times. Do you understand?"

"Yes, Daddy," Kane and Kara chorused, peeking fearfully at Janice before dashing off to the "safe" seats indicated by their father.

"Janice, behaving like this will not get you anywhere."

"You don't understand, Kevin. I need to get to New York. I need to...." Her shoulders shook at the enormity of her predicament. Not getting on the 7:30 flight meant – no job, no money, no car... foreclosure!

"Ms. Monroe, I **am** sorry," Clarissa said. "There is nothing I can do about tonight's flight but I see you're booked on the 6:00 a.m. flight. You have an assigned seat so you'll definitely get on."

"Unless that's cancelled too," Janice mumbled.

"Thank you, Clarissa," Kevin said. "By the way, why was Flight 3236 cancelled?"

Clarissa looked uncomfortable. Her eyes darted around. Spotting her manager within hearing distance, she said, "I'm not sure, sir. We weren't told the reason. The manager is right there if you wish to speak with him."

Kevin glanced in the indicated direction. The short, plump, graying man with creases on his haggard face was dealing with an incensed passenger. He let it go.

If Janice couldn't get on the flight as standby number three, he definitely wasn't getting on. He put his arm around her shoulders, and patted her back, while she sobbed into his gray polo shirt. Kara and Kane stared curiously.

Kara, followed closely by Kane, went to their father, "Daddy, why is Ms. Monroe crying?"

Embarrassed, Janice withdrew from Kevin's embrace. She excused herself to go to the ladies restroom.

Kevin took Kara and Kane into his vacant arms and explained. "Ms. Monroe is very sad because she isn't going to New York tonight. We aren't either. There was something wrong with the plane, so they cancelled the flight."

Tears popped into his children's eyes.

"What was wrong with it, Daddy?" Kara asked, struggling not to let the tears flow.

"I don't know, sweetheart," Kevin answered honestly.

"So we will not see Auntie Vette?" Kane asked in an almost inaudible voice - the most words he'd spoken in a long time.

"Not tonight, son, but we're coming back bright and early tomorrow morning and we'll get on the flight then."

"Promise, Daddy?" Kara asked.

"I can't make that promise, sweetheart. I have no control over this situation. I can promise we will be back in time to catch the flight in the morning."

"Okay, Daddy," a satisfied Kara exclaimed.

Janice exited the bathroom with red-rimmed, swollen eyes. Kane and Kara left their father's arm to hide slightly behind him.

"Are you ready to go?" Kevin asked.

"Yes, no sense in staying here."

"Get home safe, Janice." Kevin reached into his pocket and pulled out a business card. He wrote his home and cell phone numbers on the back and handed it to her. "Call me if you need anything... any time."

Impulsively, Janice reached up and kissed Kevin on his lips. "You are a godsend, Mr. Hinderblocker. Thanks for everything. Have a wonderful night. I'll see you in the morning."

Janice walked away from the Hinderblocker family towards the airport exit.

A kiss? See you in the morning? What's up with that? Kara thought... puzzled.

"Why did she kiss you, Daddy?" Kara asked.

"Oooo...Daddy has a girlfriend," sang Kane.

Boy, how things changed, Kevin thought with a smile. *I think my children will be just fine.*

"Cut it out you two," he said, laughing. "How do you feel about staying in a hotel tonight?"

Kane looked at Kara for guidance. A scowl flashed across her face. In a grown-up voice, she said, "Daddy, Kane and I want to see Auntie Vette and New York City."

Kevin knelt before his children, taking each little hand in his sizeable one. He said, "I know you're disappointed. So am I. I wanted to spend time with Auntie Vette, too." He paused. "I miss her, too," he said, referring to his deceased wife.

Yvette and Kimberly favored the most, both in looks and personality. Kevin knew the children were hoping for a piece of their mother through her sister, Yvette.

"Look on the bright side," Kevin said cheerily. "We're going to a nearby hotel where we'll be able to see the airplanes from our window."

The children groaned. More planes were the last thing they wanted to "see".

Undaunted, Kevin said, "Tomorrow, we'll get into New York early enough to spend the entire day with Auntie Vette. By the time we reached there tonight, it would have been too late to do anything, anyway. So, actually, this is working out much better. What do you say, guys?"

Kane deferred to Kara once more.

A smile slowly descended across her lips. "Sounds cool, Daddy," she said.

"Super cool," Kane cosigned.

Kevin ruffled Kane's hair. "I'll go find our suitcases. Stay put! Kara, watch your brother. I'll be right back."

"Yes, Daddy," Kara said with an angelic expression, watching their father walk away.

Stopping, he returned to his daughter. "Kara...," Kevin warned.

"We'll be right here when you get back, Daddy," Kara said, mischief pirouetting in her eyes.

"I'm serious, Kara," Kevin gave his final warning before walking towards the baggage claim area, glancing over his shoulder every few feet, until he could no longer see his children.

Kara waved each time he turned. After Kevin was no longer in sight, she counted slowly to ten. Grabbing Kane's hand, she whispered, "Let's go!"

"Where?" Kane inquired, planting his feet to their spot.

"Just come on," Kara demanded.

"Daddy told us not to move."

"No... he said to stay put," Kara clarified.

Stubbornly, Kane said, "Same thing."

With authority, Kara said, "No, it's not. I told him we'll be right here when he comes back. That won't happen if you don't come with me right NOW."

Kane was torn. He didn't want to disobey their father. BUT, he also told Kara to watch him. Kane rationalized his decision to follow his sister. *Kara can't watch me if I don't follow her, right?*

Besides, she's finally talking to me. I don't want her to not like me again. Decision made, he followed his sister.

Kara marched up to the lone ticket agent playing on his phone behind the dais.

"Excuse me, sir."

The agent looked down at the cute little girl in pigtails.

"Yes, ma'am," he answered, eyes gleaming.

"Why was the flight to New York cancelled?"

"The flight wasn't cancelled, Baby Doll." The ticket agent responded.

Kara cringed at the term of endearment.

"Yes, it was. We've been here all day. When we came, it was right after lunch. We had dinner while waiting on the plane to come. My daddy told me they cancelled it and we have to come back in the morning to catch a different, really early plane."

Kara stopped, checking to make sure their father hadn't returned.

Amused, the agent said, "Oh, you must mean Flight 3236. What a mess that was!! I'll check for you, Baby Doll. Just a sec."

He reviewed some notes on his screen, frowned, hit some more keys, frowned some more. "Hmm," he mused. "This is strange. They cancelled that flight because they didn't have a crew? That can't be right. Let me read this again." A few minutes later, mumbling to himself, he declared, "Yep, that's what's stated here – no crew. Jeez, that sucks."

"Sir, I don't understand. What does that mean?" Kara asked politely.

"What?" The distracted agent asked.

"Why can't they fly without a "crew"?"

Oh no. I can't believe I said that out loud... What harm can it do, right? She's just a little girl.

He answered, "It means there wasn't anyone to serve the peanuts."

Kara said, "Oh! Thank you, sir."

Urgently Jackson Snow said, "I shouldn't have said that, Baby Doll. The official reason listed is engine trouble."

"Then how do you know they didn't have a crew?"

Jackson Snow panicked. He never shared the real reason he was fired from his previous job. He was a computer whiz. He had the natural ability to tap into unauthorized documents accidently. He unintentionally found the email strings between corporate headquarters and the airport personnel. He wished he could control his abilities. It got him in trouble every time. He groaned.

Stuttering he said, "Um... a...uh... friend of mine... right... a friend of mine told me. It's just a rumor. The reason the flight was cancelled was because of ENGINE TROUBLE." He pronounced the last two words carefully and loudly. "Got it, Baby Doll?"

Smiling innocently, Kara said, "I sure do! Thank you, sir."

Nervously Jackson said, "Doll, it's easier to remember - cancelled because of engine failure."

"I'll remember, sir," Kara said sweetly, walking away from the counter with Kane in tow. She loathed being called Baby Doll. She was NOT a baby. She liked the way "no crew" sounded better than "engine failure". *How boring!*

Several minutes later, Kevin returned with their suitcases on a pulley.

"Any problems?" he questioned.

"No Daddy," Kara and Kane uttered in perfect harmony.

He studied his children. "Why do I get the sense you guys are up to something?"

Kara replied, "No idea, Daddy. You said to stay put. Here we are. What's the problem?"

He couldn't answer, but he knew something was amiss. He missed the wink Kara threw to Kane and the giggle Kane successfully suppressed.

"Let's go. I have to call your aunt to tell her we're not getting in until morning."

Kevin took out his cell phone as the three exited the airport.

"I didn't want to tell you before because I didn't want you to worry." Brett took a steadying breath. "I lost the Asheford Management account... two months ago."

"Two... months.... ago?" Marla fell into a vacant seat. "How is that possible? You've had that account for years. They were the first company you signed when you started your firm. I... don't... get it."

Marla recalled the joy Brett expressed while sharing his last day with the most generous technology company he worked for (well, it was the only firm he ever worked for before starting his own business).

Brett joined Technical Twin Solution (TTS) after graduating from Duke University. It was owned by two cousins - Larry and Garry Feldstein. He had great benefits, a decent salary, and was treated as an equal, even with his limited professional experiences. Brett loved the job. It afforded him hands-on experiences, new adventures, challenges, and knowledge.

Imitating the voice of his former employer, his friend, Garry Feldstein, Brett said, "You were a great manager. Thank you for your dedication, service, and loyalty. You've wanted to start your own business for quite some time, yet you never tried to steal any of our clients. That is why we're given you your first client – Asheford Management Corp."

Marla almost fell off her seat when Brett shared that shocker. She was flabbergasted.

"Why are you doing this?"

Garry explained that Brett was a great kid who they wanted to succeed. His success or failure reflected on them.

Brett didn't understand why Asheford, one of their oldest clients, would leave an established company for an upstart company.

"We informed them you could offer a much better contractual rate with great service. Always remember 'money is power'." Larry

Feldstein delivered that tidbit.

"Recently, they've undergone some structural changes. They hired a new CFO whose loyalty is to another technology company. He convinced the Board that they could save a lot of money going with the new company. I was already giving them a hefty discount. I couldn't afford to cut costs any further. If their rates are lower than mine, they are operating below cost.

"Simon, the head of the Management Group, confided that if the new technology company doesn't pan out, or their cost suddenly increases - which it will - he will campaign to get us back. He promises to recommend us to other agencies. He was very apologetic, but his hands are tied.

"Marla, we NEED the New York contract to stay afloat. Without it, we may have to file bankruptcy."

Marla gasped.

"I didn't want to tell you because..." Brett lowered his head. "I didn't want you to know that... I'm a failure."

Marla couldn't believe it. Brett was one of the most confident men she knew – 'a failure'? She tilted Brett's head up to kiss him lightly on the lips.

Emphatically, she stated, "Brett Meadows, you ARE NOT a failure. You didn't lose that account because of incompetence. You lost it because of bureaucratic hypocrisies. You are wonderful at what you do... whatever that is." She winked. "You NEED to always remember that. Why else do you think I married you? Not because you're handsome or wore me down with your puppy dog eyes. No!!! It's because you're brilliant. You're going places and I'm going along for the ride," she half-joked.

Brett felt slightly better.

Marla was disappointed that her husband hadn't had enough faith in their love to share the devastating setback with her.... a setback that could bankrupt *2B Mpact.* Now was not the time to dwell on it. However, Brett could rest assure the subject would resurface.

"Brett Andrew Meadows, we **promised** to tell each other everything, no matter how difficult."

Brett hung his head in shame. "I know Marla. I'm sorry. I hoped something else would materialize so I could say 'hey we lost that but we got this'."

"Don't worry, sweetheart. We'll make it through this. We'll get to New York. You'll blow the execs and the board members of *Multidata Infonet Inc*. away. Your company will be featured in *Forbes,* AND are you ready for this? We will dance down Easy Street, my man, my lover, my friend."

Brett loved it when Marla reverted to her cheerleading days. With her by his side, he knew he could face anything thrown at him.

Everything would be fine.

It had to be.

~7~

"Hey, Missy, ya in my seat."

Kami opened her eyes to a burly man standing above her.

"Excuse me?"

"I said, ya in my seat," the man repeated.

"That's impossible," Kami replied, annoyed her sweet dream starring Dante and their unborn child was interrupted. "I have my boarding pass right here."

"So do I and it reads seat 4C."

Kami dug in her purse for hers'. "Are you sure you're on the right flight? This one is going to Kennedy Airport in New York."

"I know where it's going, Missy and ya in my seat."

A flight attendant walked over. "What's going on?"

"Girlie here is in my seat and won't get up," the man complained.

"I have a boarding pass that states aisle seat 4C," Kami stated politely.

"May I have your passes, please?" The weary flight attendant, Candi asked.

The plane hadn't left the terminal and already there were several problems.

The two boarding passes were identical. Both had Flight 8962, 7:30, JFK, seat 4C marked on them. *How can this be?* Candi wondered. Scrutinizing the passes, she couldn't find the problem. She peeked around the curtain at the two passengers whose boarding passes she now possessed. Both wore frowns.

She picked up the microphone and announced, "Ladies and

gentlemen, we apologize for the delay. We will depart as soon as we correct an unfortunate issue."

Above loud moans, she persisted. "There are administrative problems we must handle before we can depart, but we will depart shortly. Please, let us know if we may provide you with anything while you wait. In a brief moment, we will direct your attention to the screens closest to you to watch the in-flight safety video. We thank you for your patience and for choosing WorldLine Airways for your flying pleasure."

The passengers, many from cancelled Flight 3236, were relieved the plane was not experiencing mechanical problems.

Candi took the passes to her co-worker. "Theo, look at these. I'm missing something. They have identical information, but that can't be right."

Theo examined the passes closely. Moments later, he exclaimed, "Ah, ha. Here's the problem."

Candi looked where he pointed. "Gee, how did I miss that?"

"It's an easy mistake to overlook."

"Thank you, Theo. This will not be easy. Stay close in case I need you."

"You got it."

Candi went back to Kami and the waiting man.

She said, "I'm sorry but you must leave. Your ticket is for tomorrow night's flight."

"That's impossible. I specifically requested a ticket for **tonight's** 7:30 flight."

She shrugged. "The agent booked you on the wrong flight. It's important to review all documentation carefully before leaving the counter. I'm sorry for the mix-up, but you must exit immediately. This flight is full and we are behind schedule."

Reaching under the seat in front of her, Kami retrieved her purse once more. She stood with tears in her eyes. She gazed at the man standing in the aisle next to **her** seat.

"Mr., will you please trade my ticket with yours? I really need to get to New York. My husband is being deployed and I'm preg..."

"Save it, lady. There's no way I'm giving up my seat. I met this hottie on *Singleyou.com.* We're meeting in New York. She's a rich old broad. Not much to look at, but if the price is right, it doesn't matter. It's all the same in the dark. Heh...Heh... heh. Know what I mean?" The man cackled, grabbing his crotch.

Candi shook her head in disgust. She wished she was throwing off the vile man, wiping his nose with his sleeve instead of the beautiful young woman wearing the painful expression.

Kami tried to appeal to the stranger once more.

"Mister, please! I must tell my husband I'm pregnant before he leaves for Afghanistan."

"Tell him yar pregnant? What kind of wife are ya? Are ya trying to get him killed? Ya after his benefits or ya don't love him or somethin? Ya want him fighting, thinking about ya and his brat? Come on, lady! I'm doing the chap a favor. He doesn't need to know yar carrying his child – if it's his. He can take a DNA test to prove it. I would if it were me. A hot number like yarself... faithful? Ha! Hey, you're a beauty." He said gawking at Kami as if seeing her for the first time. He stared at her chest licking his lips. "I'll give up my ticket if ya give me yar number and agree to a little sometin sometin later. We can go in the bathroom right now to seal the deal. Know what I mean?" He leered at her.

"Ya wouldn't mind waiting, right, Stew?" he said to Candi.

It took everything she had to keep the smile on her face.

Kami stared balefully at the despicable man. *Was he serious*? She was trying hard not to vomit.

"What ya think ya too good for ole Melvin here? Well, ya know what? No ass, no gas. Know what I mean? Guess ya ain't gettin to New York tonight. Heh...Heh... heh. Get to stepping, so I can sit down. Ole Melvin's legs are hurting."

Kami slowly moved out of Melvin's way so he could take the seat she'd warmed up.

Melvin flopped down in the seat. "This feels great. Hey, Stewardess," he called. "I'm willing to share my seat. Yeah, just let Missy here sit on Melvin's lap. Yeah. Right here." He pointed to his crotch, closed his eyes, and began gyrating in his seat. He opened one eye to look at Candi and Kami. “What about it, Missy? I guaranteed ya comfort. Heh...Heh... heh.”

His closest seat companion moved closer to the left to avoid contact with him. A speechless Candi turned bright red. Kami struggled to keep the bile down. It was getting difficult.

Viewing the expressions on their faces, he cackled some more. “Ya loss, Princess. Melvin’s working with a ten-inch. I bet ya husband ain’t got that. Heh...heh... heh...” snort... “heh... heh... heh...” snort... “heh.....”

Kami reached in the overhead compartment for her luggage, dazed, repulsed, and embarrassed. Eyes of pity, compassion, and Melvin’s cackling followed her descent down the aisle of the fully booked plane to the exit. Candi apologized the entire way.

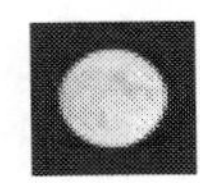

When the plane doors opened, an agent on the other side greeted a comatose Kami. She gently took Kami’s arm, escorted her down the ramp, and back into the terminal. She led her to a nearby seat and forced her into it.

Kami couldn’t believe it. She was so close to seeing Dante. Why was this happening?

Hearing the gate rumble open, Erich sat straight up in his seat. Maybe God had heard his prayers after all. He quickly jumped up to check if someone had given up their seat. One look at the gorgeous woman he’d spotted earlier that day told him something was terribly off. She looked pale - like she was about to toss her cookies.

He walked to the agent guarding Kami.

“Is she all right?” he inquired.

“No,” the agent whispered. “She was issued the wrong ticket. She and another passenger had the same seat number but different flight days. The plane was full. We had to ask her to leave.”

The crestfallen expression on Erich’s face explained it all.

"You thought she'd taken an incentive and given up her seat, huh?"

"I'd hoped."

"I'm sorry. This hasn't been an easy day." The agent sympathized. "See what provisions we can make for you. We screwed up. We have to make it right."

Dejectedly, Erich thanked her. Squaring his shoulders, he went to the counter to confirm his assigned seat for the 6 a.m. flight. Two agents were managing the desk. He peered at the first one wondering why she hadn't called Doctor Israel.

Clarissa saw the good-looking man emerge from the line. Just as she assumed he wasn't able to get on the 7:30 flight. She removed his name from that flight list, glad she had booked him on the 6 a.m. flight before it filled up. Why the cross-look? She smiled at him. He ignored her.

She watched him approach her coworker. *Humph, you do someone a favor, and this is the thanks you get. Ungrateful bas...* Then it hit her. The business card he gave her. He wanted her to telephone someone in New York to confirm his "life or death" emergency. She searched the desk. *What happened to that card? I put it right here.*

Shrugging, she went to assist the next passenger.

Erich confirmed his reservation with the second agent. There was nothing more he could do until 6 a.m. He needed to get some rest. He walked to the rental car kiosk and dialed the two airport rental car locations, only to learn that neither had available cars.

"What do you mean, there are no cars? This is an airport. You're supposed to have cars," Erich shouted into the phone.

No, we're supposed to have planes, the person at the Premier Car Rental location chuckled to himself. It had been an interminable day. The agent was slaphappy with exhaustion. "Sir, we are completely out of cars because of the flight delays and cancellations."

Erich slammed down the phone. He was filled with mixed emotions. He wanted to laugh. He wanted to shout. He wanted to get to New York. Erika's life depended on him. And he was depending on WorldLine Airways.

Taking out his cell phone, he called and arranged for a car service to pick him up and take him to Miriam's home so he could retrieve her convertible. He knew where the spare key was kept. He then left his new flight time with Doctor Israel's service. He called his parents to divulge his latest travel disaster and agreed to meet them at the hospital in the morning. Last, he called Miriam.

"Hi, my name is LaSean. May I get you some water?" The agent asked kindly.

Kami was devastated. She couldn't believe she wasn't on the flight. Twice she'd overlooked details. It was so unlike her. She didn't know what to do. She didn't have any friends in Charlotte. She just wanted to go home. She wanted out of this nightmare. She wanted to wake up in her bed with Dante by her side.

"Miss, would you like some water?" LaSean repeated.

Kami glanced at her but did not see her. A sharp pain was ripping through her abdomen, doubling her over.

"What's the matter? What's happening?" The agent asked, filled with concern.

The pain brought Kami back to the presence. "AARGH!!! Oh my God. My baby. Please, let my baby be all right."

"Are you pregnant?"

"Yes!" Kami screamed through compressed lips.

"When did you eat and drink last?" LaSean asked.

"I'm... not... sure." She couldn't remember what day it was, let alone the last time she ate. She remembered going in search of food but couldn't recall finding anything to eat.

Springing into action, LaSean grabbed some crackers and water from a nearby vending machine. She made Kami eat and drink the items offered. LaSean stayed with her while she chewed slowly and took tiny sips.

"How's that?"

The pain subsided with the fifth cracker. "Much better. Thank you," Kami said.

"You were hungry. In your condition, you must remember to eat. I don't have any children, but I was there for the birth of each of my cousin's four children. It was amazing. It's important to eat. Take your time. When you're ready, come to the counter so we can get you on another flight."

Shortly thereafter, Kami had a new ticket and boarding pass for the 10:00 flight leaving the next morning.

"Thanks LaSean. You've been very kind," Kami said.

Seated on a chair, she phoned Dante.

"Hi lover, I was kicked off the flight."

"What do you mean, 'kicked off?'" Dante asked evenly.

"I got an agent who booked me on tomorrow's 7:30 flight instead of tonight's'."

"Is Charlotte full of incompetent people?" He was referring to the mix-up at the car rental place. That was a disaster! That was the reason she wasn't in New York. "Tell me you're kidding."

"Wish I could. I asked the person whose seat I had to switch with me. Told him how badly I needed to see you. Dante, he was so disgusting. He said he would if I'd sleep with him."

"I hope you told him where to go."

"I was too embarrassed. I got my stuff and hurried from the plane. If all goes well, I'll be on the 10 a.m. flight. I checked my ticket thoroughly. It's correct. At least we'll get a few hours together before you ship out."

"I can't believe no one offered their seat. I should have followed my gut and met you in Charlotte."

"You were going to come here?"

"Yes, when we had the storm the other night in Arizona. Then I received orders to report to duty. I had already received the okay to leave from New York. I didn't want to rock the boat by requesting another change."

"Oh, lover, I wish you had. I miss you so much. My phone is dying. I'll call Jessica. The woman I did the *A Total Change* event with to see if I can crash at her place for the night. I don't want to sleep here, nor do I want to rent a car after my experience earlier today. I'll call to let you know where I end up. Love you, sweets."

"Love you, sweeter."

Kami called Jessica, "You'll never guess what happened..."

Jessica picked her up from the airport. She was fond of Kami and wanted to get to know her better. She was pleased to have her stay the night.

~8~

"This is ridiculous. Your airline screwed up, yet you won't do anything to accommodate us?"

Darryl, the information specialist and Brett had been going back and forth for the last twenty minutes.

Darryl was fed up. "What would you like us to do, Mr. Meadows, rent you a private jet?"

"Hell yeah, if that's what it'll take to get us to New York."

The two men, both with similar physiques and height, sized each other up. They stared at the other across the counter, neither willing to back down.

Directing her statement to both men, Marla said, "Enough of this macho crap. We have a situation here that needs rectifying. Darryl, what can you do for us?"

Darryl's steely glare remained on Brett a moment longer before he reluctantly tore his eyes away to focus on Marla. "I see you are on standby for the 6 a.m. flight. The next one is 10:00 but from the yelling your husband was doing, I reckon you have to get to New York before then so I have two suggestions for you."

"What are they?"

Brett, not uttering a word, glared at Darryl, silently thinking, *I can take him.*

"The first is we try to get you on a flight on another airline. The problem is, when I did a quick scan, I saw nothing leaving from here tonight. I can check surrounding airports if you're willing to make arrangements to get to New York."

"That's fine," Marla blurted, stealing a peep at Brett who was brewing and glaring at Darryl.

Darryl expertly tapped the keys. "I'm sorry, Mrs. Meadows. There aren't any flights with available seats leaving tonight for Newark, LaGuardia, or Islip. I even tried Philadelphia and Washington, but nothing. If you're willing to drive to Greensboro in the morning, I can book you on a 7:30 flight. It's cutting it close but you'll get to New York by 9:30 assuming everything runs smoothly. Also, there is another flight leaving from Columbia, SC in the morning at 7. That gives you a little more time to play with. Both flights have available seats on them."

Marla peered at Brett. From his expression, she knew he wasn't going to help her make a decision.

"Are you able to change our round-trip ticket to arrive in either Greensboro or Columbia without a fee?" Marla asked.

"Unfortunately, I can't. Since there aren't any issues with your return flight, we would have to charge you a change fee."

Seizing the opportunity to exercise his lungs, Brett screamed. "You must be kidding!"

"No, I ain't!" Darryl screamed back with attitude dripping with each word.

"Okay Darryl, let's see if I understand," Marla said calmly. The men resumed their power stares. "If we book a flight out of let's say, Columbia, we must keep our tickets returning to Charlotte or pay the difference in cost?"

"That's correct, Mrs. Meadows."

"So...although we didn't cancel the flight, we're being penalized."

"I know it sucks, but that's the policy. I can get a manager, but I guarantee she'll say the same thing."

"Get her anyway," Brett shouted.

"Wait a minute," Marla said. "You said there were two options. What's the second one?"

Darryl huffed at Brett before speaking to Marla. "You can rent a car. The airline will pay for the rental to get you to New York. You," Darryl made sure he emphasized the 'you,' while addressing Marla, "have been very patient. It's been a pleasure working with YOU. I will get approval from the manager to allow you to keep the car during your five-day stay in New York. Then you can drop it off at the airport before your return flight home."

"If you can do ALL that, why can't you waive the change flight fee? This is asinine!" Brett declared.

"That's very kind," Marla added quickly not giving Darryl the opportunity to respond. "But my husband asked a valid question. Why can't you change our tickets to return to either Columbia or Greensboro without charging a fee?"

"Mrs. Meadows, it is a lot cheaper for us to rent a car for the week, with the discounts, and incentives the airline receives than to change the tickets for a flight."

"Why is that?" Marla asked.

"My understanding is to change tickets are a bookkeeping nightmare. The airline probably loses money. But who knows? I don't. I'm just a peon."

"You got that right," Brett agreed brightly.

Quickly grabbing Brett's arm Marla said, "Will you excuse us while we discuss our options?"

"No, problem. You come back when you're ready," Darryl said, challenging Brett with his eyes.

Marla and Brett sat down on nearby chairs.

"Brett, what's the big deal?" Marla asked. "We didn't drive. We'll need to take a taxi home, anyway. Remember?"

Sheepishly, Brett mumbled, "Oh yeah. I forgot. But babe, we can't afford a taxi to Columbia or Greensboro. That'll cost a small fortune. I guess we could drive a rental **IF** the airline will pay for it AND a hotel for the night."

Marla contemplated the options quietly before saying, "Wouldn't you rather drive to New York?"

"No! That's why we got airline tickets. I'm not up for an 11-hour drive, Marla. It's after 7:30. It's getting dark. I'd rather drive into the night not into the day."

"Here are our choices. We can rent a car and drive to either Greensboro or Columbia. Stay in a hotel overnight and pray our flight isn't cancelled in the morning OR control our destiny. We can rent a car and drive straight to New York. If we leave immediately, we'll be there by 7:00. Come on. It'll be fun. I'll keep you awake with my singing."

He snickered. "Not convincing, darling. You can't carry a tune to save your life."

"Forget you." She hit his arm, then reached out and kissed him on the lips. "Honey, you will get this job. I can feel it. We will drive. I'll drive towards the end so you can get a little shut-eye. Then once we get there, you can get approximately two additional hours. You've operated on less and been sensational."

"Always the cheerleader," Brett answered with a smile.

"It's in my blood. My mama was a cheerleader. Her mama and her mama and..."

"I get it," he said, holding up his hands in mock surrender.

Marla grabbed his hands and put them around her waist. "I love you, Mr. Meadows."

"Yeah, yeah, yeah. I'll drive on one condition."

"And that is?"

"We get a full refund for the tickets."

"But we didn't even pay for our tickets."

When *Multidata Infonet Inc.* selected *2B Mpact* as one of the candidates to pitch its proposal in front of its Board of Directors, they offered to send two round-trip tickets for Marcus and Brett to use. Determining Marcus was better off manning the office, they agreed Marla would go in his place. The CEO of *Multidata* explained the tickets were strictly for business purposes. He offered to send one ticket but to put them up in the *Marriot* for five days – all expenses paid for the honeymoon they never had.

When Brett shared the news with Marla, she assumed the entire trip was compliments of *Multidata Infonet*. He didn't correct her misconception.

"True," Brett lied. "Let's say it's our first step in saving our new client money."

"I like your way of thinking, Mr. Meadows." She kissed Brett on the tip of his nose. "I'll talk to Darryl. Stay here, pleeeaze."

Brett knew not to object.

He watched his beautiful, petite wife bop to the ticket counter.

He'd felt the electricity between them as soon as he entered the Western Civilization *class they took together at* Duke University *during their freshman year of college. Her small, golden-flecked, amber eyes embedded in her kewpie doll face, followed him as he claimed the last empty seat... right next to hers. He wanted to trace the freckles lightly sprinkled along her cheeks. He longed to kiss her upturned pug nose and thin lips. But most importantly, he wanted to run his fingers through her fiery red hair, and down her compact, athletic body. He had fallen for her as soon as he crossed the threshold of that classroom.*

He learned she had a boyfriend, so he settled for being her "pal". Luckily, that union didn't last long. Unfortunately, she started dating others. He did as well. They double-dated a few times. Brett hated those dates. Watching men grope all over "his woman" and not being able to voice his objection in fear of losing her friendship disturbed him. He wished she could see him.

It finally happened Junior year. Marla was upset over her latest breakup. She asked Brett to come over. She told him she needed him (woohoo) and her roommates were gone for the night.

He had a date that evening, but as usual, when Marla called, Brett jumped. He broke-off his date, stopped at his friend's Frat house, and "borrowed" a twelve-pack of beer.

He went to Marla's off-campus apartment. When she opened the door, he noticed her swollen eyes and red nose. Her mascara had left black smudges down her face. He followed her to her bedroom. He sat on her desk chair. She sat in a lotus position on her bed.

"Can you believe Rick dumped me? I've never been dumped."

Marla was used to being the dumper. "He "reconnected" with his ex. This hurt, Brett. It really hurts."

That was difficult for him to understand. They'd only dated three weeks and four days. He kept track of how long each man lasted in her life. He tried to find compassion. He couldn't.

"Marla, he's a fool. Why are you crying over a jerk that couldn't appreciate what he had? I say good riddance!"

He threw her a can of beer. She caught it, opened it, and gulped it down. He opened one for himself. He was halfway through his first when she asked for another. He gladly threw her another. He intended to get her drunk so he could profess his love for her. He was tired of waiting on the sidelines.

"You're right, Brett. There are more fishes in the sea. I'll show him. I'll be back on the dating scene so fast I'll forget all about what's his name."

Marla, you don't have to look. I'm right here, *Brett screamed inwardly. He wished he had the guts to say the words aloud. He took a gulp of beer. After a few more cans, he'll be brave enough to speak the words he'd held back for two years.* On second thought, I don't want to be drunk. Go for it, Brett, *he urged himself.*

"Marla...."

"Brett, pass me another one."

"Don't you think you ought to slow down? You're a light-weight. This is your third one."

"Who are you? My father? Campus police? Lighten up. Let's have some fun."

Brett opened the beer and handed it to her. He moved to the bed to sit beside her. She laid her head on his shoulder. He massaged her neck.

"Ah, that feels so good," she said taking a swig from the can. "Why can't more guys be like you? Did you know...?" She started laughing hysterically.

"What's so funny?" he asked, swallowing a sip from his can – beer number two.

"I'm free," she proclaimed, jumping from the bed. She went to her stereo system and turned on the radio. She turned the dial, stopping

on a station playing slow, sensual music. "Come dance with me."

Brett couldn't. He was turned on just by rubbing her shoulders. Dancing would send him into dangerous territory. "Not a good idea, Marla."

"Throw caution to the wind. Hand me another beer." Again she started laughing. "Come on, friend. Dance with me. It'll make me feel SO good." She was slurring her words. Brett threw her another one. Who was he to try to control her drink intake? She let her hair down. Brett's breath stuck in his throat. She was radiant.

She started a slow, seductive dance, staring into his eyes.

He couldn't take his eyes from her. Her cheeks were rosy as if she was wearing blush, her lips smiling, and her eyes were half-closed. He was mesmerized and so very hard. He wanted to ravish her. He couldn't. He wouldn't.

She threw back her head to guzzle the last of the beer. She grabbed his hand and pulled him to his feet. She started to grind against him. He couldn't take it. He pushed her away.

"Marla, STOP IT! You're drunk! You don't know what you're doing."

What started as a good idea, no longer felt that way. He couldn't take advantage of her. He loved her. He wanted her to love him too. He realized this wasn't the way to do it. He didn't want to be the rebound man. He felt bad about his earlier intentions.

"Yes, I do. I'm reeeeeeee." She had a foolish smirk on her face. She snuggled next to him once more. This time, she wrapped her arms around his neck and pulled herself up so she could wrap her legs around his waist.

"Wove me, rett," she slurred.

"I do, Marla, with all my heart."

"pove it. May wove to me. I nee you. I nee you to fill meee uppppp... up up and awaaaay."

"Marla, let go. You're drunk."

"I am." She giggled. "I fill grrrreat. You may me fill batter. Make wove to me."

She released him, backing away with a sultry look. She slowly unbuttoned her shirt, staring deep into his hazel eyes. Brett couldn't move. He'd wanted to make love to her since freshman year. She slowly removed her shirt. She began unhooking her bra. Common sense slapped him in the face. He tried putting her shirt back on her. She resisted. She started crying.

"Why don't ennyone wan me?"

He was astonished. This was not the strong, confident, no-nonsense cheerleader he knew. What had that jerk done to her in the brief time they dated?

He sat her on the bed. Her shirt fell to the ground. He sat next to her. He pulled her into his arms and comforted her until her cries subsided. He tenderly undressed her and placed her under the covers. She watched him undress down to his underwear. She smiled at the erection straining against his boxers. He slid under the covers next to her naked body. She tried grabbing him. He pushed her hand away, "We're not doing this, Marla."

She protested somewhat. The beers had finally won. She stopped fighting him.

He embraced her tightly. He listened for her even breaths. "I love you, Marla Murphy. I will always protect you. I will never, ever take advantage of you. This is my solemn vow to you."

That night, he proved to himself how much self-control he had.

Later, after the hangover cleared, Marla realized the dangerous games she played that night. She could have been raped - twice.

What a man! She fell hard for Brett Meadows. They began dating. After three months, they made love. They were sober. It was unsullied.

Marla returned with a slip for the rental car and vouchers for a full refund on both tickets.

"I'm impressed," Brett said.

"As you should be. Darryl had to call around for a rental car. There weren't any available at the rental locations here at the airport. Just when he started calling places outside of the airport, a Ms. Anderson from Premier Car Rental called him back. She said she was doing the closing for the day and discovered a car that was returned earlier wasn't properly logged into the system. She said they'd experienced computer problems throughout the day, which could explain the error. Then she rambled on about being glad she caught it because the woman, who was very beautiful... why she throw that in beats me..., that returned it this morning gave them a rough way to go yadda yadda..."

Marla saw Brett's eyes glaze over.

"Earth to Brett..." She snapped her fingers. "As luck will have it, the car is ours. I also got a voucher for a free tank of gas. How you like me now?" Marla bragged, doing a horrible impression of the running man.

Brett grabbed his wife, picked her up, and twirled her around the airport's waiting area. "I likes. I likes a lot Mrs. Marla June Murphy-Meadows. What would I do without you?"

Marla gave her husband a deep, passionate kiss. They released each other to the sounds of claps, whistles, and 'ahs...'

"You're stuck with me for life, Mr."

"Just the way I likes," Brett sang, grabbing his wife's hand as they exited the airport terminal in search of the rental car location.

Darryl watched the exchange in amusement. He was pleased when he was able to satisfactorily accommodate an inconvenienced passenger.

While Meredith stood in line securing new flight arrangements, Brian called a car service. The Winthrop Family left the airport with new tickets for the following week. They stepped into the waiting car. Ian stared silently out of the window, watching the airport and his dreams... his dream of going to New York, his dream of getting the brain tumor removed, and his dream of living a normal life... fade into the distance.

He secretly swatted the tears that hit the corner of his eyes.

He didn't want his ever-watchful mother to see them.

"Ian, sweetie, what's on your mind? Meredith inquired from the seat next to him.

"Nothing, Mommy," he replied, not turning from the window.

"You're awfully quiet. Has your headache returned?"

"No, Mommy. I'm fine," Ian insisted, nervous to wipe another tear. Praying the stress wouldn't trigger a headache or the slurring.

"You're not fine. Talk to..."

"Mer, leave the boy alone. If he says he's fine, he's fine," Brian snapped, tired of the Mother Hen routine.

Thank God for Pop, Ian thought. He knew when to step in and when to say nothing. He was an honorable man. He wished his mother treated him better.

Ian loved his mother. She was overbearing at times and lax at others. She was an enigma. He didn't fully understand her. He didn't think anyone did.

"Brian, there's something wrong with our son. I would think you'd want to know what it is," she challenged.

"It doesn't take a brain surgeon to figure it out." Hearing his own words, Brian flinched. "Oops, sorry! I didn't mean to say that."

Ian broke into hysterical laughter, letting the tears flow freely.

His parents glanced at each other and shrugged. *Why bother trying to make sense out of a teenage boy's behavior?*

Catching their expressions brought another bout of hysterics from Ian. He was laughing so hard, he had to hold his side. Brian's lips twitched, watching his only son's meltdown. It was great to hear him laughing - something he rarely did these days.

With the commotion happening inside the car, the family didn't notice the Town Car pulling smoothly into their circular driveway until it came to a complete stop.

A baffled Lucinda threw open the front door and ran to the car. "Hola Ian, Mrs., Doctor Brian. ¿Qué pasó? Why you here?"

The words tumbled out before the family completely emerged from the car.

"Luci!" Ian cried, opening the car door and running awkwardly into his nanny's waiting arms.

Unable to say Lucinda when he began forming words, he called her Luci. Brian, finding it 'cute' adopted the name.

"Háblame! Dime lo que pasó, cariño?" Lucinda said.

As promised, she taught the infant Ian Spanish. As a result, he was fluent.

"Fue horrible, Luci. I had to sit in a wheelchair. Me enfermé. I threw up..."

Lucinda interrupted. "¿Estás bien, cariño?" she asked, feeling his forehead.

Brian paid the driver while Meredith enviously watched the exchange between her son and his nanny.

She pointed at her gold diamond watch. "It's late, Lucinda. Why are you still here?"

Unperturbed by Meredith's tone, she answered. "My Nando work late. I stay to make sure everything nice and fresh. I not come back for few days so I make things good until next time."

Taking some luggage into the house, Brian said over his shoulder, "It's great to see you, Luci. It's a great welcome home surprise."

"It's great to see you, Luci..." Meredith mumbled under her breath, imitating Brian. *Both of them acting like Lucinda's the second coming. What's the big deal? We just saw her this morning.*

"But what happen?" Lucinda asked, wrapping her arm around Ian to help him walk towards the house.

"I can help my son walk, Lucinda," Meredith said tersely, moving towards Ian. "You may leave now."

Where is this coming from? Brian wondered, returning for the rest of the luggage. *Why the animosity*?

"Mommy, I want Luci to help me get ready for bed... okay?" Ian pleaded, disapproving of the way his mother spoke to his caregiver, his friend.

"All right, dear, but I'll tuck you in and say goodnight in a little bit," Meredith conceded.

"That's fine, Mommy, and thank you." Although he was too old to get "tucked in" he knew the expression on his mother's face too well. *She feels unwanted, unneeded.*

He kissed her on the cheek and whispered, "You're not losing me, Mommy." He winked and tucked his arm into Lucinda's. The two walked unsteadily into the house.

Meredith stared after him in awe. Her heart swelled with pride.

~9~

JADE MORALES

Putting the key in the door, Jade was met with the familiar sounds she so desperately wanted to escape.

Damn that plane, she thought, not for the first time that day.

She should be in Puerto Rico listening to Rosario bitch about everything going wrong with the wedding.Instead of standing in the hallway eavesdropping on her father and Carmen arguing about the same old thing – women.

"These ARE NOT mine, Tony. Whose are they?" Carmen screamed.

"They're yours, Carmen. I bought them for you, remember?" Antonio replied smoothly.

"Papi, you are out of your mind. I know my underwear! Which one of those ho's did you have in our bed this time? Huh, Tony?"

"Carmen, why do you always think the worst? Why don't you trust me?"

Jade burst out laughing. Was he serious? Her father had more women on the side than a pimp had prostitutes. He was amazing. He was fifty-five years old but still couldn't keep his penis in his pants. Jade believed he was a sex addict. He couldn't be with just one woman. He tried, but it never lasted. She was surprised Carmen lasted as long as she had – two long, painful years.

"Maybe because you lie to me all the time, Tony," Carmen

spat.

Maybe, because he was screwing you and your mother at the same time, Jade thought cruelly.

"Baby, I don't lie to you. I swear these are yours. See? I even had them monogrammed. I can't believe you don't remember. I go through the trouble of doing something special for you and this is the thanks I get. Nagging! Women! You know what, Carmen? I'm leaving. I'm not staying with someone who doesn't trust me."

Way to go, Papá. Make her feel guilty for your actions.

The panties belonged to one of his side pieces – Camille Noble – who had the same initials as Carmen Nolte. Jade was with him when he bought the expensive panty and bra set. Camille must have purposely left them for Carmen to find. Jade knew her father would go off on Camille the next time he saw her. IF there was a next time. There were rules. Camille just broke one of them.

Jade had to give her father his props. He was smooth.

She heard shuffling behind the closed bedroom door.

"Let go of me, Carmen."

In a little girl's voice, Carmen said, "Oh Papi, I'm sorry. I do remember. Please forgive your Carmita. I don't know how I forgot. They're beautiful – so soft and silky."

Yuck, she can't possibly be touching another woman's smelly drawers, thought Jade. *How gross.*

"I swear I trust you. Now come to your little Carmita, Papi."

How do you spell desperate? C A R M E N. Jade would have laughed if it wasn't so pathetic. A few minutes later she heard the mattress creaking. She went into her bedroom and softly shut the door, disgusted with them both. She plugged her iPod into her stereo system, put on her earphones, and listened to one of her favorite artists – *Stephanie McKay*. She loved her music. McKay had roots in The Bronx like her, Ron K. Taylor, and J.Lo.

Blocking out the activities in the other room, Jade sang to McKay's song *'Jackson Avenue'*, becoming more and more relaxed with each lyric – *"Back in the day, on the block, we'd be playing handball, till the streetlights came on..."* Jade loved that song. It brought back sweet memories of her childhood, growing up in the South Bronx. She continued to hum to the lyrics. *"B-Boys round the way they be calling our names...."*

After the song, she promised to call Rosario.

BRETT AND MARLA MEADOWS

"Watch out!" Marla shrieked in panic.

"What? What happened?" A groggy Brett asked, jerking the car back into his lane.

"You nodded off and swerved into the next lane," Marla replied, calmer than she felt.

"Really? I'm sorry," he said. "I told you, I'm not a good night driver."

Brett and Marla were successful in renting the car and were four hours outside of Charlotte.

"I should have listened," Marla admitted. "You were right. We should have taken our chances with the flight in the morning. We'd be comfortable and well-rested in a nice roach motel by the airport, instead of having near misses with oncoming traffic."

"It won't happen again. I'll put in a Bonnie Raitt CD."

"I have a better idea. Pullover and let me drive."

"Sweetie, I'm fine. I just dozed for a sec. When we stop for gas, I'll get an enormous cup of java."

"Brett, if the car in the other lane hadn't swerved, we would have hit it?"

"Marla, are you listening? I got this. Once I get coffee, I'll be okay."

"Yeah, but then we'll have to stop every few miles for you to pee. No thanks. We'll never get to New York at that rate. Pullover and let me drive. I'm not tired. I have Taylor Swift, Dolly Parton, Billy Ray Cyrus, and Keith Urban to keep me company."

"Yikes! The woman wants to torture me. I said I was sorry. I didn't mean to nod off. I promise to stay in my lane. Please, please don't punish me."

Marla laughed. Brett was a rock-and-roll, Bluesman. Country music made his teeth hurt.

"You know I love country music, Mr. Brett Meadows. Why should you care what I listen to? You'll be asleep before your backside hits the passenger seat. Now pullover!"

Conceding, he pulled off at the next gas station exit, filled the tank, and got comfortable in the passenger seat. By the time Marla returned with two coffees and a half dozen donuts - nothing like sugar to keep you going - Brett Meadows was out like a light.

Grinning, she put Brett's coffee in his cup holder, plucked a glazed donut from the box, and placed the donut box on the back seat of the *Ford Focus*. She adjusted the driver's seat, the mirrors, put *Once in a Lifetime* in the CD player, and buckled herself in before pulling smoothly out of the gas station.

Glancing over at Brett, Marla pressed play on the CD player saying, "I guess it's just you and me, Keith."

~10~

THE WINTHROP FAMILY

"What's your problem?" Brian hissed after Meredith closed the front door behind them.

"Nothing," she answered sulkily, stomping to their bedroom.

Lucinda was always around, doing everything for her family. Her family. Her son and her husband. Brian and Ian entrusted Lucinda with everything. EVERYTHING!! They seemed to prefer the housekeeper over her. She was sick of it.

Meredith peered at her reflection in the master bathroom mirror. A violet-eyed monster stared back, asking, "*Why are you being spiteful? You relinquished the care of your family to a stranger over twelve-years-ago. You've confided just as much to Lucinda as everyone else in this house. She's kept your family going, allowing you the freedom to do your dirt, so get over yourself.*"

Deep down, she knew the real problem – Lucinda knew her secret.

Several months earlier, Meredith was in her bathroom on her secret prepaid phone, arguing with the caller about her needs. Entering her bedroom, she spotted a flabbergasted Lucinda standing inside the bedroom door. Meredith quickly disconnected the call but knew it was too late. From the shock registered on Lucinda's face, she'd heard too much of the conversation.

At first, she ripped into the housekeeper for walking into her private sanctuary without acknowledging her presence.

Lucinda enlightened her employer. "I knock and call. When no answer I come in like every morning."

Meredith begged, pleaded, and cried, trying to describe her addiction.

Lucinda sighed. "I do not tell Doctor Brian, but I worry for you. This is dangerous. You get hurt. Please stop."

Meredith looked directly into Lucinda's eyes and whispered, "I've tried, but I can't."

Then she told Lucinda everything. She was relieved. She had someone to confide in. Someone she could trust. Someone who wouldn't judge her. She was no longer alone. She felt lighthearted.

Lucinda kept her word, but her knowing made Meredith nervous.

Meredith was overwrought from the long day. She was also disappointed they weren't in New York. That's what she convinced herself of so she wouldn't feel guilty about her treatment of Lucinda.

In one week, we'll be in New York.

She washed her face and brushed her teeth. When she exited the bathroom, Brian was leaning back in the recliner in the sitting area just off the master bedroom.

"Feeling better?" He inquired, studying her.

"A little tired," she replied.

"We all are, Meredith," he said.

It didn't sound like he was talking about the day's event. She was fearful to ask him to elaborate. Instead, she said, "I'm going to say good night to Ian."

Brian didn't comment, just continued examining her.

Meredith left their bedroom with an uneasy feeling settling in her bones. *Something isn't right,* she thought, walking towards Ian's room.

She found him on his knees saying his prayers. She stood silently by the opened door, admiring her handsome son. He had gone through so much, yet he always had a ready smile for everyone. Her heart surged with the love she felt for him.

"Amen," he said, getting up slowly from his knees. "Came to say good night?" He questioned, spotting her in the doorway.

"Sure did." Meredith noticed Lucinda's absence. "Where's Lucinda?"

"She left. I told her what happened at the airport while she was helping me get ready for bed. She was furious. It was so funny. Her Spanglish is hilarious when she's upset."

Meredith smiled with her son.

"Are you okay with what's happening, Ian?"

"Oh sure. I know God has plans for me," he said slowly but deliberately, getting underneath his covers.

"How do you feel about what happened today?"

Ian stared at her contemplating the question. A scowl flashed across his face. "Honestly, Mommy, I was angry, disappointed, and confused. But I talked with Luci. She says everything happens for a reason. I can't understand why God would let them cancel the flight but like you said it has nothing to do with God. This tumor and these headaches are my crosses to bear."

"Ian, you're too young to have 'crosses to bear'," Meredith said, chuckling. "You do believe the tumor and headaches will be gone next week, don't you?"

"Absolutely," Ian replied with conviction.

"That's it! Stay positive." She bent down and kissed her son. "I love you, Ian. Sleep well."

"I will, Mommy." He gave her a tight embrace and kissed her cheek. "Don't worry about a thing. Everything will be fine."

Meredith was taken aback. Ian hadn't hugged her that tight since he was a small boy frightened of a charging dog that broke out of its yard and ventured into theirs. The dog growled and barked at them. Ian grabbed Meredith around her neck, trying to crawl into her body. Brian was successful in shooing the dog back into its yard before it bit anyone.

She smiled. He hadn't slurred during their entire conversation. Meredith was thrilled. "That's my boy. I love your attitude! God helps those who help themselves."

"I finally understand what that means."

"Good! Your father is coming in shortly to say good night. I'll let him turn out your light."

"Thanks, Mommy."

"See you in the morning."

Before she reached the door, Ian called, "Mommy, you are the best mother in the whole wide world, even with your faults."

Meredith returned to the room and sat on the bed, goose-bumps dancing on her body. "Why'd you say that, honey?"

"Because..." He drawled, "... no one's perfect. Not even you."

Meredith presented an uneasy smile. An alarm was sounding softly in her head. "Why are you saying this, honey?"

"Because, I don't tell you how much I appreciate you. None of us do. You're a magnificent person. I love you, Mommy."

Magnificent? Tears threatened to fill Meredith's eyes. *Where is this coming from*?

Fear was trickling down her spine. Something was off. She felt it. She inspected her son closely. There was a sparkle of life in his eyes she hadn't seen in a long time. Maybe she was being paranoid. She shrugged off the nagging feelings making the hairs on the back of her neck do a military salute.

Brian filled the doorway. "Hey, Bud, came to say goodnight. It's late. You must get your rest to keep up your strength."

"I think that's my cue to leave," Meredith joked. "I'll let you have your male-bonding time. Sweetheart, thank you. I love you very, very, very much."

They hugged tightly. Meredith kissed his forehead.

Ian flashed a smile.

Meredith left the room. Dread followed closely behind.

~11~

JADE MORALES

It was 11:00 before anyone discovered Jade was home. Manny tried sneaking his girlfriend, Heather, into Jade's room. Something he's done on occasions when he knew she wouldn't be home (which was rare). Her room was on the opposite end of the hall from their father's and next to the staircase, making it easier to sneak his girlfriend in and out without detection.

Manny opened the door to Jade's darkened room, leading Heather inside without turning on the light. Kissing her deeply, one hand under her half-opened blouse, the other on her round bottom, teenage hormones racing, he led her to the bed. As he laid her down, he felt an additional body underneath theirs. The three bodies jumped up simultaneously.

"What the...?" Jade hissed, stomping to the light and switching it on.

Light flooded the room, catching an embarrassed Manny zipping up his fly.

Shocked at seeing Jade, he whispered, "What are you doing here?"

Heather, red as a tomato, was busy stuffing her young breasts inside of her too-small bra and buttoning up her blouse, missing buttonholes along the way. She muttered an awkward "hello" before bolting from the house and into Manny's car to wait for a ride home.

"Uh... hey Jade," Manny said sheepishly. "What's up? Why are you home?"

"Don't 'hey Jade' me Emanuel Josef Morales," Jade spat angrily. "What are you thinking? Obviously, you're not thinking. At least not with the head on your neck," She hissed, tapping his head with her fist. "Why are you bringing Heather into MY room? ¿Estás loco? Papá's down the hall. Do you know what'll happen if he catches you having sex in his house?"

Manny was speechless. He was busted. There was no sense in denying his intentions, but he needed a good reason why he was about to get busy in her room.

Weakening under her unwavering gaze, he told the truth. "Heather and I went to the movies and started kissing and..."

"Spare me the details, Manny. Just... why my room?"

"Because, I didn't see your car, and your room is next to the stairs, and far from Papá's, and he wouldn't hear us, and I have to pass your room to get to mine so it's easier to come in here, and my room is messy, and I didn't see your car so I didn't know you were home. Stop me anytime, Sis."

Jade stared at Manny for several minutes. She wasn't as young as Manny and Heather when she began having sex, but who was she to judge. She remembered how she felt with Oscar. She blinked back the tears. She wouldn't let those emotions engulf her... not now, not in front of her brother who she wanted to get mad at but couldn't. *He **is** Papá's son.*

With a stern look, she asked, "Were you at least going to change the sheets?"

Taken aback, Manny stared at her for a complete second before breaking into a goofy grin. He hugged her. "Ah shucks, Sis. Good to see you. Why are you here?"

Jade led her younger brother to the bottom of the bed. They sat down. "The flight was cancelled. I'm booked on a 9:45 a.m. flight straight to San Juan. When I told your sister, she had a hissy fit. Yelling at ME! Telling ME I'm purposely trying to ruin her wedding. She is unbelievable. Like **I** cancelled the flight. Manny, Rosario isn't getting married for another two weeks. Give me a break."

"Did Viviana make it?"

"Sí. Ella no tenía ningún problema. She said Rosario is driving everyone crazy. She's behaving like she's the Queen of England."

Manny chuckled. "Well, we'll be there soon for support. I better get Heather home. Does Papá know you're here?"

"No, and I'm trying to keep it that way. I'm hoping to sneak out in the morning. He and Carmen argued over some woman's panties she found in their bed. You know how they get when they're making up. I don't think they've come up for air since I got in."

Manny snickered. "Yeah, boy, Papá's the man."

"Manny, don't idolize Papá for that. Remember, Papá's Mima died during childbirth and his Papá deserted him when he was ten. He was thrown into different foster homes. I believe he was abused in some of them. He doesn't talk about his past but I think that's why he treats women the way he does."

"My sister, the psychoanalysis."

"Manny, I'm serious. Women are precious. Your mother and sisters are women. Always respect other women the way you respect us."

Properly chastised, Manny kissed Jade on her cheek. "I will, Sis. Have a safe trip. Give everyone hugs and kisses from me when you get to PR."

"I will... and Manny?" Jade said as he headed for the door.

Stopping, he turned around. "Yes?"

"Make sure you wear a raincoat. I'm not taking care of any more babies."

Manny blushed. "J!"

"I'm serious! No babies!"

"I got this, Sis. I know what I'm doing."

Manny tried to escape, but Jade stopped him once again. "Man?"

Sighing, he turned around. "Yes?"

"I love you. Know that."

He looked at her peculiarly. "Ah, Sis, you're going away for a couple of weeks not dying. I'll see you soon."

"I have this weird feeling that something is going to happ...." She stopped herself, laughing nervously. Not wanting to alarm her little brother, she said, "Don't mind me. I'm tired. It's been one heck of a day."

Manny searched her face. She smiled. He relaxed. He started for the door once more. Just before completely exiting, he turned, grinned, and said, "off the record, I love you too."

Jade grinned, watching her handsome, respectable brother quietly leave the room. She was very proud of the man he was becoming.

She turned off the light, returned to bed, and once again pulled the covers over her head. Thoughts of her lost love, Oscar, penetrated her brain. With all of her might, she desperately tried to ward off the memories. They were too strong. She no longer had the strength to fight them. She relaxed.

She was transported to the first apartment they lived in when her family relocated to Charlotte ten years earlier. She snickered over the anger she felt when discovering there were only two bedrooms. She was a grown woman – nineteen almost twenty is grown, right? Manny was seven. At least they got the master bedroom. Jade chuckled.

Restlessly she flipped over.

Those sea-green-eyes, that olive skin, those deep, deep dimples sucked her back into that Riverside Terrace apartment complex.

"Jade, are you sure you want to do this?" Oscar asked for the 100th time.

"I... am... positive!" she exclaimed slowly and purposefully.

"There's no rush. We have the rest..."

She silenced him with a passionate kiss.

"I want your first time to be perfect," he declared, staring lovingly into her eyes.

"How can it not be? I'm with the perfect guy. Now please let's stop talking. I've waited for you for over a year. I'm twenty-one. I AM READY!" She announced, pulling Oscar's shirt up over his head, re-

vealing a chest sprinkled lightly with dark hair.

*"**You've** waited?" He snickered. "You've been forced to wait, my dear. How many times have you tried to jump my bones?"*

"Oscar, please!" she cried desperately. "I want you. I can't wait any longer. I'm ready. I promise. I am. I love you with everything I have."

Jade nibbled on his left earlobe, licking his quarter karat diamond earring seductively.

Oscar buried his head in the crevice of her naked, erect breasts. He felt like he would explode, but was willing to suffer to make her first time as painless and enjoyable as humanly possible.

She ran her fingers through his loose curls, kissing every inch of his face.

"Princesita?"

Jade leisurely got up from the couch, stood in front of him, legs apart, and unbuttoned her skirt. It fell to the floor, joining her blouse, bra, and underwear.

Oscar's erection struggled to get out of his jeans.

Alluringly, she started walking towards her bedroom, gesturing over her shoulder for him to follow.

Peering at her well-sculptured, hour-glass figure, he knew he had lost the war. He quickly jumped up and followed his "Princesita" into the room she shared with her brother.

Jade was already on the bed awaiting her lover.

Oscar went to the bed and gently pulled Jade to him. Her heart swelled with the love she felt for him. She wanted him to feel that love. She grabbed his head and kissed him fervently, desperately trying to unbutton his jeans.

He pulled away.

"Honey, I want your first time to be special. Let's not rush. Your father and Manny are away for the weekend and Nia is with Madison. We have two days alone together. Woman, this will be a day you will never forget. Just let me do it my way – easy like a Sunday morning."

"But it's Friday," she joked, grabbing for him.

"Woman, please! I got this."

Jade gave in. "I love you, Oscar!"

"And I you, mi Princesita."

With that, he undressed, got into the bed, and took her on a journey she would never forget.

Jade reminisced over the sweet way he made love to her – the excruciating pain, and the immense pleasure. Neither of them had to go into work. They spent the whole weekend exploring each other. She knew every inch of Oscar's body – from the scar on his knee, which scabbed over, to the birthmark on the back of his shoulder. It was the best weekend of her entire twenty-one-years of life.

She flipped over once more. The emptiness within her body was so intense she could barely breathe. She felt the emotions bubbling over. She stuck her head in her pillow and cried herself to sleep.

ϟ ϟ ϟ ϟ ϟ ϟ

BRETT & MARLA MEADOWS

"Brett, can you see? I can't," Marla declared from the passenger seat.

"Barely," Brett answered. "The rain's getting worse."

When they entered Washington DC, Marla woke Brett to drive. It was pouring. They were traveling well-lit I-95 with windshield wipers at full speed, yet visibility was difficult. The construction on the highway added to their inability to see.

"Maybe we should pull over to wait it out," the level-headed Marla suggested.

"Maybe, but that'll add more time to our trip."

"True, but it's pouring, Brett. We can't see two feet in front of us. It's starting to flood. Surely, the client will understand if you're a little late."

Brett contemplated his options: risk an accident or risk

being late.

"Tell you what...we'll pull over for about twenty minutes. Then we'll continue – rain or no rain. We're about 4 ½ - 5 hours from New York. Driving the speed limit should get us there between 8:30 and 9:00."

"Sounds good to me. Do you want to take a snooze while we're waiting?"

"No," Brett answered, expertly steering the car onto the right shoulder of I-95. "Let's talk or smooch but hand me a donut, please."

Marla reached over, grabbed her husband by the neck, and gave him a long, deep, fervent kiss.

Coming up for air, Brett said, "Whoa...what was that?"

Laughing she said, "Now that the smooching is out of the way, we can talk."

She reached in the back seat to get the donuts. She handed Brett a glazed one and his lukewarm coffee, and took a donut for herself.

Donuts completed, they snuggled and talked about their future - watching the rain plummeting against their windshield.

THE NEXT DAY

Day 2

Each decision you make is a gamble you take.

~12~

BRETT & MARLA MEADOWS

"Brett?"

"Yes, Marla," Brett said in a tone between sleep and consciousness.

"Are you falling asleep?"

"No, Marla," he said as an enormous yawn betrayed him. Thirty minutes had elapsed since they pulled off the road. He stretched, trying to wake himself. The steady, rhythmic beat of the rain against their window wasn't helping. He was extremely tired. He should have followed his instinct and checked into a hotel for the night.

"Good! I have a confession to make."

"This isn't your deathbed. Confessions aren't necessary," he joked.

"If I should die before we get to New York, I pray to Brett my confession to fork." She teased in the rhythm of "Now I Lay Me Down to Sleep". The prayer she recited as a young child every night before going to bed.

"What is it you wish to confess, my child?" Brett asked, adopting the voice of a priest. "By the way, that rhyme was awful."

They laughed.

Sobering, Marla said, "Remember the night I asked you to come over? I said what's his name dumped me."

"Ah, one of my fondest memories." He grinned.

"Why? Because you tried to get me drunk?"

"Now, now, now, darling, if we're telling the truth, let's be totally honest. I didn't **try** to do anything. I did get you drunk."

They chuckled.

"Well, I lied."

"You and Rick didn't break-up?"

"He didn't dump me. I learned earlier in the week that he was seeing me and his "ex", current girlfriend. They never broke up. I was pissed. My roommates were gone for the weekend. I invited him over. I put on a sexy, see-through, cream negligee. When I opened the door, Rick's eyes bulged from his head. He knew he was getting lucky that night. He and I never did the do. Something about it or him didn't feel right."

"Marla, I knew you weren't a virgin. It didn't bother me then or now. I don't want to hear how you slept with him. I heard enough of those stories when we were "pals".

That was true. It was why she enjoyed their friendship. She could talk freely about the men she slept with. He never judged her. He didn't talk about his sexual conquest. She wondered why but appreciated that quality.

"You need to hear this one," Marla said. "I pulled him into the apartment and pushed him on the couch. We started making out. His hands were everywhere."

"Is there a point to this confession?" Brett didn't want to hear it. Their college days were behind them.

"Please have patience. There's a reason I'm telling you this."

Brett sighed, leaned back in the driver's side chair, and closed his eyes. With any luck, he'd fall asleep.

I pushed Rick away. It was difficult. That boy didn't want to let me go. My cheerleading training helped me get away from him. I told him if he was patient, I'd be worth the wait. I had a playlist downloaded. I connected my phone to the apartment speakers. When that first slow song came on and I started dancing, I thought Rick was going to bust in his pants. It took all I had to make that boy lay there and watch the show.

"I understand how the poor slob felt. You are a master seductress."

After five minutes, he couldn't take any more. He grabbed me. He said to stop teasing him. To give him what he came for.

I played innocent. "Rick," I said. "I thought you loved me. That's what you told me last week. Are you only trying to get in my panties?"

He hesitated briefly. At the time he was sucking on my neck. "Aw, girl, you know I love you. You're the only girl I want." Now he's kissing my neck and other places, but I'll spare you those details."

"You're so kind," Brett said sarcastically.

Marla reached over and gave him a long, passionate kiss. "I'm almost at the good part."

"Make it quick. I don't like this story!"

"Am I really the only girl for you, Rick? Really and truly?" I asked him.

"I'm a darn good actress. I may be a redhead but ditsy blonde is my specialty." She smiled in the dark before continuing.

"Why are we still talking?" Rick grumbled. "There's no one else. Trust me, babe."

"What about Vicki? I heard you two are still hooking up."

His lips paused - briefly. I moaned like I was enjoying his filthy lips all over my body when in fact my skin was crawling.

"Who?" he asked. His voice was muffled.

"Vicki," I said in a low sultry voice and moaned again for good measure.

"I broke up with that bitch a while ago. It's you I want, not her. Enough talking."

He reached for the straps of my gown to pull them down.

"So... you broke up with this bitch a long time ago, huh?" Vicki said, storming from my bedroom.

"Rick moved away from me like I had leprosy. I was tired of playing his game. When I found out he was seeing both Vicki and me, I got her number from a mutual friend. I called her, told her

Rick was seeing me, but she didn't believe me. I explained that we had a date that evening and if she wanted to know the truth, to come to my place. Reluctantly, she agreed, but only to prove me wrong. She said Rick told her he had a fraternity meeting that evening and he didn't lie to her. It took everything I had not to laugh. I made her hide and promise not to come out of my room until she had proof of his cheating. Begrudgingly, she agreed. Back to that night."

Vicki jumped in his face. I could tell she'd been crying. "I wish this bitch had known that this morning and last night when she was screwing your brain out."

Rick was speechless. I felt bad for her. She actually cared for the jerk.

"Vic..."

"Save it, Rick. This bitch, the one you don't want, don't want you either. We're through. I mean it this time. I saw you with my own eyes. I heard every disgusting word." She stormed towards the door.

"Vic, let me explain."

"Explain what Rick?" Vicki stopped, turned, and put her hands on her cute little hips. "Explain how Marla is the one you really want?"

Rick stuttered. He really screwed that one up.

I saw the tears sliding down her attractive face. I saw the pain. I felt guilty.

"Save it." Vicki opened the door.

"Wait!" I screamed after her. "You're forgetting something."

"He's all yours, honey." She slammed the door with so much force I thought it was going to fall from its hinges. Rick and I were both speechless. I found my voice first.

"Well, it's been fun. Time for you to follow your girlfriend."

Rick grabbed me. "You conniving little slut. I can't believe you set me up. You just screwed up my life. I love Vicki."

"Then why are you here, Rick?"

"Because, I'm a man. God didn't intend for us to be with only one woman."

Yet he only gave you one penis, *I wanted to shout, but I didn't want to debate with him. I just wanted him gone.*

"I may have lost her for good this time. It's all because of you and your little game, you conniving tramp."

"So none of this is your fault? I didn't even know you were still seeing her. You told me you two were done."

"Would you have screwed me if you knew I was still with her?"

He knew the answer. "Rick, please, just leave," I begged.

He laughed. "She got jokes. You're crazy if you think I'm going to let you fuck up my life then leave without getting what I came for."

"He grabbed me and threw me to the floor like I was a ragdoll. He straddled me. I kicked him in the balls and scurried backward on my hands and feet. Like I said, cheerleading taught me skills. I stood up, ran back to him while he was doubled over, and punched him in his back. He fell to the ground. He recovered quicker than I expected. I tried to run, like I should have done when he was down instead of thinking I was Bruce Lee. He grabbed my hair. We fell back to the floor. He straddled me again. This time he trapped my legs with his. He tried ripping my gown. That sucker wouldn't rip – thank God. It was one of my favorite negligees. I ended up throwing it away, anyway. It was a reminder of that night. My panties weren't as durable. He ripped those things right off. I was fighting and screaming like a crazy person. I think I broke his nose. I hope I did. There was a lot of blood.

"My roommate, Kendra and her boyfriend, Wayne heard the commotion. They rushed through the unlocked door. Wayne grabbed him off of me. He whipped Rick good. Kendra held me in her arms. I cried. She made Wayne stop. Wayne said, "If you so much as look in Marla's direction, I'll finish you off **and** report this attempted rape to the proper authorities. You'll not only lose your lacrosse scholarship, but will get kicked out of school, AND go to jail. I promise you. Now get to running, scumbag."

"One of his eyes was swelling. It was half-closed. His nose was dripping blood on our hardwood floor. He was holding his side when he limped out the door."

~13~

Tears slid down Brett's face. "I'm sorry you went through that, honey. Why didn't you tell me?"

"Because, I couldn't risk you getting kicked off the basketball team, out of school, or going to jail. Your mother already hates me."

"She doesn't hate you," Brett said weakly.

"I've accepted it," Marla said, returning to the subject at hand. "Brett you would have done more damage than Wayne. I'm glad Wayne was a third-degree black belt. He knew how much pain to inflict to get his point across without impacting Rick's livelihood."

"I have to thank him next time I see him."

Marla shrugged. "Like you said – it's in the past. We've never talked about it after that night. I must tell you how much I admire Kendra. Remember, I'm wearing a skimpy, little see-through gown with no underwear on. Kendra didn't bat an eye when I hugged Wayne. I was so emotional I didn't give a thought to what I was wearing or rather not wearing. I told Wayne he was my hero, kissed him on his lips, and hugged him tightly. Kendra's response was, "We're glad we came home when we did."

"I agreed, Brett. That maniac would have raped me if they hadn't shown up when they did."

Brett was furious. It was a good thing Marla chose now to confess. He tried letting it go. "Kendra is amazing. If that had been Alice and her boyfriend, she probably would have slugged you if you hugged him dressed like that."

Alice was their other roommate. She was a pretty, spoiled, insecure, rich girl. She created drama wherever she went.

"True," Marla said. "He would have tried to cop a feel while I was hugging him. Those two were made for each other."

Brett never revealed the stunt Alice pulled when he waited for Marla one day in her apartment. He and Marla were going to a play. She had a late afternoon class so she asked him to meet her at her place. He agreed, hoping Kendra would be there. He enjoyed talking with her. As luck would have it, Alice was there alone.

When Alice let him in, she was wearing sweat shorts and an oversized men's shirt. He told her he was meeting Marla and she'd be home shortly. Alice was all smiles. She offered him a drink and turned the television on for him. He sat back with the bottle of soda in his hand, watching a Law and Order *rerun.*

Fifteen minutes later, Alice screamed from inside her bedroom. He ran to see why. She was spread eagle on her bed buck naked. She told him she'd seen a spider. The smile on her face belied her words. He turned to leave. She bolted from the bed, closing the door to block his exit.

"What are you doing?" he asked.

She threw her arms around him and tried to kiss him. He pushed her away.

She said, "You may as well kiss me. I'm going to tell Marla you did. I won't be able to live with the guilt." She smirked. She grabbed his hands and put them on her ass. "Get a feel of how good I am. Why get into an argument over innocence? Make it worth your while." He snatched his hands away as if scorched. She started laughing. She had a beautiful smile.

Brett stared at the 5'3" platinum blonde beauty in disgust before pushing her aside. He yanked open her door, walked out of her room, and right into Kendra.

Alice came to the door, naked... smiled at Kendra, winked at Brett, and said, "Come back anytime you want some more." She closed the door behind her.

Brett was nervous and embarrassed. He grabbed Kendra's hand and led her to the couch. Kendra hadn't uttered a word.

"I swear on my life, Kendra. I didn't do anything with that girl. Please, believe me. I know it looks bad. She said there was a spider in her room. That's the only reason I was in there. I didn't know she was naked. She had on clothes when she let me in. Please, believe me. I swear I'll tell Marla everything."

"Tell me what?" Marla asked, entering the apartment.

Brett was terrified.

Kendra got up from the couch, hugged Marla hello, and grabbed a pillow from the couch. Alice entered the living room, fully clothed once more. She leaned against the wall. Brett squirmed with fear. She sneered.

"Will someone tell me what's going on?" Marla questioned, looking from one to the other.

"Oh nothing," Kendra said, casually. "Brett was trying to kill a black widow in Alice's room. He knows how much you hate spiders." She threw the pillow at Alice, winked at Brett, and walked out of the room.

"Did you get it?" Marla questioned.

"Not yet," Alice answered, throwing the pillow at Brett. "But I'm sure he will... next time." She switched back into her room.

Marla kissed Brett then went into her room to change, not giving the scene in the living room another thought.

Kendra returned to the living room. Brett thanked her.

"No worries. She tried the same thing with Wayne."

"You are amazing," he said and meant it.

"So are you," she said. "You and Marla are perfect for each other. Just sorry it took the two of you so long to see what Wayne and I have known the whole time."

Brett gave her a hug. They never spoke of that moment again, and he never went to Marla's apartment if she wasn't there.

Marla said, "That's not my only confession."

"We don't need to tell each other EVERYTHING," Brett said, having no intention of ever telling her the Alice story. "If we reveal all of our secrets now, there won't be anything to talk about in our golden years."

Marla grinned. "Please, I've got to do this."

At Brett's nod, she said, "Rick wasn't the only one I set-up that night."

At first, he was puzzled. Realization struck harder than Hammerin' Hank Aaron hitting his 30th home run. "Me?"

"Yes, you. I was a mess after everything that went down. Kendra and Wayne weren't supposed to come home that day. They were heading for the mountains for the weekend. Kendra left the lodging information and her phone in her room. For an entire year after the incident, I thanked God every night for sending them back. Alice and her boyfriend had gone to his parent's house for the weekend. No one was going to be around. Neither Kendra nor Wayne wanted me staying there alone in case Rick was foolish enough to come back. Honestly, I wasn't too keen on the idea either, but I told them I'd be fine. They wouldn't listen. They were prepared to cancel their trip to babysit me. I couldn't let them do that."

"I'll call Brett to come over."

"I noticed the exchanged glances. Wayne had a weird look on his face."

Kendra said, "Brett has a date tonight. He's unavailable."

"I could tell she didn't like divulging that information. Something in my face must have told them my genuine feelings for you."

Brett sat straight up in his seat. "Your... your... true feelings for me? You mean..." Marla shushed him once more.

"How do you know?"

"I ran into him at Starbucks. *I asked him what his plans were for the weekend. He said he was taking Marsha O'Neil to the movies."*

I was a little put out. YOU never told ME you had a date

with her. Marsha O'Neil, of all people. She was the biggest slut at *Duke*.

"She wasn't the biggest slut, Marla," Brett amended. "At least I knew where I stood with her. There was no pretense."

"Well, you should thank me for saving you. She probably had a disease."

"I wore a condom every time I slept with anyone, my pet."

"Not every time," she remarked snidely before continuing her confession.

"Why are you upset, Marla?" Kendra asked. "Aren't you and Brett just 'friends'?"

"Weren't you just in a relationship with Rick?" Wayne asked.

He and Kendra couldn't keep the humor from their voices.

"What's so funny?"

"Come here. Sit down," Kendra said. Wayne sat beside me on the couch. Kendra knelt before me. They each took a hand.

"Why don't you admit you like Brett Meadows as more than a friend?" she asked me.

I started crying again. "Because he doesn't feel the same about me."

Brett sucked in a breath.

"I have loved Brett Meadows since he walked into my Western Civilization class. He came in full of confidence. Not a strand of his straight, honey-blond hair out of place. He's so handsome."

"I couldn't hide my smile from them. You are still very handsome."

The blush creeped up his boyishly attractive- face settling in his beautiful hazel eyes. Although only 6'2", he was a force to be reckon with on the basketball court. He'd maintained his physique by working out on a regular basis.

"Once I got to know you, I fell in love with you. You were the whole package. That's why I broke it off with Gary, but then you started seeing Helen. I could not NOT be in a relationship when you were in one, so I started dating Tanner."

"Honey, don't you see what the two of you are doing?" Kendra asked. "Brett doesn't want to miss out on those double dates with you, so he makes sure he always has a date when you have one."

"But he has someone even when I don't," I said.

"Not for long." Wayne pointed out. "Marla, I see the way he looks at you. That boy has it bad."

"Call him," they urged. "If he comes running over, that'll prove what we're saying is true. The boy likes you... a lot. If he doesn't, we aren't going anywhere this weekend."

Kendra took my hands. "Honey, trust us."

"What am I going to say?"

"Tell him you dumped Rick, the bastard."

"Brett won't come over for that. I've dumped lots of guys."

"She's right, Wayne." Kendra thought for a moment. "I got it. Tell him Rick dumped you."

"He'll never believe that," I said. "I don't get dumped."

Kendra rolled her eyes and Wayne laughed.

"There's a first time for everything, darling," Wayne said, handing me the phone.

"I called you and you fell for it. When I told them you were coming they high-fived each other, patted each other on the back, and told me to clean myself up. Kendra yelled, "Don't wash your face. Let him see the tear tracks."

"Once they felt I was presentable and knew you were definitely coming, they left. I love those two."

Brett was silent for so long, Marla thought he was angry with her.

"Are you mad?"

"Hell no! I'm glad you finally let your feelings known. I was tired of pretending I was okay with being just your friend. Those double dates killed me."

"Me too," Marla admitted. "Watching those girls feed you and wipe your mouth with their tongues. I'm surprised I never puked all over the table."

"Come here, you."

Marla met Brett in the middle of the console. They kissed hungrily.

"There's one more thing," Marla said when they came up for air.

"What now?" He asked. "I'm done with hearing confessions. We wasted two years because neither of us had the guts to tell the other how we really felt. I thank God for Kendra and Wayne."

"Ditto. I wish we could see them more, but with our busy lives and the birth of their third child, it's so difficult to get together."

"Especially now that they're living in Boston."

"Marla, once we get settled in New York, why don't we arrange to see them. Hopefully, they're not on vacation."

"What a marvelous idea. We owe them so much, and we haven't seen our godson, Jax, in over a year. He must be about four now."

"I think so. Jax may be in school. Call them while I'm meeting with *Multidata Infonet Inc*. It'd be great to see them. But first I want to see you... all of you."

"Wait!" Marla said, blocking his kiss. "There's one more thing."

Brett was getting irritated. "What is it, Marla?"

"I heard your promise when you thought I was asleep."

"What promise?"

'I will always protect you. I will never, ever take advantage of you. This is my solemn vow to you.'

"I thought you had passed out. I never intended..."

She silenced him with a kiss. "I will remember those sweet words for the rest of my life, Mr. Brett Meadows. After the day I had, that promise couldn't have come at a better time. That's when I fell completely head over heels in love with you." She kissed him again.

All these years... she never once mentioned she'd heard him.

He crawled into the backseat. He moved the empty donut

container to the front passenger side floor and pushed the front seat up. He pulled Marla on top of him in the back.

"I meant them, Marla. You are my everything. There is no life without you! I love you, Mrs. Meadows."

Their need for each other was over-powering. They made love like two starving people who hadn't eaten in months. Their hips matched the rhythm of the rain pounding on the roof of the rental car.

~14~

JANICE MONROE

Janice walked through her house for the second time, making sure the windows and doors were secured.

After returning from the airport the previous evening, she spoke with her three sons. They'd arrived in Austin to spend the first month of their summer vacation with their estranged father without incident.

They rambled on and on about the wonderful city their father lived in and the many excursions he'd planned for them.

"Texas has beautiful homes, friendly people, a statue of Texas Blues Guitarist, Steve Ray Vaughn, the Ziker Park Summer Musical, and The Austonian," The boys informed her.

Bruce was taking them rock climbing and kayaking at Hippie Hollow Park, swimming in the Baton Springs Pool, to the Texas Memorial Museum, and to the Fourth of July fireworks and symphony at some park.

They were going to the Ann W. Richards Congress Ave Bridge, where 1.5 million Mexican tailed bats lived and flew out at sunset in search of insects. How gross, *Janice thought, listening to the excitement pouring from her youngest son, Devon's, mouth explaining the emergence of the million bats.*

Bruce didn't bother to call their sons regularly, was upset they were spending a month with him, yet made an itinerary so they could have BIG FUN! Janice was quietly steaming.

Devon said, "They have bumper stickers that say, "Keep Austin Weird." Isn't that cool, Momma? This place is awesome."

Ding, Ding, Ding - so that's why Bruce picked Austin – a weird man in a weird place. The puzzle was now complete.

Her middle son, Levon, said, "When I graduate, I'm going to The University of Texas at Austin *to study Computer Science.* Dell's *headquarters is here. I can apply for an internship that could lead to a possible job."*

When horses fly, *she shouted inwardly. Aloud she calmly stated, "We'll discuss that at another time."*

Levon was entering high school. His college choices would change numerous times before his high school graduation, but that didn't stop her silent prayer. Please, Lord, let me get this job.

The boys couldn't stop raving about the mini-mansion Bruce lived in with the indoor Olympic size pool.

Janice was livid. How dare he live high on the hog – barely giving me child support while I'm struggling to make ends meet? I'm knocking on welfare's door, while he's living in the lap of luxury. I need to contact Family Court to get my child support payments raised. This isn't right. *Even as she thought it, she knew she wouldn't do it. She had too much pride.*

What happened to the sulky children I forced on the plane? *She pondered, listening to the excitement in her boys' voices. They'd never been separated for more than a weekend. She missed them terribly.*

Regrettably, she admitted she was envious. The five of them should be together as a family. No matter how Bruce treated her, she still loved him. Apparently, it wasn't reciprocated. He was living with a supermodel half his age.

It was her oldest son Kevon, who broke the news of Mona, the gorgeous, long-legged, twenty-six-year-old, live-in-girlfriend. Janice knew of her existence, but hearing it from her son's fifteen-year-old mouth made it all too real.

"Hey Momma, she's tight," Kevon announced. "I see why Dad is too busy for us. If I was doing her, I wouldn't want my kids around either."

Janice was floored. "Kevon Bruce Monroe! May I remind you that I am not one of your boys? You better watch your damn mouth."

"I'm sorry, Momma. YOU said we can talk to you about ANYTHING. My bad."

When the boys were growing up, she instilled in them that if there was anything they wanted to know or try anything at all, to discuss it with her first. She didn't want them learning the wrong information or experimenting on the street. When Kevon told her he was ready to have sex, they spent hours discussing it. When she felt he was knowledgeable, she bought him a pack of condoms. What have I created? *Janice searched the heavens for answers.*

"I am not amused, Kevon," She stated firmly.

He mumbled something that sounded like an apology. He added, "But seriously, what can a young girl like that see in an old man like Dad, except the Benjamins?"

And I hope she takes him for every dime he has, *Janice thought harshly,* as long as she leaves enough for child support.

Unfortunately, Kevon wasn't finished. "Mona is gorgeous, Momma, with a capital G. She has a beautiful ebony complexion, sorta like yours. She's tall... supermodel tall with legs..."

"Listen Kevon, I need to go," Janice interrupted with a voice full of tears and a heavy heart.

Deep inside, she'd hoped she and Bruce would find their way back to each other, but with Supermodel Mona hanging around, that possibility was slim. She didn't know why she wanted to reconcile with her husb...ex-husband, who treated her cruelly towards the end of their marriage.

"I love you, son," she professed, trying not to let her voice crack. "Take care of your brothers."

"I will, and Momma... that Mona chick... has nothing on you. Dad's a fool."

Janice chuckled slightly.

Kevon knew she was upset. He and Janice were close. He tried to take up the slack after his father's impulsive decision to leave. He knew the divorce had devastated her. He urged her to date. He even tried hooking her up with some of his friend's divorced fathers. She wouldn't entertain the idea. He couldn't understand why she wouldn't let go and move on. Especially knowing his father had.

"Thank you, son," Janice whispered so he wouldn't hear the hurt in her voice.

They hung up.

Kevon wished he could take back his words. He didn't like it when his mother was sad. He went to confront his dad.

C'est la vie. Janice wished she meant those words. If only she could be like Bruce or any man who could so easily throw out the old wife for the new chick on the side. Sorry... young, new chick.

"He took the best years of my life," she complained to the air. "I was fourteen years old when I met the handsome Bruce Monroe. I always thought we would live happily ever after... together."

She shook her head. She would not dwell in the past. She had a job to get... a future to secure for her and her sons.

"Who needs a man? Not me," she asked and answered in the empty house. "Unless that man is Kevin Hinderblocker. Now that is one fine brother...YOUNG brother. If Bruce can do it, so can I." Although she spoke the words, she knew that her jerky ex-husband would always be the only man for her.

"But Kevin will make a wonderful friend," she concluded.

That was last night. Today, she was double-checking doors and windows before leaving for the airport. She said a silent prayer that the morning flight would depart as scheduled. She set the house alarm, opened the garage door, stepped inside, and checked her watch for the time.

"4:15... I better get a move on it. I don't want to miss the 6 a.m. flight."

She clicked opened her car door, buckled up, and settled in for another trip to the airport.

~15~

ERICH COPPENHAUGE

Erich sat on the balcony, looking out at Lake Norman, eating his breakfast. Fragments of daybreak had not yet started to break through but he could tell the water was rough, the humidity was high, and he smelt rain in the air.

Just what I need, he thought sarcastically, removing his glasses to wipe the condensation from its lens.

After the fiasco at the airport the previous evening, rain was the last thing he wanted to encounter.

Before leaving the airport, he called to check on Erika. He was told her condition was stable, but he needed to get to New York ASAP as if he didn't already know that.

He put the last of his eggs and bacon into his mouth, then leaned back in his chair with a cup of coffee. Glancing at his watch, he swallowed the last few drops.

"4:15," he sighed. "I better get moving. I don't want to miss the 6 a.m. flight."

KEVIN HINDERBLOCKER

"Rise and shine and give God your glory glory. Rise and shine and give God your glory, glory, children of the Lord." Kevin sang, in lieu of shouting, to wake his children.

"Daaaddy! It's still dark out. What time is it? I'm tired." Kara complained, wrestling with the overhead light pouring into her eyes.

"4:15."

"In the morning?" Kara asked.

"Of course in the morning. We have a 6 a.m. flight. Chop, chop. Wake your brother. We have to get to the airport by 5."

They had plenty of time to make their flight. They'd spent the night at a hotel ten minutes away from the airport. The children showered the previous evening, got into the double size bed, and fell asleep so fast Kevin missed kissing them goodnight.

He wasn't as fortunate. After his shower, he snuggled under the covers in the other double bed. Sleep was not his friend. His mind kept replaying the events of the day – the trip to the airport, his memorable meetings with the funny, fiery, delightful Marla Meadows, and the more explosive Janice Monroe.

"What a woman that one is," Kevin whispered into the night, smiling. He didn't know why any man would want to leave her. She was beautiful, intelligent, and her body – humph. But that mouth...what a mouth. He chuckled. He'd just figured out why her husband probably left – that potty mouth.

He laughed out loud. *I'm telling myself jokes in the middle of the night. Kevin, man, get some sleep.* He couldn't. He continued to reflect on Janice Monroe. She wasn't a bad person, he rationalized. She was hurt and terrified. He promised to protect her as much as humanly possible.

Kimberly used to say, "Kevin, my love, one day you are going to get in trouble trying to protect these damsels in distress." She said it without jealousy or malice. He smiled sadly at her memory. He missed her very much. She was the glue that kept them together... that kept him going. Her beautiful smile comforted him on many occasions.

His brain finally turned off, filled with Kim's smile, letting sleep find its way in.

A few hours later, he was awake and waiting for his children to brush their teeth and wash their faces.

Thirty minutes later, the Hinderblocker family were dressed and on their way to the airport – once more.

Little did Kevin know Kim's words would come to fruition.

ϟ ϟ ϟ ϟ ϟ ϟ

THE WINTHROP FAMILY

Meredith Winthrop awoke with a start. She thought she heard a noise. She looked at her clock – 3:50. An uneasy feeling was lining the bottom of her stomach. She glanced at Brian. He was asleep. She turned on her back and stared at the cloudy sky through the bedroom's skylight. The clouds glared menacingly at her. A storm was coming.

She turned on her left side, facing her husband. He was still a handsome man. His thick curls were thinning, but the salt and pepper hair made him look distinguished. His face had adopted wrinkles, but they only added to his handsomeness.

Where did our love go? She silently questioned.

They were so busy in their own lives they forgot to include the other.

Meredith sighed. Brian stirred.

She thought about the secret prepaid cell phone she had hidden in the back of her closet in a hat box. She knew it was wrong, but she was addicted. She could no longer control her desires. She would retrieve the phone in the morning now that the surgery was pushed back a week. She had to get one, maybe two more fixes before they left for an unspecified amount of time in New York. She didn't know how she'd survive.

Of course, you do. She mentally chastised herself. *You will revel in your child being healthy and free of pain for the first time in months. You'll be the doting mother and dutiful wife… a role you've perfected.*

She glanced at her husband again. They hadn't made love in

so long she couldn't recall the last time. They'd had sex a couple of times. It was quick, unfulfilling, and boring.

She remembered how passionate they used to be – how free – how loving. She wished.... well, it didn't matter. After twenty-four years, passion was expected to die, wasn't it?

Meredith turned away from her husband. She couldn't sleep. There was something wrong. She sensed it.

She sat up in the bed, threw her legs over the side, and prepared to check on Ian. Maybe once she knew he was safe, she'd be able to sleep.

Quietly, she eased to the door as not to disturb Brian.

"Where are you going, Mer?" Brian asked.

"Sorry, I didn't mean to wake you. I heard a noise. I want to check on Ian."

"What kind of noise?"

"It was strange. Maybe a whimper or strangling sound."

"And you think it could be Ian?" Brian asked suspiciously. "He's on the other side of the house, Mer. There is no way you would hear him 'whimpering'."

A long hallway separated Ian's bedroom, two guest bedrooms, and two full bathrooms from a kitchen, dining room, living room, and the parlor. The master bedroom suite was tucked away in the back of the spacious ranch house.

"What if he fell out of his bed again?"

"Then you would have heard a thump, not a whimper, if anything. Besides, he won't hurt himself on that plush, expensive carpet you insisted on putting in his room."

Brian was ultra-conservative where spending money was involved. He was a well-to-do doctor. Yet, he counted every penny. He grew up in a lower-middle-class family where every penny was watched. He never outgrew that practice.

"Mer, the boy is thirteen-years-old. When are you going to stop babying him?"

"What if he has another seizure like the last time he fell out of bed? What about a fever? Aren't you concerned, Brian?"

"If I felt there was reason for concern, I would be, but I don't.

I'm a doctor, Mer. The boy is fine. He had a long day. He's probably sleeping soundlessly. Come back to bed...unless there's another reason you're leaving."

"What? Don't be silly. What other reason could there be?" she asked nervously.

Brian said nothing. He tried to see his wife's expression in the dark room.

"Now who's being paranoid?" Meredith added, slipping back in between the satin sheets, hands trembling slightly. She didn't understand her nervousness. There was no way Brian knew her secret. Unless Lucinda.... No, she promised. She wouldn't tell.

"Good night, Mer." Brian flipped over, falling instantly back to sleep. Meredith could hear his even breaths.

The alarm inside her head was telling her to check on their son, but she didn't like Brian's non-accusations.

Ian was probably all right. She was wound-up from the day's chaos.

She glanced at the time on her nightstand - 4:15.

Meredith Winthrop fell into a fitful sleep.

BRETT & MARLA MEADOWS

Completely spent, Brett and Marla straightened their clothes before climbing back into the front seats of the car. The rain had not let up. It was worse. It resembled a monsoon. Several cars had joined them on the side of the road. Others were braving the storm, inching slowly on their way. Some others, posing as Mario Andretti, were slipping, sliding, or fishtailing, hitting hard to see puddles.

Brett glanced at the time on the dashboard – 4:00 a.m. They had to go if they wanted to make the meeting on time.

"What's the verdict, counselor?" Brett asked Marla.

She noticed the relaxation draining from his body. It was being replaced with anxiety and stress. She had to do something.

"Sweetheart, the law firm is doing well. My clientele is growing. I can keep us afloat until you find other resources."

Brett thought about it. He stared into the eyes of his freckle-faced wife and remembered the vows they made to one another – 'for better or worse – this is worse; in sickness or in health – they were healthy; until death do we part – they were alive and happy.' Yeah, yeah, yeah. That was fine but he was the man of the house. It was his job to support and provide for them as his father had done.

Brett and his siblings grew up with the upper echelon in Norwalk, Connecticut. *His father was an anesthesiologist and his mother was a real estate broker. They were members of several country clubs. His family was constantly on the Norwalk society pages. He grew sick of that life. When he received the basketball scholarship from* Duke University *(his escape), he eagerly accepted it, to his parents' dismay. They wanted him to accept the offers from the Ivy League schools that were heavily recruiting him and closer to their home.*

Marla was a breath of fresh air. She was unlike the debutants he was "forced" to date while growing up. She was at Duke *on academic and cheerleading scholarships. She was down to earth. She was the reason he turned down the high-paying job his mother procured for him in Connecticut to remain in North Carolina. His mother blamed and despised Marla because of his choices.*

Brett studied the crashing rain from the window, cursing *WorldLine Airways*. They should be in New York, cozy in their hotel room, making sweet love. Not sitting on the side of the road making life decisions.

"Can I let Marla support us until Marcus and I figure something else out?" he pondered.

Marla took care of her parents. She was quite aware of the

hardship they endured to give her life and the sacrifices they made throughout her life.

Angela Murphy discovered she was pregnant at forty-one years old. It was a difficult pregnancy. She was placed on bed rest during her first trimester. She was fired from her job. Marla bounced into the world when her mother was seven months pregnant. Angela was unable to have any other children. She became a stay-at-home mom. Her parents worked hard to give her a good life.

Although her father had a great pension and benefits, and their home was paid for, their medical bills weren't completely covered under their insurances. Marla helped in various ways, including financially.

Marla said her firm is doing well. Will she be able to continue taking care of her parents and keep her business and mine afloat? Brett questioned. It was a lot to ask.

"Honey, I appreciate all that you're willing to do for us, but I need to try to get this job. Marcus and I worked hard on the account. It's not just about the money. This contract will bring a new element to *2B Mpact*. We will have challenges like we had at TTS. We'll be able to hire more people, ultimately helping the Charlotte economy. All I have to do is get there."

Marla gazed at her husband of six years with pride. Nothing was going to stop her from getting him to New York, even if it meant driving through the torrential rains herself.

"Go for it, hon," she encouraged. "We got this. We can do this."

"Always the cheerleader." Beaming, Brett turned the ignition, started the car, and signaled that he was re-entering I95. "Full speed ahead," he charged.

"Slow down, cowboy," Marla joked. The speedometer displayed five mph. "Let's take it nice and slow… this time." She had a devilish smirk on her face.

"Wait until I get you in that hotel room, my beautiful bride. I'll show you nice and slow." Brett turned and grinned at Marla.

In that split second, Marla, with eyes on the road, shouted, "Brett, watch out."

It was too late. When Brett refocused on the road, the high beams from a tractor-trailer coming towards them from the opposite side of the highway blinded him. The rental car hit a water-filled ditch. The car spun out at a 180-degree angle, stalling across two lanes of the highway. A car riding at a safe distance behind them carefully maneuvered around them.

Nervous and shaky, Brett turned the ignition. It cranked but didn't catch. He waited a few seconds, then tried again... and again and... finally, it caught. With a sigh of relief, he cautiously straightened out the car, setting it in one lane facing the right direction.

"Nothing is worth risking our lives. If we don't make it to New York, I'll let you support us for a while."

Brett was astonished at how Marla kept her cool. She didn't blink or utter a word. She let him handle the situation. The next words from her lips solidified his love for her.

"Honey, come out of the dark ages. We are ONE. We got EACH OTHER! All things are possible. Always remember that."

She was willing to stick by him through any crisis. He was very happy she chose him. He loved her with everything he was. It was Marla and Brett against the world.

Brett noticed construction blocking them on both sides. The previous mishap was worrisome. "I'm pulling over the first chance I get," he stated, eyes fixed on the road.

Marla's brave front was just that... a brave front. She was just as shaken. "Good idea. It's 4:15 and we still have a ways to go, but that was too close. I thought we were a goner for sur...."

The impact that came from behind was so powerful it sent their car careening into the newly, halfway, constructed concrete wall with a loud bang. The silence was followed by darkness.

~16~
THE AIRPORT

Although the airport was bustling with many passengers, Janice Monroe spotted Kevin Hinderblocker and his two children as soon as she entered the packed waiting area. How could she not? He stood out in his light blue polo shirt, black fitted jeans, and blue and white stripe *Jordans*.

That man is too fine.

"Can you believe this madhouse?" Janice asked in way of a greeting.

"Sure can. Think about it – at least thirty people didn't get on cancelled Flight 3236 or the 7:30 flight last night. Throw in the people originally scheduled for the 6 a.m. flight, and voila, you got a crowd. How are you, Janice?"

Overwhelmed by the crowd, she didn't hear the question.

"This is insane."

Kevin agreed. "Airlines toy with people's lives all the time. They have no remorse over their decisions and how it affects another's life. They demand we get here one to two hours before departure, yet they have no qualms making us wait or cancelling flights. Honestly, I'm sick of it. Something must be done."

"Preach, brother." Janice grinned.

Kevin appraised the petite, ebony beauty. Her large soulful eyes were sprinkled with red lines. The dark circles under them hinted at a restless night. Her full lips, devoid of lipstick, were pursed together in a tight line. Her *Toni Braxton* haircut was neatly in place. Her mint green jersey top fell neatly over her tan jeggings, accentuating her brick house figure. Her 2" mint green sandals added a little height to her 5'2" stature.

"How are you this morning?" he asked again.

"I'm tired and anxious. I most definitely need to get this job. I spoke to my sons last night. Get this, they were happy. Very Happy! Can you believe it?"

"Happy, huh? I thought they gave you grief about leaving. Didn't you say something about forcing or bribing them to go to uh...Texas?"

"Wonderful memory. That was YESTERDAY MORNING!" Janice exclaimed.

The previous evening, she'd shared her financial burdens, her failed marriage, her sons' troubled relationship with their father, and her desperate need to get the job at *Bess House of Designs*. She also confided that she was still in love with her ex-husband and was heartbroken he'd moved on with his life without bringing his family along.

Kevin listened and asked the appropriate questions at the appropriate times. He was easy to talk to. She felt comfortable with him. After their talk, she felt lighter. She hadn't shared her financial hardship with anyone – not her father, brothers, or best friends. She was too ashamed.

Kevin offered to look over her finances when he returned from his cruise. He promised to help her with a budget. Janice was grateful and relieved. A burden was lifted from her shoulders and a friendship formed. Peace entered her body – a peace that was non-existent for over four years.

Erich arrived at the airport at 5 a.m. He parked Miriam's *BMW* convertible in long-term parking and took the airport shuttle to the *WorldLine Airways* terminal. He retrieved his ticket from the kiosk. Pulling his carryon, he proceeded to security check where he was met with a very long line. Twenty minutes later, he stood at Gate 10... staring. There was a lot of activity.

Where did all these people come from? He wondered. *Were they left over from the previous night? It's 5:20 in the morning. I hope they're not all waiting for the 6 a.m. flight? How big is the plane?* These thoughts flashed through his mind as he strolled over to the only available seat he saw. Confident he had his ticket with a seat number, he opened the newspaper he'd brought and began reading.

Newspaper thoroughly read, he glanced at his Rolex - *6:15 a.m.* He did a double-take. *The plane should have been here. Been here? It should be on its way to New York!*

Erich was facing the window but did not see the plane.

He heard a microphone being picked up. "Ladies and gentlemen, may I have your attention, please?"

And then the dreaded words: "I regret to inform you..."

Kevin and Janice sat side by side in the airport awaiting their flight, talking like old friends. A spectator would not have guessed the two had met the previous day. Janice admitted to being nervous about the job, even though she knew she was well qualified. Kevin was giving her verbal support when the first devastating news hit.

"Ladies and gentlemen, may I have your attention, please?" The airline representative asked politely.

"Oh, hell no, not again," Janice exploded, getting up from her seat.

Kevin grabbed her, pulling her back down.

"Let's hear what she has to say," he whispered.

"We KNOW what she's going to say. This is fucking déjà vu."

"No, it isn't," Kevin insisted.

"Humph!" Janice scowled, folding her arms across her

bosom.

"I regret to..."

Tears filled Janice's eyes.

"...inform you that Flight 1618 is delayed because of inclement weather. We have received word from the air traffic tower that Kennedy airport in New York has closed. They have grounded their planes. We will update you as information becomes available. We apologize for the delay."

The representative clicked off her microphone before returning to the dais to attend to the first furious customer of the morning.

Janice stared at Kevin with an "I told you so" expression on her tear-stained face. She was going to lose EVERYTHING. Her children may as well stay in Texas because they wouldn't have a home to return to.

Kevin stroked her shoulders as she sat numbly, staring into space.

After a few moments of silence, he said soothingly, "Janice, this may only be temporary. The weather may clear up, allowing JFK to reopen. Have faith."

"Faith?" she screeched. "Faith? I've had faith, Kevin and where has it gotten me. Nowhere. I had faith in my marriage... I had faith my mother would grow old before she died...I had faith my brother, my hilarious brother, would live to be an uncle to my children. We were very close." A tear ran deceivingly down her face. "I had faith I'd be in New York by now. Faith? Ha. What's the fucking point?"

She laid her head in her hands and cried.

Kane and Kara watched. They didn't understand what was going on. They were tired of sitting around the airport. The excitement of taking a plane or going to New York was fading. They wanted to cry too.

Kevin patted Janice's shoulder. "Sit tight. I'll be right back."

Janice didn't move. *It was just not meant to be.*

Kevin went to the dais. He waited his turn. When the passenger before him left, he assumed her position. "Excuse me. What time is the next plane leaving for New York?"

"10:00," the representative answered.

"Is it a full flight?"

"No, it isn't. Would you like to switch your reservation?"

"How many available seats are there?" Kevin asked.

The representative checked. "There are twelve, sir. Would you like to change your reservation?"

"What are the chances of getting on the 6 a.m. flight?" Kevin asked, noting the time was 7:10.

"Sir, I don't know but I'll tell you this, it's looking slim. The 6 a.m. flight will most likely get cancelled within the next thirty minutes or so. The command center at JFK has not given the signal to proceed. If you look out that window, you'll see the plane is ready. Since the weather is so bad up north, we're waiting for instructions."

"What's going on?"

"I'm not sure. Check out the news." The representative pointed towards the monitors. "From what I've heard and seen it's hurricane-like conditions."

Kevin looked at a screen turned to CNN. His mouth dropped open.

"Thank you," he said dejectedly, returning to Janice to direct her watery eyes to the television screen.

Janice gasped.

There was flooding everywhere. The rain was pouring down like buckets being over-turned. The whole northeast was being plummeted. The winds were 70 miles an hour, picking up everything in its midst. The announcer was calling it a Tornado like Hurricane, and it was heading straight down I-95. It had already hit Maryland and the DC area and was continuing south-east.

Straight towards the Carolinas.

~17~

KAMI PHILLIPS

After Jessica picked Kami up from the airport, they spent the evening eating, drinking (non-alcoholic beverages), and talking into the wee hours of the night. Kami enjoyed herself. She was unhappy with the circumstances that led to their bonding but was glad she could spend time with the very entertaining event planner.

Before going to sleep, Kami called both Dante and Debra. She updated Debra on her latest travel debacle and gave Dante her lodging info.

He spent his time in the hotel room watching television, not wanting to explore New York City without his lovely wife by his side. Hearing the sadness in his voice prompted Kami to share the news of their pregnancy. Her cell phone battery died. That last interference convinced her that she needed to tell him in person. Too many factors kept preventing him from hearing her incredible news over the telephone lines.

The following morning, Kami was awake, dressed, and ready to meet her husband. She didn't want to wake Jessica or leave without thanking her gracious host. She tiptoed into the living room where Jessica was asleep on the lumpy, pull out, second-hand sofa bed. She insisted Kami sleep in the very comfortable, queen-sized bed because of "her condition".

Kami checked the time – 8:15 a.m. She'd gotten approximately four hours of sleep. Jessica... even less. She would sleep on the plane. That would alleviate her fear of flying. Her taxi was due any minute. Taking a deep breath, she called Jessica's name. Not getting a response, she called again. Still nothing. She walked to the sofa bed and shook her host.

"Huh? What's wrong?" Jessica asked, jumping up, startled. Fog lifting, she recognized Kami. "Oh, hey. Leaving so soon?" She asked, leaning against the sofa with a huge yawn and hair spread out all over her head.

"I am but didn't want to go without thanking you for your hospitality."

"Oh, please. It was nothing. I'm sure you would do the same for me if I get stuck in Arizona. I do wish you'd let me drive you to the airport."

"Thanks. You've done so much for me already. I've called a cab. I'm grateful you were available because honestly, Jess, I don't know what I would have done. The only other person I met in Charlotte is the gentlemen I told you about, Karl Stewart," Kami stated, already forgetting the reunion with her childhood friend, Michelle Green.

She and Michelle reunited at the Arizona airport on their way to Charlotte. Michelle was responsible for Kami's cautiousness with friendships. They were tight growing up... Thelma and Louise. When Michelle's family moved to Charlotte, they promised to write each other. Kami kept that promise. Michelle did not. Kami's ten-year-old heart was shattered and a wall built.

"Karl Stewart?" Jessica asked trying to recall what Kami told her about him. "The one who helped with the rental car fiasco?"

"That's the one. I'm very fortunate he wasn't a psychopath. That situation could have ended much differently."

"So true," Jessica agreed.

While Kami was sharing the rental car incident with her, Jessica held her tongue. She couldn't believe how lackadaisical

Kami had been. She silently thanked God her new friend wasn't harmed.

"Mr. Karl isn't even in town. He was on his way to Los Angeles when we met. I don't think his wife would be too understanding if I called her house and said, 'hello, I met your husband at the rental car office. He said to call if I needed anything. Well, my flight was cancelled and I need a place to stay for the night.' I don't think so."

"I know that's right," Jessica stated. "Especially... a gorgeous woman."

Kami blushed.

Jessica was an average looking woman but Kami was 5'5" of gorgeousness. Her heritage of Japanese and African American mixed contributed to her unique features. Her coal-black, almond-shaped eyes had men drooling. She had long, jet black hair, butterscotch-colored skin, thick naturally shaped eyebrows, straight nose, dimpled cheeks, heart-shaped mouth, long dancer legs, a small waist, a nice round ass, and a c-cup chest. Her appearance captured the best of both races. Men couldn't help but flirt with her (women too).

"I'd have so many questions for him when he got home, he'd wish HIS flight had been cancelled," Jessica joked.

The women laughed. Jessica was a lot of fun. She was witty and bright. Eventually, with the right training and direction, she would make a fine event planner.

When their laughter subsided, Kami said, "I guess I could have gotten a room somewhere or camped out at the airport, but this was so much nicer, so again, I thank you."

"You are welcome. I had a great time."

"Me too," Kami stated honestly.

She promised to call Jessica as soon as her feet hit the New York soil.

They embraced.

Kami rushed outside into the waiting cab.

JADE MORALES

The next morning, Jade left the house undetected. Not wanting to chance being discovered, she put her make-up on in the car, using extra concealer to camouflage the bags under her eyes.

By 8:25 she was ready to go.

She could barely see the street in front of her. She finally understood the term 'raining cats and dogs'. It was beyond pouring.

Maybe I'll wait it out, she considered. *Nah…with my luck that "side of town" will have clear skies, the plane will get clearance to fly, and I'll miss it. Then I'd have to contend with the wrath of Rosario. No, thank you.*

Jade phoned the airline to check the status of the flight. The circuits were busy. *The weather must be bad all over*, she concluded.

She contemplated waiting once more. The argument that met her when she entered the house yesterday evening jumped into her head. She started her slow drive to the airport in the horrendous weather conditions for a self-absorbed sister. The airport was normally a twenty-minute ride, but driving at her speed, she was looking at a minimum of an hour. There was no way the plane was leaving at its 9:45 scheduled departure time. She turned on the radio to relieve the building tension.

The radio announcer was warning everyone to stay indoors. "If you don't have to go out – don't."

"Too late for that," Jade muttered.

"There are hazardous conditions out there. Only emergency vehicles should venture out. If you must go out, use extreme caution," the radio announcer advised.

"Did you hear that, Rosario?" Jade screamed in the empty car. "I shouldn't be out in this weather."

She considered her choices – disappoint her sister, deal with Carmen, drive in the atrocious conditions. The weather was the safest of the three options.

Her wipers were on full, but it didn't make a difference. She couldn't see directly in front of her. After reciting the *Lord's Prayer* and two *Hail Marys*, she carefully merged onto the highway.

KAMI PHILLIPS

As the cab reached the end of Jessica's block, the skies opened up, releasing a downpour. The driver threw on his brakes to slow down the car, skidding slightly.

"Whew, where did that come from?" Kami questioned.

"The sky would be my guess," The cocky cabby retorted.

No crap, Sherlock. Kami bit her lip. It wouldn't do to piss him off. It was bad enough the trip to the airport was going to take longer with the rain. She didn't need him taking the scenic route to raise the price of the fare.

Sweetly, she asked, "Will you please turn on the radio so I can listen to the news?"

"Suit yourself, lady. If that's your pleasure, fine. It's your dime."

Did someone wake up on the wrong side of the bed this morning or what? Kami wondered.

He was the rudest person she'd met since the guy on the airplane. Oh, and the women at the rental office. Kami heard Charlotte was a friendly city filled with wonderful people. That was proving incorrect. Then Jessica popped in her mind, and the couple who helped her when she thought she'd missed her flight, and the airline rep who gave her crackers, and her all-time favorite, Karl Stewart – rental car hero. Kami smiled at the thought of him. He was a very sweet gentleman. She hoped she and Dante would have time to socialize with him and his wife someday.

Okay, so maybe Charlotte was a friendly city with some bad trans-

plants, Kami conceded.

"My guess is it's a Nor'easter." The radio announcer was saying.

"A Nor'easter?" His sidekick asked. "I thought they only happened when it's cold."

"It can happen at any time of the year," The first on-air personality stated with authority.

"Okay, but don't they usually travel from the South to the North?" The second one asked.

"Hmm... good point. It usually picks up power in New York or New England. This one is doing the exact opposite – traveling from the north to the south."

"So maybe it's a So'easter," the radio personality mused.

"Good one! Yeah, let's go with that. There you have it our listening audience. Stay locked in your homes today because a So'easter is headed our way. We'll have more information on the storm after this commercial break. Time to pay some bills."

"Hey lady, you still want to go to the airport?" the cabby asked.

"Yes."

"Figures!" he huffed, pressing the gas a little harder than necessary causing the car to skid.

Kami sat back and closed her eyes. This was going to be a long day.

THE WINTHROP FAMILY

"OH MY GOD!" Lucinda screeched. "Oh, Dios mío! Lo siento! Lo siento mucho. Por favor, perdóname. Lo siento."

The Winthrops turned to find their housekeeper/nanny standing a few feet from them, hands twisting, and tears sprinting down her face.

Meredith yelled, "What is it, Lucinda? What is it? Please tell me."

Lucinda gulped in air, "He call me...." Another shriek escaped from her lips. "Lo siento."

"What happened?" Meredith tried to speak calmly, but the words came out in a gurgle.

When no more words exited Lucinda's mouth, Meredith ordered Brian to get their housekeeper a glass of water.

Brian immediately went to fulfill the demand... tears blurring his vision.

Meredith knelt before Lucinda, who'd fallen onto Ian's desk chair. She spoke slowly but firmly to her employee, her friend. "Please... tell me what he said."

Lucinda began stealthily, staring bravely into Meredith's violet eyes. "Last night, he call me. He say he very upset about the flight. He say it cancel because of engine trouble."

"That wasn't the reason but go on," Meredith urged.

Brian returned to the room with a bottle of water. Handing it to Lucinda, he said, "Here you go, Luci."

Hearing Ian's nickname for her brought a fresh bout of tears and a glare from Meredith.

Brian was clueless. What had he done to cause harder tears to fall from Lucinda or the agitated look from Meredith?

Ding dong, saved by the ringing doorbell. He went to answer it, admitting the Fire Chief, two police officers - O'Kelly and Malone, and the EMT workers.

When did it start raining? He wondered, briefly watching the rain pour onto the streets, before closing the door. He led the group down the spacious hallway into Ian's room. He peered at their wet, unprotected shoes, and thought how upset Meredith was going to get when she saw the dirt tracked into her home. He knew the thought was irrational. Under the circumstances, Meredith wouldn't care or notice the dirt on her rugs, but crazy thoughts helped deflect the real ones threatening to invade his mind.

The police officers forcefully removed Meredith and Lucinda from the room, depositing them into the parlor, to let the EMTs do their job. The fire chief quietly retreated from the home.

His expertise was not required. With the raging storms and accidents developing throughout the city, he was needed elsewhere.

"Can you call a doctor to prescribe a sedative for the ladies?" Officer O'Kelly asked Brian in a raspy voice.

"I am a doctor," Brian responded absently.

"I see," Officer O'Kelly acknowledged, catching the eye of his partner. Although the two had only worked together for a short time, Officer Malone knew what his partner's eyes asked.

Excusing himself, the younger officer left the room. He returned with an inconspicuous nod, indicating "it" was "done".

Officer O'Kelly smiled his response.

Officer Malone noticed the women had quieted down since his absence. The doctor stood with his back to the room, gazing at the plummeting rain through the large picture window.

The doorbell sounded.

Brian moved to answer it. He was stopped by Officer Malone. "Let me, sir."

Brian nodded at the twenty-something-year-old police officer.

Opening the door, Officer Malone was confronted by a short, round Hispanic man jabbering in Spanish. The rain was soaking through his unprotected clothing.

"Please, slow down. I don't understand. My high school Spanish is not that good."

Fernando did not smile. "My wife is here."

"Wait here, sir." Officer Malone said, closing the door behind him, leaving Fernando in the rain.

Returning to the parlor, he said, "There's a Mr....." Realizing he hadn't asked for a name, he said to Brian, "Sir, please come with me. There's a gentleman at the door claiming his wife is here."

"It must be Fernando Garcia," Brian said, rushing from the room. "I didn't think to call him."

Fernando was being blocked by another officer standing vigil on the other side of the door. Brian noticed several police cars parked by the curb. A handful of neighbors stood in a cluster in the middle of the street, hiding behind umbrellas, pointing towards his home. It no longer felt like home. Not with... it was just a house.

"Let him in," Brian ordered. Fernando was shivering from his rain-soaked clothing. "Why are there so many police cars out there?"

Brian's question was ignored.

The officer stepped aside. Fernando hurried in.

"Doctor Brian... what hap?"

An unmarked police car skidded to a stop by the curb, before the officer closed the door, causing a bigger commotion amongst the neighbors and Fernando to stop in midsentence.

"What the...?" Brian bellowed. "What is this - a three-ring circus? Why are there so many police cars here?"

Again - no response.

They watched an over-weight, ruddy-faced man heave himself from the driver's seat and a much younger, clean-cut, good-looking man extract himself from the passenger side. Both men dashed towards the house.

"Who are they?" Brian questioned.

Reaching the door, the men extended their hands, exposing their identifications. The older heavy-set man made the introductions. "Hello sir, I'm Detective Foley and this is my partner Detective Lawrence."

Brian did a double-take. This wasn't happening! He looked at the gray skies and the pouring rain. He clearly misunderstood.

"Excuse me," Brian said.

"I'm Detective Foley and this is my partner, Detective Lawrence." The detective yelled so Brian could him over the beating rain and raging wind.

"What? Detectives?" Brian exploded, glancing briefly at their ID's but staring intently at the younger detective. "What on earth for?"

Detective Foley explained. "Whenever there are questionable circumstances, we must investigate."

Brian was astonished. "Questionable? Investigate? What are you talking about? Are you seriously going to drag us through an investigation?" he shouted.

The neighbors shook their heads at the sadness of it all.

"Sir, may we come inside? We will try to protect as much of your privacy as possible," Detective Foley assured him, peering over his shoulder.

It was then Brian spotted the television vans pulling up to the curbs in front of his neighbor's homes. He wished he had listened to Meredith and bought land in a gated community. They could afford it but he didn't want Ian to feel as if he was unattainable or better than his peers. He wanted his son to remain as grounded as he and Meredith were.

Fat chance of that happening now, he thought bitterly.

"Besides, we're getting drenched," Detective Foley added.

Brian stepped aside to let them enter. He glanced once more at the heavens, muttering to himself, "You really do have a sense of humor."

Turning from the closed door, his eyes fell upon a family portrait taken a few months earlier. It was Ian's thirteenth birthday. Ian was smiling. His grey eyes sparkled. Peering closer at the photograph, Brian detected a haunting sadness just beyond the shine.

Why didn't I notice that before? Surely, I wasn't that busy.

Overwhelmed with guilt, his legs buckled. He fell to his knees in tears. Fernando knelt beside his friend, a puddle forming around them. He took Brian into his arms and held him. Their tears mixed together as they fell.

The law enforcers stood awkwardly inside the doorway, wiping their rain-soaked bodies with the towels Officer Malone provided. No matter how awkward the situation, the detectives had a job to do.

"Why, Lord, why? What did we do to deserve this?"

Brian couldn't grasp that his son, so full of life yesterday, was gone today. He cried as images of Ian's lifeless body soared through his head.

He would never understand why Ian Winthrop, his thirteen-year-old son, chose suicide.

~18~
THE AIRPORT

Kevin and Janice reserved seats on the 10:00 a.m. flight to JFK. Everyone was hoping the rain would end, so travel could resume. After the fiasco with cancelled Flight 3236 the previous day, none of the airlines, especially WorldLine Airways, wanted to cancel more flights. But at 8:32, it was necessary to cancel the 6 a.m. flight. JFK had not resumed its operations. Charlotte, along with other airports along the east coast, temporarily grounded its planes going to the northern states.

Janice called *Bess House of Designs*. Nate Hill, the CEO and co-owner, was aware of the weather conditions. New York was getting hammered. He had to close his company. Yet, he agreed to meet with her whenever she made it in for the interview.

"Ms. Monroe, I am looking forward to meeting with you. If you can garner the same success with my boutiques that you had with your businesses and pass my tests, you'll have a glorious future with this company," Mr. Hill expressed. "If for any reason you don't foresee making it in today, tell me, so we can make other arrangements. My gut tells me you are perfect for this job."

That was high praise coming from the perfectionist, Mr. Nate Hill. Janice was ecstatic. Employment with *Bess House of Designs* was every designer's dream. She was determined to get to New York... by any means necessary. Things were going to work out!

ϟ ϟ ϟ ϟ ϟ ϟ

Erich was stunned that his flight was cancelled - again. He secured the last available seat on the 10 a.m. flight and called Doctor Israel with his latest flight situation.

"As we speak, a horrific rainstorm with all the evidence of a hurricane is trouncing New York," Doctor Israel informed him. "The hospital is experiencing on and off power outages. Erika had a slight fever and temporarily lost consciousness. We revived her. The fever is breaking. Currently, her condition is stable. However, she could go into shock at any moment. She must have the kidney transplanted as quickly as possible. We hope to see you soon, Erich. Keep me abreast of your travels."

"I will. Thank you, Doctor Israel, for everything you're doing for my sister. She is fortunate to have you. I will get there... somehow. If anything happens to Erika, I could not live with myself, knowing it was my fault."

"Erich, you have no control over what is happening." Suddenly, Doctor Israel asked, "Do you believe in God?"

Erich hesitated. That was a tough question - especially under the circumstances. His numerous prayers had gone unanswered; his sister was infected with a disease he could barely pronounce, Glomerulonephritis – who names these diseases? *Why Erika? She's the nicest person I know. She's harmed no one. So why her?*

The doctor waited patiently for Erich's answer.

Although Erika's suffering was hurting his soul, there was a lot of good in his life. He was loved, he was healthy, and his kidney matched. Erika could be much worse – and his kidney didn't have to match just because they were twins... but it did! God was using him to save his sister.

"Yes, I do," Erich replied with conviction.

"Then have faith and believe that everything happens for a purpose and a reason. Goodbye, Erich, safe travels."

Doctor Israel disconnected without waiting for a response.

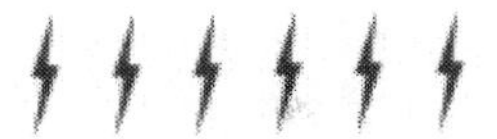

Kami exhaled deeply after escaping the confines of the cab. She was so relieved to finally arrive at the airport safely, she gave the rude cabbie a thirty percent tip. The money was well worth it.

She didn't think she would make it alive. They slipped and skidded; they fish-tailed and hit a parked car; they fell into two potholes – both filled with water. For the second one, Kami steered the car while the cab driver pushed them out. That did not improve his mood.

The airport was more crowded than the previous day. She checked in and went to her departing gate. The plane sat on the runway. She took a seat, pulled out her cell phone, and called Dante. He answered on the first ring.

"Talk to me, pretty lady."

"Hi, lover. I'm at the airport waiting for the weather to clear up."

"The airport? Really?" Dante asked, astonished. "How did you manage that in this mess? There are a lot of warnings around here. Is it not bad there?"

"Oh, it's bad all right. I made it here on a wish and a prayer," Kami said, half-joking. "I had the cab driver from Hades. He was awful and rude. When the car got stuck in a water-filled ditch, I thought he was going to make ME get out and push. He used expletives that would make an inmate's toes curl."

Dante chuckled listening to Kami recreate her experience.

"I must have said 50 Hail Marys. YOU KNOW I'm not Catholic. Anyway, I'm here and once again waiting for a boarding announcement. It's 9:45. The airport is packed. I overheard some people say they cancelled the first flight to New York."

"Another cancellation? That's incredible."

"Tell me about it. But this time it's unavoidable. There's no way the plane can fly safely in these conditions."

"I hear you, but I miss you so much, Kam. It feels like ages since I've seen you. I'm bored. I'm losing my mind in this room."

"Then go out and see some sights. I don't mind. Besides, when I get there, we are NOT leaving the room until it's time to get you on the plane tonight. Trust me. You'll be glad you rested for me."

"Don't hurt me now," he joked. "I'm out." After a pause, he said, "Who am I kidding? I can't go anywhere. I'm stuck here until the weather breaks. Guess I'll get some rest so I'll have the energy to keep up with you."

"You're going to need it," Kami said seriously. She enjoyed making love to her husband. Once they closed their hotel room door, she was planning to make love to Dante like never before. Then, while they were recuperating before session two, she would tell him about their baby. Kami smiled at the thought.

"I'll see you soon, lover," Kami whispered into the phone.

"I'll be waiting, pretty lady." Dante hung up with a huge grin dancing on his face, visualizing the scene that would play out in a few hours. He hurried to shower so he could take a few tours once the weather cleared, then get back to the hotel in time to take another shower and surprise Kami at the airport. He couldn't wait to begin creating a new life inside of his wife.

He went humming into the bathroom, closing the door behind him.

Jade was trembling when she finally pulled into and parked in the airport's long-term parking lot. She laid her head on the steering wheel and cried body wracking sobs. She was very thankful to have reached her destination in one piece. She cursed Rosario as her car did the *Tango* along the wet streets of Charlotte.

She contemplated turning around many times but couldn't do it. The wedding was important to Rosario. If the roles were reversed, her sister wouldn't think twice about putting her safety above Jade's important day. Jade was different. Nothing was going to stop her from being a part of one of the most important days in her sister's life. As much as she complained about Rosario and her selfish tendencies, she loved her younger sister dearly and would do everything humanly possible to make her happy.

She searched for the airport shuttle bus. Her plan was to jump out of her car when she saw it approaching – hoping she'd notice it in time. Her watch read 10:03. She was late for her 9:45 flight, but with the pouring rain, she didn't think she missed it.

With her window cracked, the rain was pouring in. She strained to hear the sound from an approaching bus. Within minutes she thought she heard it. She rolled up her window, popped the trunk, and grabbed an umbrella. The umbrella flew inside out, the car door slammed on her jacket, and her hood flew off her head. Frustrated and wet, she opened the door to remove her trapped jacket, threw the broken umbrella onto the back seat, shut the door, and ran around to the trunk – which was drenched with water. She pulled out her wet luggage, slammed the trunk shut, locked the car remotely from her key chain, and ran to the shuttle pickup location to discover it was not the airport shuttle but the rental car shuttle. Jade screamed in frustration, stomping her feet on the ground, splashing water everywhere, including on herself.

The rental shuttle driver, witnessing the tantrum, pulled over to let her on. Although it was against the rules, the driver couldn't leave the poor woman in the rain.

Besides, he reasoned, *I don't think the airport shuttle is running anymore*. There weren't many people braving the weather.

The driver opened the doors. Jade rushed on, soaked to the bone, with words of gratitude.

Arriving at the airport terminal, she thanked the driver profusely. She hurried inside and checked in. As suspected, the plane was grounded. She went into the restroom to dry off using the restroom dryer. She washed her face, reapplied the concealer, eyeliner, and lip gloss. Feeling slightly better, she proceeded to the waiting area and miraculously found a vacant seat. She sat down, looked around, and instantly recognized several passengers from the day before. The bald guy was there again with his wife and children.

What a lucky woman, she thought. Then chastised herself. *Why did I think that? There will never be another man for me. Oscar is and always will be my only love.*

He is cute, she acknowledged. He was about 6'4", 215-pound hunk of muscles. He had a dark, rich, chocolate complexion with small mesmerizing eyes, and a sharp chin. His bald dome shone brightly as if polished. He had thick, juicy lips. He sported a goatee that fit nicely under his wide nose.

Sighing, she put her iPod buds into her ear to relax to the smooth sounds of *Kenny G's Breathless*.

Her heartbeats sped-up... slightly.

~19~

THE WINTHROP FAMILY

Meredith, Fernando, and Lucinda remained seated in the parlor long after everyone left - the detectives, the police officers, the neighbors, the news vans, and the EMT's carrying Ian's lifeless body. Brian got up. He walked to the window.

The parlor was Brian's favorite room in the house. It had an old-time, manly feel. Walking into the room transported him into simpler times. A time when men hunted for food and women prepared it. The room resembled a log cabin with slate walnut wood panels on the slanted ceilings and the four walls. A wood ceiling fan hung in the middle of the cathedral ceiling. The floor was made of Brazilian wood, with area rugs strategically placed throughout. A wood-burning oven sat in the center of the room as if it were accidentally dropped there. A small round table with a burgundy and cream cloth sat proudly under an oil-burning lamp. Two Queen Anne chairs sat on either side of the table. A coffee table sat in the middle of the room, separating a four-legged couch, an over-sized wing chair, and a love seat from the chairs. The chairs faced two large picture windows covered with heavy burgundy drapes held opened with tie-backs, giving an amazing view of Brian's colorful spring garden just on the other side of the windows.

The rain was coming down stronger. The Garcia's were not in a rush to leave. The incessant ringing of the phone was being answered by the machine. Many of the callers were news people wanting a story.

The group sat together recalling the events from the day.

Fernando massaged Lucinda's tensed neck.

"Lucinda, please forgive me. I was horrified by what you told the police. I'm sorry doesn't make up for slapping you."

Lucinda smiled sadly at Meredith. "It all right, Mrs. I know you no mean it. Emotions are raw on all of us. No worry no more." She started shaking. "You were right," Lucinda mumbled. Fernando gathered her into his arms.

"No! I was wrong. Very wrong! I had no right to say those cruel things to you. You didn't know Ian's plan. I didn't either. He told me he loved me too before going to bed. The boy never says the words "love" and "you" in the same sentence unless he wants something." Meredith chuckled sadly. "That and the strange feelings I felt should have been a warning, but I didn't pick up on it, either. Please don't feel guilty. There's nothing anyone could have done," Meredith said passionately.

Fernando jumped up. "Yes, there is. The airline! If those stupid idiots hadn't cancelled the flight, your boy would be alive and well, right now."

"Fernando, this isn't anyone's fault," Brian said, staring out into his beautiful, soaked garden. It was the first time he'd spoken since the house emptied.

"Forgive me, sir, but you're wrong," Fernando said emphatically. "Ian should be in the hospital recovering from his surgery, but because the airline cancelled the flight, that didn't happen. The boy was tired of living with the headaches. Ask Lucinda. He didn't like worrying you, neither of you, but especially you." He pointed accusingly at Meredith. "He thinks you're unhappy all the time. He didn't want to add to your sadness, so he kept his pains to himself. Well, he didn't. He shared it with my Lucinda."

Fernando, usually a reserved man, watched the Winthrops accuse Lucinda of knowing Ian was going to take his life and said nothing. He watched Meredith strike his wife and again said nothing. He watched his wife cry but didn't defend herself against the attacks of the people she'd grown to love like family.

Still, he said nothing. He thought back a few hours.

Pulling himself together, Brian escorted everyone into the parlor. He made the introductions. Detective Foley took the oversized wing chair, proving he was the in-charge officer, forcing the others to sit on the couch, love seats, and the Queen Anne chairs.

"We know this is a troublesome time for everyone. We'll be as quick as possible. I've spoken with the EMT's and CSI who are conducting preliminary tests to determine the cause of death. We won't know for sure until an autopsy is conducted." He surveyed the room. "I'd like to ask some questions. I will record your responses. If anyone objects, please tell me, and I'll take notes the old fashion way." He grinned. No one joined him. He pulled a tape recorder from the inside of his wet jacket pocket, placed it in the middle of the coffee table, and spoke clearly into its microphone.

"My name is Detective Roland Foley, it's June 22. I'm at the home of Doctor and Mrs. Brian Winthrop, 908 Locust Valley Lane, Charlotte, NC, 28511, where their thirteen-year-old son, Ian (no middle name) Winthrop, was found dead this morning..."

A loud cry escaped from Meredith and Lucinda simultaneously.

The detective waited a beat before continuing, "... found at 8:09 a.m. on the floor of his bedroom by his mother Meredith (no middle name) Winthrop."

Turning to Meredith, he said, "Would you like a glass of water before you begin?" Shaking her head no, the detective said, "Please, walk us through the events that took place this morning. State your name for the record and speak as clearly as possible. Any details you can remember will be helpful."

Meredith cleared her throat a few times before beginning. Her voice was shaky but clear. "My name is Meredith Winthrop. This morning I went into Ian's room to check on him. Ian's my son.... was my son." She paused to regain her composure. "He's been having severe headaches. He doesn't sleep well. When I entered his room, he was on the floor. That was unusual. He loved his bed. He commented on the comfort of his mattress. I knew something was wrong. I yelled for Brian."

Detective Foley interrupted, "Why did you yell for Doctor Winthrop?"

"I was scared. I thought he may have fallen off of the bed. It's happened before. The other time he had a seizure. I needed Brian."

Brian cringed. She **needed** me. Strong, independent Meredith, **needed** me. *Sadness tightened its grip on him.*

"His room is on the opposite side of the house. I wouldn't have heard him fall. I was also nervous. I had a very sleepless night. I felt, in my bones, that something wasn't right."

"Did you check on him?" Detective Foley asked gently.

"No!" Meredith screeched through tears, pointing accusingly at Brian. "HE told me Ian was fine... that I was over-reacting. OVER-REACTING! Me, a mom! I wish to God, I had followed my instincts and NOT listened to HIM."

Brian flinched.

Meredith broke down again.

The detectives watched Brian even closer, finding it odd that he prevented his wife from checking on their child.

He's hiding something, *Detective Foley thought, making a mental note to revisit that topic.* I wonder what it is.

Detective Foley sent Detective Lawrence a silent message with his facial gestures to watch the doctor closely. His partner nodded in understanding.

Guilt flooded Brian's body. Maybe if I'd believed her, Ian might be alive. Oh.my.God - could I have saved my son's life? *That question would haunt him until his dying day.*

Detective Lawrence saw the guilt trot across the doctor's face. It piqued his interest. What are you hiding, you bastard?

He evaluated him. Brian weighed about 210 pounds, thinning salt and pepper hair, bent nose, thin mustache, grey eyes, some wrinkles splattered on his face, and a little round in the midsection. I guess some women might consider him handsome, eh, that's too strong of a word – maybe attractive. *The detective thought enviously.*

He scrutinized the exquisite Meredith Winthrop oozing of class, even though her world had been shattered. She was a very attractive 51year-old woman. She kept her short chestnut hair tapered at her neck, full on the top, neatly trimmed on the sides, and tucked behind her ears. Her violet eyes were nestled in a heart-shaped face - void of wrinkles and 'character lines'. Her cheekbones were symmetrically placed on either side of her aristocratic nose. Her thin lips framed perfectly straight white teeth. She was 5'9" and very slender. Clothes fit her like they were designed specifically for her, giving her success as a fashion model for several years.

The Winthrops seemed like an odd couple - worlds apart – oil and vinegar. What does she see in him? *Detective Lawrence wondered, searching Meredith's face for the answer.*

Through her tears, she caught Detective Lawrence studying her. He smiled encouragingly.

Detective Foley did the same.

Pull it together, *Meredith advised herself.* I must be strong... I must be strong. Ian was strong. I must be strong, *she chanted over and over in her head. And try she did. Still, it took ten minutes before she was composed enough to continue.*

Officer Malone handed her a box of tissues.

The two officers, Malone and O'Kelly, stayed in case the detectives needed their assistance. The reality was they were in no hurry to go out into the hammering rain. The weather conditions were causing mayhem around the Queen City. They were safer in the Winthrop's home or so they thought.

Things were about to get heated.

~20~

Meredith took a tissue from the box offered from Officer Malone to wipe the tears from her face.

"I called Ian's name. He didn't move. I screamed it... nothing. I panicked. There was something wrong. I shook him. I called Brian... again. Ian was a hard sleeper but can usually be aroused when shaken."

The soft cries from within the room stopped her reverie. Fernando was comforting his wife. Meredith understood how difficult this day was for Lucinda. She, too, lost a child. Lucinda helped raised Ian from infancy. She was there for all of his firsts. Impulsively, Meredith grabbed the box of tissues and sauntered over to her. She handed her friend the tissues and gave her a heartfelt hug. The two mothers clung to one another for what seemed like an eternity. The lawmen were visibly uncomfortable.

Detective Foley cleared his throat. "Whenever you're ready to continue, Mrs. Winthrop," he prodded gently, wanting to end the interview quickly. The weather was worsening. He wanted to run to the security of his home.

"Right," Meredith said, returning to her seat on the couch. "Brian finally came. He too tried to arouse Ian. He checked for a pulse, a heartbeat, any sign of life." Meredith stopped. This was difficult.

"Brian finally came." Interesting choice of words, *the detective mused.* What were you doing, Doctor? *Suspicion was written all over Detective Foley's face as he said to Brian, "Would you like to continue?"*

"Sure, I heard Mer scr...."

"Sorry to interrupt, sir, but please state your full name for the

record," Detective Foley instructed.

Brian tossed him a hard look. Doesn't he realize how difficult this is? Doesn't he care? *Brian vented in his head.* Why would he? It's not his life, his family, his son. It's just a job for him.

After another prompting from Detective Foley, Brian spoke in a clear, concise voice. "My name is Brian Richard Winthrop, Jr. I am Ian's father." The detectives watched him closely. "Ian was named after me. I'm a Junior but hold little regard for Brian Senior. I didn't want Ian to be the "third" yet, I wanted to give him a part of me. Meredith and I took the Br off, and voila Ian was born. We agreed not to give him a middle name. His mother doesn't have one, and I don't have an allegiance to mine. What's its purpose? Meredith lived just fine without one, and I hardly use mine."

Brian was aware he was rambling but sharing the origin of his son's name made him feel closer to him.

He smiled at one of the many memories of the two of them discussing Ian not having a middle name.

"But Pop," Ian complained, "all the really cool people have a middle name which they turn into initials like LL Cool J."

Brian tried not to smile. "Those are not his initials, bud. That's his professional name. His initials are TJ."

Wrong example to use. Ian's smile grew wide. He knew everything about his favorite rapper. Brian realized a bit too late that he'd been conned. "You've just proven my point, Pop." Ian laughed victoriously. "Todd James is a super cool name – TJ for short. And my friend James...everyone calls him JR – James Robert and Michael Jerome, the kid on my baseball team is called MJ... "Lookout MJ, the ball is coming. Steal that base MJ. You got this MJ." Ian mocked the parents yelling from the stands during their baseball games. "And my best..."

"Okay, okay, okay," Brian relented, laughing. "So what should your middle name be? Richard – IR. How about Peter, IP, or Dave – ID? I got it... Steven IS. That's it. We'll call you IS. Is, come here. Is, hand me the remote... Is... is your homework done?"

They fell back against the car seat laughing. Brian could

barely see through the windshield from the laughing tears clouding his eyes.

"You win this round, Pop but not the war. I'll be back with a super cool middle name to go with Ian."

Brian pulled up to the curb, stopped the car, and let Ian out for baseball practice.

The detectives waited patiently for Brian to rejoin them from his trip down memory lane.

Visibly shaking the sadness away, Brian continued. "I was in the bathroom when I heard my wife screaming for me. I ran into Ian's room. He was motionless on the floor. I tried waking him, but he didn't budge. I checked his pulse, his heartbeat, and his breathing. I gave him CPR. I ran back to my room to get my stethoscope. I listened to his heart again. Then I called 911."

"How did your son die?" Detective Lawrence asked, speaking for the first time since entering the house.

"Isn't that what the autopsy will determine?" Brian snapped.

Shocked, everyone looked at him oddly.

"I'm tired," he explained, running a hand through his hair. "I don't enjoy being a suspect in my child's death. I see the looks passing between you as you "watch" me. I know the question burning in your brain – why didn't he want his wife to check on their son?"

Detective Foley raised an eyebrow. Detective Lawrence waited to see where the conversation was going.

Detective Foley used the opportunity to address him. "Well, sir, since ***you*** *brought it up... why didn't you want your wife to check on your son?"*

Brian hesitated. How could he explain to these people why? It was none of their business. He said as much. "It's none of your business."

Detective Foley studied him. Hmm... interesting response. *"Doctor, is the reason you didn't want your wife checking on your son because you already knew he was dead?"*

Gasp and mutters swept the room.

The calm Brian Winthrop erupted. He stood up and charged towards the detective. "You no good, insensitive jerk. How dare you?"

He pulled his arm back to punch the detective but was restrained by Officer Malone, who'd reached him first.

"Doctor Winthrop, I understand this is very emotional. This is not the way to handle this. Please, sir, get a grip." He gently urged Brian back to his seat. He didn't sit down.

"How dare that pompous ass insinuate that I killed my boy," Brian shouted. "I was just as shocked as my wife (he emphasized the word wife staring at Detective Lawrence) to find Ian… de… unresponsive this morning." He couldn't say the word "dead".

"Doctor, as I've stated, we are trying to find out what happened to your son. I apologize if you misunderstood my question. I only wanted to know if you knew your son was dead."

"And how would I know that, Detective Foley? What I'm hearing is…" Brian said evenly. "You believe I killed my son. Got back in bed with my wife. Made love to her." He threw that in casually. Meredith's eyes shot wide-opened.

"… then went to sleep knowing she would find Ian in the morning. What kind of a monster do you think I am?"

"I wasn't implying YOU had anything to do with his death." Detective Foley fringed innocence. "I'm here to investigate, not accuse anyone of wrongdoing."

Brian knew the detective was lying. He could tell by the way he was scrutinizing him.

Officer Malone urged Brian to reclaim his seat. He did. He took in a few deep breaths. He let them out slowly.

"You people don't seem to realize we are mourning. We shouldn't be here. We had a scheduled flight to New York. Our flight was cancelled yesterday and my son is gone today. How the hell am I supposed to know what happened?"

For the second time since finding Ian's lifeless body, Brian exploded. The tears ran like lava. As hard as he tried, he couldn't control them. Fernando and Lucinda rushed to his side, comforting him. Lucinda handed him the tissues. Meredith could not go to him. Her legs felt like bricks, weighing her down, keeping her trapped in the seat. Or maybe it was her guilt that immobilized her. Why did he say we made love? Does he know?

"I'm sorry, sir. We didn't mean to upset you," Detective Lawrence said.

Brian did not acknowledge the young, good-looking detective. He directed his response to Detective Foley. "I noticed an empty bottle of pain pills by Ian's bed."

"Did you prescribe the pills, Doctor?" Detective Foley asked gently.

Brian tried not to get upset again. He gave himself a pep talk before answering. He's only doing his job. He has to ask these difficult questions. Answer him, get rid of THEM. Grieve in peace.

"No, I did not," Brian answered. "His physician – Doctor Jake Lafayette prescribed them for his headaches. I will give you his telephone number."

"That will be helpful, sir." Glancing over his hand-written notes – the ones he wasn't going to take – the detective said, "You stated you were going to New York – why? And why would not going make Ian so upset he allegedly took his own life?"

Brian cringed at the word "allegedly".

"I think I can answer that." Everyone turned towards Lucinda.

~21~

"Why can **you** *answer that, Lucinda?" Meredith asked suspiciously.*

"What haven't you told us, Luci?" Brian inquired.

"Please state your name and position or relation to Ian Winthrop," Detective Foley instructed.

Wringing her hands together, Lucinda glanced at her husband for support. He nodded and whispered, "¡Puedes hacer esto!"

"My name is Lucinda Lourdes Nicolette Perez Garcia."

"Is there any room left on the tape?" Detective Lawrence joked.

No one found humor in his statement. He received icy glares.

"I'm going outside to warm up. It's a little chilly in here." The investigator stated jovially, rushing towards the door.

"Excuse my partner. He's a little green," Detective Folly explained.

Stopping at the comment, Detective Lawrence re-entered the room. "I am not green. I was a street cop for six years before becoming a Sergeant. I was a damn good Sergeant for over eleven years. Then I threw my hat into the detective ring and got stuck with this Bozo." He smiled fondly at his partner, his mentor.

Snapping, Brian said, "Didn't realize you were applying for a job. I thought you were investigating the "circumstances" surrounding my son's death."

All eyes turned on Brian.

What has gotten into him? *Meredith pondered for the second time.*

Detective Lawrence blushed a deep crimson. "I'm sorry, Mr. Winthrop. You are...

"DOCTOR," Brian said harshly. "Doctor Winthrop. As you so unabashedly recited your credentials, here are mine. I've worked damn hard, for thirteen years, to earn the title "doctor". I've established **several successful** practices. I am a member of the Board of Trustee for the American Medical Association. I've been featured as one of the best orthopedic surgeons in the United States by US News for eight consecutive years. I will not be disrespected in my own home. If you can't respect that, I politely ask you to remove yourself."

"Whoa, Brian. Take it easy." Meredith cautioned. "What's going on?"

Brian remained silent, waiting for Detective Lawrence's next move.

The detective cleared his throat. "I think we got off on the wrong foot, 'Doctor'."

Brian winced. He didn't like the way the detective said "doctor". It sounded like a curse word.

"I apologize, 'doctor'. I did not intend to disrespect anyone in this room. This is a delicate situation. My credentials are only important to me. My qualifications shouldn't have been questioned, but I apologize for my insensitivity."

Brian did not acknowledge the apology.

Detective Foley also apologized before returning to business. "Please continue, Mrs. Garcia."

"Gracias Señor. I am nanny to Ian and housekeeper to Mrs. and Doctor Brian. The Winthrops take Ian to Sloan Kettering Hospital in New York, where specialist perform brain surgery on him. Ian have very bad brain tumor. The tumor it diagnosed several weeks ago but it grow fast. The only way to save him life was surgery."

"Why go all the way to New York when we have fine doctors right here? Isn't flying with a brain tumor dangerous?" Detective Foley questioned.

Brian spoke up. "Again, my name is Brian Richard Winthrop, Jr. I am an orthopedic surgeon." He glared briefly at Detective Lawrence who had retaken his seat. "Ian was diagnosed with Craniopharyngioma... a noncancerous rare brain tumor. There are less than 200,000 diagnosed cases in this country. As Lucinda stated, it *was spreading quickly. This was strange because characteristically, this particular tumor doesn't spread. It had to be removed in case it turned cancerous.*

"If we drove twelve hours to New York, Ian wouldn't have received the proper rest required for a successful surgery. His headaches were progressively worse. Frankly, the long drive may have resulted in an aneurysm. Yes, sometimes flying is dangerous. The flying time to New York is quick. The risk was nominal and his doctor cleared him to fly. We had to get Ian to New York. Flying was our best and fastest solution.

"Charlotte has many first-rate doctors. However, Doctor Brunn, a specialist, flew in from Germany to personally perform Ian's surgery. His success rate for removing difficult brain tumors, such as Ian's, is 100%. Doctor Brunn isn't affiliated with any North Carolina hospitals. We didn't have time to wait for him to receive the necessary licenses. He is affiliated with Sloan Kettering, which has state-of-the-art equipment." Brian wiped his eyes. "Surgery was set for early this morning, but the flight was cancelled."

Lucinda picked up the story, after restating her name. "Ian call very early this morning. I think like 2 or 3 a.m. He not able to sleep. He cry on phone. Break my heart. He say he can't live with pain no more. Say it was unbearable. His words were slurring. He needed a wheelchair. He hated it. He say boys his age should be free to run and play ball with friends not stuck in wheelchair. He loved baseball and soccer. They were his favorite sports.

"He say he looking forward to surgery. He would finally be free from headaches. But he say maybe the Lord have other plans for him. Why else would flight get cancelled? I tell him his parents will make other arrangements. He snap at me. He say they been through enough. He couldn't watch them suffer no more. He say his mommy sad all time, his pop work all time. That no way to live. He say he was a burden. He say if there is a God, he wouldn't put him and his family through 'this torture'." Lucinda made quotes with her fingers.

She spoke the next words slowly. "He tell me he love me. He say he always love me. Not to feel guilty for his decisions. I ask what he mean. He say, "I love you, Luci. Take care of mommy and pop. They need you. Tell Nando I love him too. Thank you, Luci. Goodbye.

"I say, Ian, what you mean? What you talking about? But he crying and hang up phone."

Meredith was in Lucinda's face before she could take her next breath. "You stupid, stupid woman. My son says goodbye to you, and you don't think to call me... to warn me or his father so we could watch him. My son would still be alive if you weren't so damn stupid."

Lucinda flinched as if she was kicked in the gut. "I know Mrs. and I'm..."

"Don't you dare tell me you're sorry! Sorry, will not bring my son back. How could you be so stupid?"

"Mrs. I not think..."

"You're damn right you weren't thinking."

The room was quiet except for Lucinda's sobs.

A woman from the coroner's office entered. She handed a paper to Police Officer O'Kelly, who was standing closest to the door observing those in the room. He scanned the paper, let out a whistle then handed it to Detective Foley. He read it then passed it to Detective Lawrence.

The officers looked at Detective Foley for direction.

Clearing his throat, the detective said, "The preliminaries show that the cause of death may not have been the pain killers your son ingested."

All emotions seized. An eerie silence penetrated the room. All eyes turned on Detective Foley, ears tuned on high volume.

He paused, staring intently at each of the four adults in the room but focused on Brian.

"Which one of you concerned loved ones murdered Ian Winthrop?"

~22~

THE AIRPORT

By twelve o'clock the weather had not cleared. It was amazing how many people made it to the airport in the dreadful weather. People were everywhere – sitting on chairs, standing in corners, sprawled out on the floor or on luggage, standing at counters but no matter where a person was physically – they were all doing the same thing - staring at the television monitors. The scenes were mesmerizing.

This was one of the largest storms experienced by the east coast in recorded history. There were mudslides, floods, power outages, and blocked roads. It was reported that in one New York City neighborhood the water level was so high, people were paddling through the streets in boats - leave it to New Yorkers!

The storm wasn't slowing down.

Suddenly, the airport was engulfed in total darkness. Pandemonium ensued. The passengers went nuts, pushing and screaming, trying to get.... nowhere. Security came rushing from everywhere to take control and prevent rioting and looting. Several minutes later the back-up generator kicked on, casting the airport in an eerie glow.

The microphones were inoperative. An industrious ticket agent climbed on top of the ticket counter with a bullhorn to announce all flights for the day were cancelled. The Charlotte airport was officially closed and would reopen in the morning, weather permitting. Nothing could be done without computer systems, lights, or telephone service. Once the airport was fully operable, new tickets would be issued.

Before putting the bullhorn down, the agent added, "A state of emergency has been declared. The police and emergency workers are pulling everyone off the streets. The airport is on lockdown - meaning no one may enter or leave until further notice. This is for your safety. You are inside, you are safe. When there's a change, we will make an announcement. Thank you for your cooperation."

The agent stepped down from the counter, placed the bullhorn behind the desk then turned to address the waiting mob at the counter.

ϟ ϟ ϟ ϟ ϟ ϟ

Kami was lonely. Her cell phone wasn't getting service. Her novel was finished, her iPod needed charging, and she was hungry. The bookstore was closed, the restrooms full, food lines were long, and restaurants were running low on food.

She didn't know what was happening in New York. Was the weather still bad? Was Dante waiting for her? Was he gone? She was in a panic. She couldn't think straight. She couldn't leave the airport – not that she had anywhere to go.

Damn those car-rental agents. Because of their incompetence, she was placed on Flight 3236, a flight she shouldn't have been on... a flight **she** didn't book.

And damn Mother Nature for getting her cycle when Kami so desperately needed to see her husband.

She prayed she wouldn't be too late.

After the 10 a.m. flight was cancelled, Erich planned to drive to New York. What other choice did he have? Who was he kidding? *CNN* showed the disasters occurring along the east coast. The rain was making its mark and leaving chaos in its exit. Miriam's BMW convertible would not make it and there were no rental cars available. He wished he had his Hummer. Nothing could stop that tank, but Miriam had driven it to Florida for her "girls" vacation.

He was at a standstill. If only Erika and Lenny had taken him up on his offer and moved to the Carolinas when he'd found the perfect home for them. It was a five-bedroom colonial style house right on the lake. It was beautiful, in a great school district, and only five miles from his place of residence. The couple refused, stating their life was in New York near their aging parents.

What was he to do? Erika's life was dependent on him and he was dependent on WorldLine Airways. He couldn't get to her without transportation. Hopelessness descended heavily upon him. Erika was not just his sister, she was literally a part of him. How could he exist without his twin?

He recalled her visit to *Alfred University*, where she met and fell in love with his best friend. He thought about his nephews, Erika and Lenny's twin sons. They were handling their mother's medical condition like brave young boys. His eyes misted when he thought back to when his parents broke the news of Erika's medical condition.

"Erika has Glomerulonephritis," his father stated.

"She has what?" Erich yelled.

"Glomerulonephritis. It's a disease that damages the kidneys' filtering units called glomeruli," explained his father.

So they can just give her some pills and she'll be okay, right?" Erich asked hopefully.

"I'm afraid it's not that simple, son." His father answered. "Erika has an 'end-stage kidney disease'. About 90 percent of her kidney function has been lost."

"Dad, are you saying Erika's dying?" Erich asked.

His father never answered his question. Instead, he spoke of Erika's options and told him she and Lennie chose the kidney transplant.

"We agreed it is the most efficient solution. Then we discovered The United Network for Organ Sharing kidney transplant waitlist was 108,017..."

Although they lived very separate lives, they were very close. He had to save her. But how? He sat immobilized. Watching the rain pounding the windowpanes of the airport terminal, he recalled his visit to New York to have his kidney tested to see if it matched Erika's.

He was shocked when he saw her. Her cheeks were sharp-boned and sunken. Her hair once thick and full of bounce was thinned and laid dull and lifeless on her head. Her skin was a yellowish gray. As she reached to hug him, he tried to avert his eyes from her hands, which were like skin-covered bones. He put on a brave face, but inside he was an emotional mess. He was comforted that her sense of humor had not dissipated. She somehow kept smiling, even when in pain.

He groaned at the memory when his parents met Miriam... his Nubian queen... his breath of fresh air... in person. *That sure didn't go over well,* he chuckled. Miriam didn't find humor in the situation.

Erika waited until he was leaving for the airport to broach the topic of that visit.

"Mother told me about Miriam. She asked why I hadn't mentioned she was African American. I'm not sure she believed me when I said I didn't know. You and I never discussed her race."

"Are we discussing it now?" He asked. His voice was soft in sharp contrast to his foreboding expression.

"Erich, I don't want to upset you. I have nothing against Miriam. I don't know her. I can tell **you** *love her.* **I** *can accept that. It's Mother who has the problem."*

Erich explained why Miriam meant so much to him.

Erika felt the passion in her brother's words. It touched her deeply. She threw her arms around his neck and said, "I am happy for you, Erich. I cannot wait to meet Miriam in person. I know I will like her."

Erich dropped his bomb. "I hope the two of you get along because whether or not Mother likes it when I return to Charlotte, I'm asking Miriam to marry me."

His mother was livid when she learned about the engagement. She tried a multiple of things to convince Erich he was making a terrible mistake.

Her final words to her son on the subject were, "Erich, I do not approve of your decision. She is not the right girl for you. I will never accept her as your wife."

Erich said three words to his mother, "So be it."

Erich did not divulge that conversation with Miriam. He did share it with Erika, who already knew. Richelle Coppenhauge called her daughter crying. She was furious that Erich chose "that black girl" over his own mother. Erika warned Richelle that if she didn't accept Miriam she risked losing Erich.

Richelle stated, "That's a chance I may have to take. I will never give that union my blessing."

Erika was too weak to fight.

She didn't tell Erich about the conversation with their mother. Instead, she said, "Send her a wedding invitation."

Miriam and Erika spoke on the phone a few times. They got along fabulously. They couldn't wait to meet one another.

Erich could not believe what was happening. He felt like he was in a poorly directed "B" rated horror movie. He was trapped in an airport. What else could go wrong? Was he here for the night? Was the chair he sat on his sleeping quarters? He felt helpless. He needed to regroup.

He rose and walked towards the men's room, pulling his carryon behind him. Noticing the never-ending line outside the women's bathroom, he was thankful he was a man. Entering the men's room, he found an empty stall, went inside, and sat on the toilet with his pants intact. He weighed his alternatives, knowing his only option was to call Doctor Israel. He'd put the call off for as long as he could.

With trepidation, he punched in the numbers embedded in his brain. His hands trembled slightly, his forehead broke out in a cold sweat, and his heartbeat escalated. He felt in his being that something had changed in his sister's condition. Suddenly, he was terrified of speaking with the doctor. The phone rang. He had service!!! That meant he was destined to speak with the doctor. *Why am I nervous*?

"Doctor Israel here."

"Hello, Doctor. It's Erich. Thank God you answered. I couldn't make this call again. I have bad news." His voice cracked. "My flight was cancelled because.... because of... of the weather. No planes in or out. The airport has lost power and is closed... closed until... tomorrow," Erich paused.

Doctor Israel could hear the tears in his voice.

"I cannot... um... I can't... I... um... make it to New York. Driving is impossible. I... I... cannot save Erika. I..."

"Erich, listen to me," Doctor Israel interrupted. "You're no longer needed. Erika is..."

The line went dead.

"Hello? Doctor Israel?" Eric removed the lifeless phone from his ear. He frantically dialed Doctor Israel's number – nothing. He hit redial – still nothing. He scowled at the phone in his hand. Missing signal bars.

No, no, no, no, no. This is not happening. Doctor Israel's last words rambled inside his head. "Erika is... what, Doctor? Erika is what?" Erich screamed from the stall, banging his fist against the wall. The man in the adjacent stall hurried to finish his business, flushed, and ran out of the bathroom without washing his hands.

Doctor Israel's earlier words vibrated in his head: *slight fever, temporarily lost consciousness, revived, shock at any moment, kidney transplanted ASAP.*

Erich covered his ears to silence the words. He rubbed his head. "What was the doctor trying to tell me?" He shrieked trying to block out the reverberating words. "Erika is..." *Oh God.... What could it be? Did she lose consciousness again? Spike another fever? Went into shock? He said I wasn't needed anymore. Why? His tone was so... hushed... sad... morbid? Oh, God, no. It can't be. But what else fits?* "Erika is... dead."

His entire life spent with Erika flashed before his eyes.

The wail was long and loud. It sounded like a wounded animal ensnared in a trap. The remaining men in the bathroom fled. The wail was heard inside the waiting area. Numerous people turned towards the eerie noise. Their hairs stood on end.

Several police officers stationed in the waiting area entered the men's room with weapons drawn. The squeals continued.

"It sounds like a Bobcat," one of the police officers stated. "But how could an animal have gotten into the airport, then into the men's bathroom, without being seen?"

"It is kind of dark," another officer offered. "Nothing surprises me. Lately, strange things have been happening at this airport."

Nervously, the first policeman knocked on the closed stall door where the sound was emitting. The second officer cast a glance at him that asked, "*Really?*"

Reaching across him, the second officer pushed against the unlocked door. It swung open to reveal Erich sitting on the toilet fully dressed with his head leaning sideways against the stall's wall. Bucket size teardrops fell from open, wild, blank eyes. His left arm rested in his lap. His right arm was hanging towards the floor with his cell phone dangling from his hand. The officers regarded each other. There was no question in their minds. This man had cracked. Taking the phone from him, the two officers slowly and carefully lifted a catatonic Erich to his feet, leading him away with the anguish cries emanating from his mouth. A third officer followed, pulling Erich's carryon luggage.

~23~

"Daddy, we're scared," Kara spoke for her and her brother. "We want to go home. We don't want to go to Puerto Rico or New York anymore. This isn't fun. We just want to go home."

Kevin studied his children. He definitely related to their feelings. As the adult, he had to remain optimistic - for them and for Janice. Her conversation with the famous Nate Hill no longer had her on top of the world. A man of his status wouldn't wait on her forever. People would kill to get that job. Mr. Hill had many options. She felt so lost, so broken. She was tired of her life... tired of taking one step forward and three steps back. She sat in her chair, rocking back and forth, humming a non-rhythmic tune, staring off into space, trying to lose herself from her situation, from her life.

Janice's reaction and the squeals from the bathroom were scaring his children.

"Why are those policemen carrying that man?" Kane asked, staring after the entourage leaving the men's room.

"I don't know," Kevin answered. "He looks sick."

"He looks crazy?" Kara returned frankly.

Ah, like mother, like daughter. Kevin grinned.

"What's the matter with Ms. Monroe?" Kane questioned.

"She looks crazy too," Kara interjected.

"Kara, don't be rude," Kevin reprimanded.

Kara shrugged. She was calling it as she saw it.

"She must get to New York," Kevin explained to Kane. "She's

very sad that we're stuck here."

"Us too!" Kara stated bluntly. "And we want out."

Kevin spoke slowly, "We can't leave. The airport is closed. We are stuck here for the night."

"But we don't wanna stay here, Daddy," Kara whined.

"No one does, Kara," he snapped. "But that's just the way it is. We don't have a choice. We are sleeping on these chairs tonight. Now stop whining."

Kara and Kane burst into tears. Kevin felt horrible. He gathered them in his arms and apologized. He explained he was tired and frustrated, but there was nothing anyone could do because of the dreadful weather.

ϟ ϟ ϟ ϟ ϟ ϟ

Jade watched an expensively dressed man, about 6'1", average weight, in his early thirties, resembling *Christopher Reeve* as *Clark Kent,* being led from the bathroom. She wondered what his story was and where they were taking him. According to the "bullhorn" employee, the airport was on lockdown.

The man looked familiar. But then again, everyone was looking familiar. He looked like he used a gym membership on a regular basis. His head, full of brown curls, was leaning to the side. His black-framed glasses couldn't cover the crazed look in his brown eyes.

She probably had a similar look in hers. She was about to lose her mind - sitting and waiting – sitting and waiting. If she didn't get on a plane soon, she too would be escorted out, only not by police officers but by people wearing white coats.

Jade didn't know what to do. She couldn't call anyone. There was no service. She didn't know what was happening in the rest of the world. All she knew was it was afternoon. Although the airport's dreary lighting and the darkness outside made her question the time on her watch. She wanted to get up and go somewhere, anywhere but didn't dare leave her seat for fear of losing it. Since she was stuck in place, she searched for a friendly face, someone to talk to. Everywhere she looked, people were wearing scowls.

Kami noticed the attractive Hispanic woman with the amazing blue eyes scoping her surroundings. She wondered who she was searching for.

Jade felt someone watching her. Continuing her search, she caught beautiful, almond-shaped eyes of an Asian, no wait – African American – uh that wasn't right either, possibly Puerto Rican... uh no, Persian - maybe. The beautiful woman's ethnicity was difficult to discern. Her jet black hair complemented her butterscotch-colored skin.

She smiled at Jade. Jade shyly returned one of her own. A family sitting nearby moved. The beautiful woman swiftly left her seat for the vacated ones. She motioned for Jade to join her before anyone grabbed the seats. Jade quickly followed suit.

The usually reserved Kami sensed a vulnerability, a sadness about Jade that drew her to her.

"Hello, I'm Kami," she said.

"Hi, I'm Jade."

Kami had an innocence that made Jade want to protect her.

Awkwardness followed. Neither woman knew what to say. What seemed like a good idea at first no longer did.

"I'm sorry," Kami said, hoping to shatter the awkwardness. "I don't know anyone and saw you sitting by yourself, searching for someone, and since we are stuck in the airport... I don't know.... I saw you sitting by yourself. Are you waiting for anyone?"

Jade shook her head staring at Kami peculiarly.

"I'm by myself, too. I may have already said that. You're by yourself... Anyway, I just thought... maybe..." She stopped. *Why is she staring at me like that?*

Realization hit her like a dropped egg to the floor. Kami

laughed so hard her stomach hurt.

"Oh my goodness," she said between giggles. "You didn't... you do. You think I'm hitting on you, don't you?"

"Awkward, but it crossed my mind," Jade answered honestly. "I mean, you're gorgeous. You look like a model – except you're not that tall. What are you... about 5'4"?"

"And-three-quarters!" Kami said pouting. Her height was a sore subject. She generally stated her height at 5'5". *What's a 1/4"?* She usually rationalized. She wished she was a tad bit taller – about Jade's height – 5'6"/5'7".

Oblivious to the stranger's feelings, Jade continued. "I've heard some models swing both ways."

"OMG! That's too funny. You thought I was hitting on you!" Kami chuckled harder, drawing stares from the frustrated people around them. "I can't wait to tell my husband."

Whew! She's married... to a man. Jade also laughed.

The awkwardness was broken.

"I needed that," Kami admitted.

"Me too," Jade agreed, wiping the tears from her eyes. "This stinks." She said, returning to reality.

She told Kami the reason she was on her way to Puerto Rico. "I should have known something was going to happen. This is the year of my thirtieth birthday."

"You're turning thirty?" Kami asked. "You look much younger."

"Gosh, thanks," Jade gushed. "Yep, in November I'll be an old maid." She shuddered.

"What do you mean... something happens? Is it something bad?"

"Usually."

"I mean turning thirty is a milestone. You may want to hide in the closet with a huge bottle of wine but I wouldn't call it 'bad'."

Jade chuckled. "It's not the turning 'thirty' part. It's the five-year part. Every five years something tragic happens to me, except once, when I turned twenty." She smiled at the memory.

"I met the most amazing man – Oscar Livingston." Jade shared little snippets of their life together. Withholding tears, she explained the tragedy that had befallen her late fiancé the year she turned twenty-five.

When she completed the tale of her life with Oscar, Kami exclaimed, "How very awful for you." She wiped the tears from her face. Impulsively, she embraced her new friend. Jade didn't resist. Each was surprised at her reception of the other.

Jade excused herself. Kami saved her seat while she went into the bathroom... cried, washed her face, glared at her reflection, and scolded herself. *You should be able to talk about Oscar without falling apart. It's been five years.*

Maybe Dante can introduce her to one of his friends. Kami thought sitting alone, waiting for Jade to return. She was very attractive, even devoid of make-up and light dark circles under her small slanted eyes. Her jean skort accentuated her hourglass figure making men take notice. Kami was sure Dante wouldn't have a problem fixing Jade up with one of his buddies.

Kami was astonished that in five years, Jade had not found anyone worthy of dating. But truth be told, if anything happened to Dante, she too would remain alone for the rest of her life.

Refreshed, Jade rejoined Kami. She told her about the Oscar Livingston Foundation started by his lawyer friend, Marla Murphy-Meadows. Kami surmised that Oscar had to be a very special person. She made a mental note to research the foundation then send a sizeable, anonymous donation when she returned to Arizona.

Kami told Jade she was an event planner. "I work for my best friend, Debra, who owns an event planning company called, "An Affair to Remember".

"Catchy name. I like it," Jade said.

"Two nights ago, we had the official kickoff event for a non-profit organization called *A Total Change (ATC)*. Its mission is to help young women who age out of the foster care system become a viable, functioning part of society, by providing housing, resources, education, and the skills needed for them to function on their own without becoming a product of 'the system'."

"Hmm... interesting," Jade mused. "I must look them up. My papá grew up in the foster care system, so that's a cause dear to my heart. I'd like to donate money to them."

Jade took a pen and paper from her handbag and wrote the name of the organization, *A Total Change (ATC).*

Kami shared the news of her pregnancy and explained that her wonderful husband was waiting for her in New York.

"He doesn't know yet. I'm going to tell him when I get there."

"Ooh, that's awesome, Kami. That will be the best surprise!" Jade pushed away the melancholy and memories trying to smother her.

This isn't about you. Stay focused on your new friend, she told herself

"You don't think I should have told him over the phone?" Kami tried hiding her anxiety.

Jade scuffed. "Over the phone? Are you nuts? That news should ONLY be shared in person."

Kami hugged Jade super tight. Jade was astonished.

"Oh, thank you. You don't know how much your words mean to me."

"I think I do," Jade teased. "You tried to squeeze the life out of me."

Kami laughed. "It's just that I am very anxious. A childhood friend told me I should have told Dante as soon as I found out." She tried to maintain her sense of peace, but she could feel the anxiety creeping in.

"What fun would that have been? Obviously, that friend doesn't have children. This way, you get to see his expression when you tell him. Nah, this is way better."

Kami went to hug Jade again but was stopped. Jade held out her hand. "I need to breathe to see my baby sister get married."

Kami laughed.

"I'm teasing. I'm a hugger too."

The two women hugged each other... Kami, not as tight as the last time.

Soon they were laughing and swapping stories. Time was flying, but it didn't matter - they had nowhere to go.

Eventually, a comfortable silence settled between them.

"Do you think Fight 3236 was cancelled because you're turning thirty?" Kami asked a short while later.

Jade mulled over the question. "It makes sense. This is the time for the five-year curse."

"But Jade, all those awful things that happened in the past directly affected you. The plane getting cancelled affected a bunch of people – including me."

Jade thought about that. "Hmm... that's true. But it fits. The five-year curse... the plane getting cancelled, the storm, everything... it fits. What else could it be?"

Unfortunately, the answer will destroy Jade's world.

~24~

THE WINTHROP FAMILY

No one moved. Shock held them pinned in place.

Detective Foley read the note aloud. "Ian Winthrop has handprints on the sides of his neck consistent with choking or strangulation."

An audible gasp echoed throughout the room. Disbelief followed, with anger closely behind.

The room exploded.

Detective Lawrence knew what his partner was aiming for, so he closely monitored each person's reaction.

Brian was lost in his thoughts, wondering how he missed the bruises on Ian's neck.

Lucinda's eyes were wide with shock, tears streaming down her face.

Meredith and Fernando were livid.

Fernando sat quietly steaming.

Meredith shrieked. "How dare you come into MY/OUR home and accuse us of murdering our son? Are you insane? Have you lost your little pea brain, Detective?"

She glared at Detective Lawrence. He refused to meet her stare.

"I'm only here to investigate, not to accuse," Meredith mimicked Detective Foley's earlier comment. She stood. "We're done. I want you and your partner out of my house right now. We have nothing more to say to you. GET OUT NOW!"

"Ma'am, take it easy. I..." Detective Foley tried.

"Take it easy? Take it easy?" Meredith wailed. "First, you accuse my husband and then all of us of killing my child. My son. My son is dead, Detective. D.E.A.D and you want me to take it easy? Have you ever lost a child? A thriving, healthy, beautiful child? Huh? Have you?" She waited for the answer.

Detective Foley squirmed. Detective Lawrence wished he had gone outside. That storm was safer than the one in the room.

"I'm waiting, Detective. Have you ever lost YOUR child?"

The detective blanched. "No, ma'am, I have not," he admitted quietly.

"Do you **have** *children?" Meredith's voice was calm, but the overflowing tears belied her emotions.*

"Yes, ma'am."

"How old?"

Detective Foley cleared his throat. He wished he could withdraw his question. Usually, when he pulled that stunt, a guilty party emerged – either with a confession, a flicker of guilt across the face, a flash in the eye, posture change, etc. That wasn't the case here. None of the people in the room appeared to have "choked" Ian Winthrop. He regretted his impulse. Now he was in the hot seat.

"How old, Detective?" Meredith asked again.

"A daughter seventeen and two sons fourteen and nine."

Meredith's eyes didn't waver from the detective's face. "A fourteen-year-old son, huh?"

She swallowed her pain, violet eyes blazing. She would never again hear the laughter or wipe the tears of her thirteen-year-old son, while this person got to go home to his. Her family would never be the same, yet his was intact.

"Is this fourteen-year-old son of yours alive, Detective? Was he well the last time you saw him? Is he healthy? Waiting for you to get home? To give him a hug or a high five?" At that moment she resented the detective for the family he had waiting for him. She had to fight the hate... the envy seeping into her body.

Harshly, she asked, "When you go home to your nice, healthy family, Detective, will you murder one of them?"

"That's absurd," the detective spat.

"Yes, about as absurd as one of us murdering Ian," Meredith responded calmly. "I've asked once, now I'm telling you – get the hell out of my house.... NOW!"

Detective Foley said, "I really must finish this investi..."

"Your investigation **is** *finished. Officer O'Kelly, these men are now trespassing. If they are not off of my property in the next minute, I want them arrested."*

Brian was in a daze. Why didn't I notice the marks?

Fernando was seething. All Ms. Meredith has to do is ask me to throw them out. I will do it with pleasure. How dare they? And the nerve of that one showing up here. Just say the word, Mrs., just say the word, *he begged silently.*

Lucinda was twisting her hands, wishing she had her Rosary beads between her fingers.

Officer O'Kelly told the detectives to wait outside the room while he tried to repair their damage.

The detectives complied.

Officer O'Kelly knelt before Meredith. "Mrs. Winthrop, the detectives are only doing their jo..."

"By accusing us of killing our child?"

"Yeah, that wasn't smart," the officer admitted. "But Detective Foley is a good detective. One of the best. He has caught a lot of perps using that tactic. Why he used it now is beyond me. I am asking you to allow them to return so we can conclude the investigation, leave, and allow your family peace to grieve. Plus, the weather is pretty bad. We're probably needed elsewhere."

Meredith inspected the senior cop. He took her soft hands into his over-worked ones. "Please, Mrs. Winthrop. If he oversteps his boundaries again, I will personally escort him out."

She saw sincerity oozing from his intelligent blue eyes. She trusted the police officer. She nodded her consent. Officer O'Kelly left the room. He returned a few minutes later with a beet-red Detective Foley and an obnoxious-looking Detective Lawrence.

Detective Foley approached Meredith but addressed everyone in the room. "I apologize for my insensitivity. It was uncalled for. We have not confirmed the cause of death. I am a trained professional who has acted anything but professional today. Please, accept my sincere apologies, all of you."

Meredith, always the lady, accepted graciously. Fernando refused to budge. Lucinda kept fidgeting. Brian was in a world all his own.

"May I?" The detective asked humbly, indicating the seat he once occupied.

Meredith nodded. Each of the detectives resumed their previous positions.

The mood in the room was charged with negative energy, making everyone tense.

Nervously, Detective Foley flipped opened his notebook and reread his notes. He changed the tape in the recorder.

He cleared his throat. He proceeded with caution. "Doctor, you stated earlier that you performed CPR on your son after you found him. Is that correct?"

Brian slowly emerged from his trance. Detective Foley watched the many emotions flashing across his face.

"Is that correct, sir?"

"Is what correct?" Brian asked, frustrated. What was the man talking about? When were they leaving? He had a lot on his mind.

"Did you give Ian CPR?"

"Yes."

"Then... sir," the investigator prodded gently. "Why didn't you see the bruises on his neck?"

"I DON'T KNOW!" Brian barked. "What kind of doctor doesn't notice the... especially on his own son? Oh, God, I can't do th...."

He rushed from the room into the nearby hall bathroom. He paced back and forth, berating himself for his carelessness, letting the tears stream down his face. He assumed the empty pill bottle lying next to his son was the cause of death.

"Stupid, stupid, stupid!" Brian shrieked, banging his head against the bathroom door.

Fernando knocked on the door. "Doctor Brian, it's all right. You didn't know. It's not your fault. Come on, buddy. Don't do this. Not here and not now."

Fernando was right. This was not the time to show his emotions

– not in front of ***him.*** *He washed and dried his face and eyes before reentering the parlor with his head held high, and Fernando by his side. All eyes were on him.*

They each went to their previous seats.

"I apologize, Detective Foley. You must understand how difficult this is."

The detective quietly acknowledged the doctor's words. "I do sir, and again, I am sorry for your loss."

The woman from the coroner's office was still in the room. She witnessed the entire scene. "May I explain why the doctor may have missed the fingerprints?" She asked the law enforcement personnel.

"Please," Detective Foley assented.

"Doctor, your son's pajama's had a high collar. When you checked his neck for a pulse, you most likely checked the front. The bruises were towards the back. Unless you were examining his body, you wouldn't have seen it." Softly she added, "He was your son. Your impulse was to save his life. You saw the pill bottle." She shrugged. "It was an understandable mistake. Don't beat yourself up."

Brian was grateful she understood his feeling.

"One more thing," she added. "The fingerprints found on Ian Winthrop's neck were child size. No one in this room could be responsible ***if*** *choking is the cause of death." She shot Detective Foley a sharp look.*

He shrank back into the chair. He already knew he'd screwed up.

"But I don't under..." Meredith began.

Reality hit Lucinda Garcia like a Mike Tyson *punch. A siren-like sound escaped from deep in her throat. "Oh Lord, noooo! He promise me. He say he no... never.... he say he no do it.* Él me prometió. Dijo que él no haría!"

"DO WHAT? What are you saying? Speak English!" Meredith roared.

"Oh, Mrs. I so sorry. I not know he try it. He say he never do it."

"DO WHAT?" Meredith shouted.

"Lucinda, tell us what you're talking about right.this.minute," Brian demanded, harshly, emphasizing his last few words.

Startled at Brian Winthrop's sharp tone, Lucinda nervously twisted her dress with one hand. With the other, she brushed away the tears rolling rapidly down her saddened face with the crumpled tissue.

"A few months ago," she explained haltingly. "Ian went to party. He say it boring. His friends suggest they play choking game."

Brian gasped. He and his colleagues witnessed numerous teenagers rushed into the ER from playing the foolish game. "Lucinda, why didn't you tell us before now?"

"Ian say not to."

"Don't you know when to use judgment and when to keep a confidence? What's wrong with you, woman?" Meredith screeched. "Ian is thirteen years old. He doesn't dictate what you can and cannot tell us."

"Ian, tell me he no play. Say he no like it. Don't like what happen to friends. He promise he not play game like that and if he at party where they do, he call me or Nando to get him. He promise me."

Meredith rushed to Lucinda and slapped her, leaving her handprint on Lucinda's fair skin. Lucinda cried out in pain.

"You idiot. My son is dead because of YOUR stupidity!!! YOU COULD HAVE STOPPED HIS DEATH. IF YOU HAD JUST OPENED YOUR MOUTH, IAN, THE BOY YOU CLAIMED TO LOVE, WOULD BE ALIVE RIGHT NOW," She screamed hysterically.

Anger crept up Fernando's body. It took every ounce of self-control not to send Meredith Winthrop to join her son.

She turned towards Detective Foley and pointed at Lucinda, "Guess you're correct after all. There's your murderer."

Lucinda flinched. Meredith's accusation stung worse than the slap. She hid her weeping face in her husband's tensed shoulders.

Fernando gently rocked Lucinda to comfort her and keep from jumping up and returning Meredith's slap. He sat silently, equating Lucinda to Jesus Christ. On Sunday, they praised Him, calling Him a King, and five days later, they crucified Him. Isn't that what these people were doing to his Lucinda? Just a few minutes ago, Meredith Winthrop had her scrawny little arms wrapped around Lucinda, comforting her. Now those same arms inflicted pain on his sweet, dear, undeserving wife. Fernando was fuming.

The unexpected event dumbfounded the officers.

Officer O'Kelly recovered first. "We know this is a volatile time. But please settle down, everyone. You are upset, Mrs. Winthrop. I get it, but as an officer of the law, I must warn you if Mrs. Garcia wishes to press charges against you, I will have to arrest you for assault."

Meredith didn't care. She needed to get away from that house and the tragedy that took place within it. It irritated her to think Lucinda could have prevented Ian's death. Deep down, she knew her emotions were misplaced. SHE could have STOPPED her son's death, if only....

"Mrs. Garcia, do you wish to press charges?" The officer asked.

Holding her bruised cheek, Lucinda shook her head no. Fernando started to speak. Lucinda placed a hand on his cheek to silence him.

Officer O'Kelly said, "Okay, ma'am, if you're sure..."

Lucinda remained silent.

Detective Foley said, "We are done, for now. The coroner will determine if the handprints are Ian's. Once we get the report, either Detective Lawrence or I will contact you. We are sorry for your loss and for the part we played in unnecessarily upsetting you."

The law officers left their cards on the table as they exited the house into the storm.

~25~

Fernando would not sit quietly any longer. His wife did not deserve the hostile treatment she received from Ms. Meredith, of all people. It was his turn to speak. "Now, there are some things I must say."

"Nando, don't! Está bien, querido," Lucinda insisted.

Fernando got up. He paced back and forth. "No, it is not all right, mi amor. You have been nothing but good to these people. From the moment you met this woman crying in the grocery store until now. You have done everything she's asked of you: you taught Ian fluent Spanish; you helped **raise** him; you held her hand, and helped her with her life. Questioning nothing, she asked of you. Never telling **her** secrets..."

Brian raised his eyebrows.

"...yet she's upset with you for displaying the same loyalty to her son... tu hijo, Ian." Fernando addressed Meredith. "That's right, Ms. Meredith, Ian thought of my Lucinda as a second madre. No disrespect to you, but he has known her almost as long as he has known you and Doctor Brian. I sat and listened to the two of you act as if my Lucinda was nothing more than hired help. Maybe to you she is, but not to Ian. He loved her."

Fernando watched the tears cascade down Meredith's cheeks, but forgiveness was not on his agenda. They had hurt his wife unnecessarily. They had no right to make her feel like she was unimportant or responsible for Ian's actions. Couldn't they see the pain his death was causing her?

"Ian told my Lucinda every chance he got how much he loved her. It was her arms that comforted him when he couldn't bear the pain. He ran to her when he scraped his knee, got his report card, or made the honor roll. It was she who knew when he made a new friend or fought with an old one. Ian called her at night when he had a nightmare and couldn't sleep. And it was my Lucinda who he told of his first kiss. Don't you dare sit there and act like she meant nothing to him. She was more than a Nanny. She was more than a friend. She was a grandmother to him. When they were alone, do you know what he called her? Of course not! You're too busy with your charity work, helping your husband with his business affairs, and having your own..."

"Fernando enough," Lucinda ordered sharply.

Meredith was crying louder. Brian hadn't moved from the window nor uttered a word. He surveyed the people in the room. They had known each other for over twelve years, yet they were like strangers.

"We all upset," Lucinda said. "We say things we don't mean. We all love Ian the same. He love us all the same. He was special. We will all miss him. What happen is tragic. We need each other now. We need each other's strength."

Fernando gazed proudly at his wife. Always so kind-hearted. He loved her so much. After all these people had put her through, she was still so sweet and caring towards them. That was his Lucinda – always turning the other cheek.

Lucinda asked, "Can I get anything before we leave? This is long day. We all need rest. The days ahead will be muy difficult."

Brian glared at his wife, who was crying shamelessly. "Luci, Fernando, we owe you both an apology. Fernando, you're right. We had no right to treat Luci the way we did. Our behavior would disgust Ian. Luci, will you please find it in your heart to forgive us? You're more than a housekeeper. You always were. I, too, have confided things to you I couldn't share with my wife."

That gave Meredith pause. Her crying slowed. She stared at her husband, listening closely to every word.

"I knew no matter what, I could count on you. Ian knew it too." Turning to Fernando he smiled. "I knew what Ian called Luci when no one was around - *abuelita.* One day, I heard him and asked what it meant. He said, 'grandma'. I asked, "Why do you call Luci 'grandma'?" He replied, "Because I have a mom. Luci is like an older mom – a grandmother.

"I'll never forget the glow on his face the day he explained it to me." Brian's smile grew wider at the memory. "Ian said, "She's the only grandma I know. Luci is more my grandma than Mommy's Mom and I didn't know your mom. Let's keep this between us, okay, Pop? I don't want mommy to get upset." Then he ran off to find Luci to share his school day with her."

They heard Meredith's intake of breath, "He never told me. I wouldn't have been upset." She smiled slightly. "Lucinda is more of a mother to me than my mother has ever been."

Meredith's mother was a cruel monster.

~26~

MEREDITH WINTHROP – THE PAST

Meredith was raised in Myers Park, not far from her current residence. She was the youngest of three children. Her youngest brother, Norman, was ten years older than she and the oldest, Lollan, was thirteen. Her mother and father doted on her when she was a child. She was the only girl and cute as a button. Her older brothers despised all the attention she received. In her early years, she tried to do things to make them happy, to make them like her. Knowing this, they took advantage of their little, innocent sister.

Lollan would corner her when no one was around and touch her in places she didn't think was appropriate. He was always so happy and relaxed when he was "done" so it must be all right, she thought. She loved the way he smiled at her when he was through and gave her anything she wanted as long as she kept "their time together" a secret. She did whatever it took to keep him smiling.

A few times, Lollan made Norman watch. That sickened Norman. Lollan used to "love" him the way he "loved" Meredith. Now Lollan only '"loved" him when SHE wasn't around.

Norman detested Meredith. He was cruel to her. He called her names she didn't understand. He'd give her things so he could have physical fights with her to get them back. He always did it when they were alone. He told her it would get worse if she told anyone. Once, he hit her very hard. Her leg was black and blue for days. She wore long pants so her parents wouldn't find out. Only Lollan knew. He taught Norman how to hit Meredith so bruises weren't left. He didn't want his "most prized possession" marred. Lollan loved beautiful things.

When Meredith turned ten, she knew they were abusing her. She used their abuse to control them. She let Lollan continue to molest her, but she no longer cared about his happiness. It was her way of getting things from him.

At thirteen, Meredith was stunning. She moved on to the boys at school and in the neighborhood. Lollan had taught her the power of her body. She used it to get what she wanted. She rarely let Lollan touch her. His touch disgusted her, but he was their mother's favorite. To get things from her mother she had to go through him. Norman loathed the control she had over Lollan. He told lies about her.

The lies didn't fool their father, Bartholomew Jackson Montague. He believed Meredith every time. He doted on his only beautiful, intelligent daughter. Sara, her mother, was jealous of their daughter's beauty and her husband's affection towards her. She believed Norman and punished Meredith based on his lies. At first, she took away Meredith's "play dates" for weeks, even months. This made Lollan happy. It gave him back his "private" time with his beautiful sister. Norman was miserable.

He persuaded their mother to choose a different reprimand. His mother agreed. By then, she'd figured out what was happening between Lollan and Meredith. She blamed Meredith. Her handsome son was too perfect to participate in such filth unless provoked. He was a man and men were easily tempted. She locked Meredith in her room without food until close to when Bartholomew was due home from work. Meredith knew if she told her father, things would only escalate. Her mother made sure of that.

At fourteen, Meredith stopped Lollan's advances completely. He no longer had anything to offer her. She preferred the soft, clumsy touches of the boys her age, not the hard, experience touch of her twenty-seven-year-old biological brother. The thought of the vile things he had done to her and made her do to him for years made her angry. He took her innocence away. His only saving grace was he never took away the one thing she could never get back – her virginity. Still, her anger festered. Her brothers became afraid of her. Their mother couldn't protect them. They would NEVER reveal the role they played in taking away Meredith's innocence. They never suspected

Sara knew some of what they'd done to their sister.

Meredith grew tired of her brothers living with them. They were a constant reminder of the sins they all committed. She demanded they move out. They refused until she played the only card she had – their father. If she told Bartholomew of their many depravities against his precious daughter, he would write them out of his will, possibly press charges, or even worse. They were too young to die.

Bartholomew was a fair, kind, and just man, but he was powerful. He was feared by many... especially his sons. He was also a handsome, intelligent, extremely wealthy man who could be a tyrant when provoked. Meredith was certain none of the things done to her would have happened if she had been brave enough to tell him.

She persuaded Bartholomew to let her brothers join the family business - The B.Art Winery. The added responsibility limited their visits "home" to Meredith's relief. It also freed up Bartholomew's time to spend with his beautiful teenage daughter. That incensed Sara.

In her twisted mind, Sara believed Meredith was having sex with her father. She watched the things she did with Lollan. If the Slut could do those awful things with her brother, why wouldn't she do them with her father? *In Sara's demented mind, she assumed it was the only way Bartholomew could love the "little tramp".*

Sara's resentment grew. Her harsh treatments of Meredith escalated in Bartholomew's absence. She continued to lock her daughter in her room without food. When possible, the cook would sneak her food. Sara wouldn't let the housekeeper clean her room. She wouldn't give her an allowance or money for anything.

She demanded Meredith provide for herself. If one of the domestics informed Mr. Bartholomew of what was happening in the home, Sara would deny it then invent a reason to fire that employee. The domestics rarely got involved. They needed their jobs. The Montague's paid extremely well. Discretion was worth a lot.

Complaining to her father increased the abuse. Sara was a great manipulator. She had an explanation to combat Meredith's claims.

When asked why Meredith wasn't treated with the same benefits afforded the boys, she explained. "Bart, Meredith is a beautiful, young woman. We need to arm her with independence. She needs to know how to cook, clean, and earn her own money so she'll be able to stand on her own two feet. We want our daughter to conquer the world, not be defeated by it. I'm not doing these things to be mean, Bart. I love our daughter just as much as you do. I know what a girl needs to survive. Trust me."

He did. He openly admitted to spoiling Meredith. He wasn't a woman. He didn't know what women needed to survive. He didn't want his daughter to depend on men. Besides, it made sense. He was tough on the boys for similar reasons.

Meredith dreaded when her father went on long business trips. It gave her mother free reign to do whatever she pleased. Sara knew the domestics wouldn't dare reveal what they've seen or heard, so she didn't hide the abuse.

Meredith tried to persuade her father to take her with him on his five-week business trip or allow her to stay with a friend during his absence.

"Honey, you need your edchamucation," Bartholomew joked. "You know the rules. When there is school, there is no travel."

"Okay Daddy, I understand. May I please stay with Dawn while you're gone? The house is just not the same when you're not here."

Meredith saw her mother's eyebrows rise. She needed to get out of that house. Her father would be gone for too long. She didn't know if she'd survive his absence.

"Please, Daddy." Meredith tried hiding her fears.

Bartholomew said, "Come here, pudding."

Meredith did. He wrapped his daughter in his arms. Sara seethed.

"Honey, when it comes to staying at a friend's during school that is your mother's department."

"You know Mother, Daddy. She doesn't let me do anything." Meredith knew she was going to feel the wrath of Sara if she stayed in the house regardless of what she said. She pushed the envelope. "Please, Daddy. I don't want to stay with her." She pointed an accusing finger at her mother.

Bartholomew was bewildered. "Sweetheart, why doesn't Mere-

dith want to stay here?"

Sara laughed nervously, warning Meredith with her eyes to cut her crap. "That's typical teenage girl behavior, darling. They all hate their mothers and adore their fathers. Besides, the last time I gave her permission to stay at Dawn's, her parents weren't home. Those kids threw a wild party with alcohol. Underage drinking took place. She's not allowed to go over there anymore." That was a lie, but Bart didn't know that.

"Then let the girl come here. This way you can supervise the visit."

"That Dawn is a sneaky little thing. I can't be with them 24 hours a day. The last time I let her stay she brought weed into our home. It fell out of her jacket." Another lie.

"Honey, you didn't tell me that."

"Because it's not true. You've met Dawn. Does she seem like she would do any of those things? She's a good girl and smart too. She's always on the honor roll. Her parents are really strict. They don't let her do anything fun."

"Meredith is right. You are painting a different picture than the Dawn that has gone on vacations with us, Sara."

If steam could blow from someone's head, Sara's would be exploding. Wait until I get that hussy alone, *she promised. Meredith knew she was in trouble.*

Sara shrugged her shoulders nonchalantly, "Like I said, the girl is sneaky."

Releasing Meredith from his arms, he knelt before her. "Honey, what's really going on? Why would your mother lie?"

Meredith bit back the tears threatening to surface. She wanted to scream, "Because she's a devious bitch." *She threw her arms around her father's neck and hugged him tightly. She didn't think she would ever see him again once her mother was done with her.*

She made one last attempt. "Then can I stay with Joyce, Jane, Julie, Ann, or Torrie? You met them all, Daddy. They are ALL good, respectful girls. Mother even hangs out with some of their Moms."

Sara was fed up. "School is still in session. We do not allow sleepovers on school nights. I am not discussing this any further. Those are the rules of this house. This conversation is over."

Bart gave Meredith a final hug. Something wasn't right. He sensed it but there wasn't time to explore his trepidations. If he didn't leave immediately, he would miss his flight.

"We'll talk when I get home, okay, pudding," he said kissing Meredith on the cheek. "Honey, don't cry."

A tear had slipped through Meredith's closed eyelids.

"I'll be back before you know it." He wished he could cancel his business trip. Something wasn't right.

"Goodbye, Daddy. I love you." Meredith turned and ran to her room.

Bart turned to Sara. "What is going on? I've never seen her so frightened."

"Barty, it's probably her hormones acting up. They make us women very emotional. I'm sure she'll be fine in a few days."

She is not a woman! She's my little girl, *Bart thought to himself. "Take care of our baby, sweetheart. Promise?"*

"Oh, I promise!" Sara said sweetly. She gave Bart a passionate kiss then ushered him out to the waiting driver. She stood in the doorway, smiling, and waving until the car was no longer in sight.

She turned from the door, looked up the stairs, and slammed the door behind her.

The Domestics winced.

~27~

Sara charged up to Meredith's room. She was furious! She would make the conniving slut pay for her actions.

She tried pushing open Meredith's door. It was locked.

"You better unlock this door, right now."

Meredith was shaking so hard, she could barely breathe.

Silence.

"If this door isn't opened by the time I count to three, you will be sorry."

Silence.

Sara ran to her bedroom and grabbed a screwdriver. The little wench was going to pay dearly for locking her door.

She returned to the door, removed the knob, and pushed it open with so much force it hit the doorstopper and slammed shut.

That infuriated Sara even more.

She reopened the door and stormed in.

Meredith was quivering in a corner of her room.

The housekeeping staff knew what was about to happen. Many prayed for the "poor, foolish" girl.

Sara grabbed her by her hair and threw her on the bed. Meredith heard of crazy people having super bionic strength. She didn't think she'd ever experience it. Her mother threw her around like a hand puppet. Straddling her daughter, she pummeled her with punches. Meredith tried protecting herself from her mother's rage.

"How dare you lock me out AND try to turn your father against me? You want him all for yourself, eh? It's not enough that you're fucking your brother. Do you need to fuck your father, too? How deranged are you, you little slut?"

Meredith froze. She stopped protecting herself. She knew what

Lollan was doing to me but never stopped him? *Hatred built. And something else. She couldn't put words to the feelings engulfing her, thawing her.*

Sara saw something in Meredith's eyes. She stopped hitting her. She got off the bed. She stared at her child. Her beautiful child, with the busted lip, and swelling eyes. For a brief moment the guilt of what she was doing brushed lightly against her.

What am I doing? *She questioned silently.* This girl does not deserve this.

Meredith was too caught up on the knowledge that her mother did nothing to stop her brother's abuse, to notice the remorse seeping into Sara's still body.

She screamed, "YOU KNEW!!!! YOU KNEW WHAT YOUR CRAZY SON DID TO ME AND YOU DIDN'T STOP HIM? Thank God he never FUCKED me as you implied. Did you get your rocks off watching us?"

Repentance gone, Sara was back in crazy mode. She slapped her. Meredith didn't care. She knew by the end of the night she'd be dead.

"You self-indulging tramp. Do you have to sleep with ALL the men in this family? The little boys in the neighborhood are not enough for you?"

Meredith's eyes widened.

Sara grinned, slyly. "Yeah... I've watched you! I've seen you screw so many boys, I kept score. You're getting better at it."

Meredith was appalled and humiliated. Until that moment, she didn't know how sick her mother really was. Something snapped inside of her. The hatred was slowly being replaced with sadness.

"Oh, Mom! How could you? You're sick! You need help."

"DON'T you dare patronize me. This is about you NOT me." Her mother's screams were shrill. "I haven't been able to catch you with your father, but I will. You're a little sloppy sometimes."

"Daddy and I have never had sex of any kind. It's all in your sick mind. Daddy's a respectable, honorable man who sees the good in everyone... including you. Daddy would NEVER do what you're implying... unlike your sick sons."

Sara paused. She lowered the hand that was about to strike Meredith. "Sons? Norman too?"

Meredith nodded shamefully.

An odd smile graced Sara's lips. "Maybe there's hope for him after all," she mumbled to herself.

Meredith heard. It repulsed her. "MOTHER! You crazy bitch!"

"Crazy bitch, huh? I'll show you crazy."

"You already have!"

"Get in the bathroom and take off your clothes."

Sara didn't want the carpet in Meredith's room ruined. She wouldn't be able to explain it to Bart.

"Why? Do you want to bathe, molest, or show me how to do it right?"

Wrong thing to do, Meredith – provoke your mother.

Meredith tried protecting herself. Her mother was too strong. She ripped off Meredith's clothes and shoved her in the bathroom. She grabbed the switch she kept hidden in the linen closet for such occasions. She was beating Meredith mercilessly.

Lyola, the housekeeper, couldn't stand anymore. She ran up the stairs two at a time. She intervened.

"Ma'am if you don't stop beating that child, I will report you to the authorities," she said, calmly.

Meredith could barely stand. There was blood all over the bathroom.

"Who the hell do you think you're talking to Lyola? I am your master. You take orders from me. Not the other way around."

Lyola shook her head firmly. "You're wrong, ma'am. I take orders from no one. I am not a slave and you are NOT my master. I work here because I am fond of Mr. Bart and Miss Meredith, and am compensated well for my services. I will NOT let you hurt this child, any more. She cannot stand. She probably has a concussion. You are killing her. Drop that switch." At Sara's defiant glare, Lyola yelled, "NOW!"

Please... just let me die, *Meredith screamed in her head. She was too weak to speak. She couldn't take any more. She would miss her father, but she couldn't live with the abuse and the knowledge that her mother did not protect her against her vile brothers.*

Sara raised the switch to strike Lyola, but the housekeeper's words stopped her.

"I wouldn't do that, ma'am, unless you're prepared to meet your maker. I am not Miss Meredith. I will drop you where you stand. Now please leave us so I can clean up her and the blood before it sets."

Sara looked at Lyola with a mix of disgust and awe. She couldn't believe a lowly servant was speaking to her in the tone Lyola was using. NO ONE had ever stood up to her.

Lyola stood her ground. "If you don't want Mr. Bart to learn what you've been doing to this child, get Minnie, so we can clean up this mess. Then leave us be."

"What makes you think you can speak to me this way?"

"The video recordings I have of this and a few other incidents. Now, please hurry. Miss Meredith needs medical attention."

Lyola was a nurse in Nigeria. When she came to America, the Medical Board did not accept her credentials. She didn't have the financial resources to return to school. Having to care for her family "back home", she became a domestic.

When Sara returned with Minnie who carried a sponge and a bucket of formula to clean away the blood, she simply said, "Lyola, I am not sure what you think you saw but this child had to be disciplined."

Lyola said nothing. She and Sara stared at one another until a silent resolution was reached. Sara did not lay hands on Meredith while Lyola was on the premises. Lyola did not reveal the video recording evidence.

Under Lyola's and Minnie's care, Meredith's bruises were gone and she was much stronger when Bartholomew returned from his trip.

It was a grueling trip. All concerns he had when he left were stricken from his mind once he saw his fifteen-year-old, unharmed daughter.

Sara made a silent vow to make Lyola pay for her insubordination.

~28~

Sara persuaded Bart to hire Minnie as a receptionist for one of his smaller corporations.

She explained, "Minnie is smart, beautiful, loyal, and dynamic. She's a hard-worker, Bart. She shouldn't have been a domestic. No one else would hire a smart, young, Black woman with six children and an alcoholic husband, so she took this job."

Bart hired Minnie. The job cost Minnie her silence and indebtedness to Sara. She had mouths to feed. The salary was great. The work easy. She didn't have to break her back. "Besides," she consoled herself with, "what happens in other folk's home is their business."

Lyola was livid when she learned Minnie had sold her soul. She forgave her... eventually.

Sara offered to fund Lyola's nursing education. She refused.

"I am not for sell. I am not Minnie. You cannot buy my silence, Ms. Sara. I won't allow you to continue abusing that sweet girl. You'll get rid of me when Miss Meredith goes off to college, moves out, OR over my dead body."

Everyone had their price, except Lyola. She refused EVERYTHING Sara offered. Sara was pissed. She didn't like the maid around, watching everything she did. She didn't like the power she held over her. She couldn't risk Bart finding out her sins. There had to be a way to get rid of her.

Meredith loved Lyola to pieces. She was saddened and angry when Lyola left for her day off never to return. It hurt. Her "friend" never said goodbye.

With the absence of Lyola and Minnie, the physical abuse returned. It wasn't as bad. Her mother never came close to killing her.

She couldn't risk Bart finding out. He would never forgive her. Also, Meredith was older. She avoided her mother whenever possible.

When Meredith turned seventeen, Sara refused to buy her a car or fund her college education. Although she paid every cent of the expensive universities her sons attended and funded both of the $100,000 sports cars they each drove.

Between her part-time jobs and modeling, Meredith saved a large sum of money, but it wasn't enough to pay for college. Sara warned her not to ask her father for the funds.

Meredith was resourceful. She went to the family lawyer. She couldn't touch her trust funds until she reached twenty-five. Thanks to Lollan's "teachings", she was great at persuasion. She seduced the lawyer into giving her part of the trust fund left to her by her paternal grandfather. She didn't dare touch the funds from her maternal grandfather. That required authorization by Sara.

Meredith was heartbroken when her father died in his sleep at sixty-five-years-old. Her mother was also until the reading of the will. Bartholomew left Meredith an estate totaling one billion dollars. Sara was left the house which she was allowed to live in until she was no longer capable of caring for herself or died, whichever occurred first. It then reverted to Meredith. Sara was livid. He left his sons The B.art Winery and his jewelry. They were angry. They felt they were entitled to more. The business was worth twenty-three million dollars, and the jewelry was valued at hundreds of thousands of dollars. They continued to complain. She grew sick of their bickering. She elegantly informed them that if they continued to protest, she would do everything in her power to take the business from them. She knew their secrets. Lollan was not only a pedophile but had a passion for cocaine. Norman was hidden so deep in the closet, his wife couldn't find him. If the company's conservative board of directors knew those little secrets, they would gladly hand over the controlling shares to Meredith - another condition in their father's will.

Meredith placed her mother in a nursing home when she showed early signs of dementia. Knowing she wasn't in her will, she refused to spend a dime of her inheritance on her mother's care. She instructed her brothers to write a check every month out of Sara's bank accounts to cover her expenses. The greedy bastards were quite miffed at the demand. They were the sole heirs of her forty-five million dollar estate, yet they struggled to part with the five thousand dollar monthly payments for the nursing home expenses.

Putting her childhood home on the market, Meredith hired the Taylor-Durham Consulting Firm *to advise her on the selling of it and its contents. They took care of everything. The Montague's house and all its contents sold quickly. She was left with the daunting task of cleaning out the family safes. Her brothers refused to assist her. It was just as well. She only spoke with them whenever it was necessary.*

Her father's safe held $50,000 in cash, his gun and bullets, important business papers, a few pieces of jewelry and pictures of family vacations. Many of the arts and crafts she'd made him in kindergarten were placed in a folder. She found the programs of the band recitals and plays she was in. The first fashion magazine she was featured in was earmarked to her page. She was sixteen. There were also pictures of her during various stages of her life: her sonogram, her first birthday, first day of kindergarten, first days in middle and high schools, her senior prom, and a few of her with her first love. Meredith cried. She didn't know her daddy was such a sentimentalist.

She stared at the photo of her with her first love... Dylan Bates.

"You were the only boy daddy was fond of," she said to the boy grinning at her.

She cried some more. She packed all the contents from her father's safe and took them to her apartment.

Two days later, she returned to her childhood home to clear out the contents of her mother's safe. It contained some pieces of jewelry and $10,000 in cash. She planned on donating it all to charity. She didn't want anything of her mother's.

She found an envelope with a flash drive, folded newspaper clippings and a blank business card displaying two words – "It's done."

She pushed the envelope aside, cleaned out the remaining contents, packed everything in a box, and brought it back to her apartment.

The house was officially vacant.

Later that evening, over a glass of wine, Meredith took the envelope out of the box. Her hands began shaking as she dumped the contents on her kitchen table. Her nervousness was odd. She took a sip of wine to calm her nerves. Some of the red liquid spilt on her beige top. She grabbed her Tide *stain remover and dabbed at the stain.*

Relax Meredith, how bad can it be? Knowing mom, she videoed my activities with some boy to show daddy. She loved trying to sabotage our relationship.

Though Meredith thought the words she had a feeling it was a whole lot deeper than that. With shaking hands, she put the flash drive into her computer. The scene displayed made her vomit. She was grateful to have made it to the toilet in time.

She wept for hours.

She'd found the evidence Lyola threatened Sara with years before. The first newspaper clipping reported Lyola was missing. Several others were updates on the investigation. Meredith learned her father offered a $100,000 reward for any information leading to the whereabouts of his daughter's friend.

"Oh, Daddy!" Meredith shed a new batch of tears. "I miss you so much! Thanks for knowing how much Miss Lyola meant to me." She never shared the love she had for her protector with her father.

The final newspaper article stated the investigation was closed. "After interviewing several close friends and her employer, Sara Montague, a pillar in our community, we have concluded that Lyola Abebe, the African Domestic for the Montague family, "ran away from her life", stated Chief Investigator O'Hara. "Mrs. Sara Montague told us that Ms. Abebe confided to her that she was "tired of her life".

"What a liar you are, Mother dear." Meredith screamed into the room.

"Co-workers have backed up Mrs. Montague's claim. One in particular, Minnie Johnson, a really good friend of Ms. Abebe, stated that on many occasions Ms. Abebe confided to her that she was saving money to "live the life she deserved." She was tired of supporting her family in Nigeria and being a maid. She wanted to disappear, wipe

the slate clean, and start anew."

"How much did you sell your soul for Minnie?" Meredith asked bitterly.

"With the recent developments we have no reason to believe there has been any foul play."

Meredith recognized the names of some of their domestics who "collaborated" Sara's and Minnie's stories.

She stared at the business card with only two words on it – "It's done". She knew, without a doubt, Sara had Lyola, her protector and friend, assassinated.

"How much did this elaborate scheme cost you, Mother?" Meredith screamed into the empty room.

She cried for days for her missing friend and the role her mother played in it. She wrestled with doing the right thing. She should turn her mother over to the police, but no matter how cruel her mother had been, she couldn't. Two words on a business card wasn't proof of foul play, was it? Meredith knew the truth. Didn't Lyola's family have the right to know the truth as well? Sara was locked away in a nursing home with her thoughts. She prayed that would be her punishment. She hoped her mother lived a long, painful life.

Meredith took the funds from the sale of her mother's jewelry, the $10,000 and half the money from the sale of her parent's house and its contents and sent it to Lyola's family in Africa. It was blood money, sure, but it was the only thing she could think of at the time. She sent a quarter of the proceeds to Ireland and the balance was placed in a trust fund for Ian.

She put the "evidence" in her bank safe to control her mother or her brothers, if needed. The Montague name meant everything to them. They would sell their souls before they had it tarnished.

Lyola Abebe's body was never found.

~29~

THE WINTHROP FAMILY

Meredith exhaled. "My mother doesn't recognize me on my rare visits to the nursing home." She shook her head sadly. Deep down, she craved her mother's love. "I truly am sorry, Lucinda. I didn't know."

Infuriated, Fernando yelled, "That's because you're self-centered. You think the sun rises and sets on you. This is your world. We're all taking up space in it. Well, let me tell you something – this world owes you nothing and neither do we. You are a...."

"Nando, no!" Lucinda shrieked. "This no right. Enough, por favor."

"Let him finish, Lucinda. Let me hear exactly how Fernando feels about me. The woman who invested in a start-up business of a perfect stranger..."

"The stranger who came into your house and helped when you were in a jam. The stranger who didn't ask for anything in return," Fernando stated emphatically.

"The stranger I gave a job because he was unemployed. We didn't need a gardener. My husband enjoys gardening. It's his therapy. I bullied him into giving it up to keep you and your wife off of welfare. Don't you sit there and call me self-centered, you ungrateful..."

"¡BASTA YA!!! BOTH OF YOU!" Lucinda cried. "Please, stop it. What wrong with you? You act like you not know each other...

like you no like each other when I know that no true. Stop it. We all hurt. Fernando and I leave for night. We come tomorrow."

"You're welcome to stay. It's pretty nasty out there," Brian stated.

"I'd rather be in that storm than stay another minute with your wife."

"Fernando!" Lucinda squealed. She needed to get Fernando out of that house before World War 3 broke out.

"No one's stopping you – GO!"

Lucinda saw Fernando's hands ball into fists. It shocked her. Fernando was not a violent man. Grabbing his arm, the petite Lucinda marched to the parlor door, opened it, and dragged her grumbling husband down the hall to the front door. A chastened Brian followed close behind.

"Luci, come back whenever you're ready. Take all the time you need. Thank you both for everything. I really am sorry about what happened. Be safe out there." He hugged each of them before closing the door behind them. He said a silent prayer for their safety.

ϟ ϟ ϟ ϟ ϟ ϟ

Brian stayed at the front door a little longer than necessary before returning to the parlor. Apprehensively, he pushed open the double doors.

An angry Meredith was pacing around the room in a huff. "Can you believe the nerve of that man? Self-centered! I've never! And after everything we've done for him and his wife. Self-center indeed!"

"Struck a nerve, eh?" Brian asked calmly, scrutinizing his wife with unwavering eyes.

Meredith halted her steps. She reeled around. "What did you say?"

"I said, did he strike a nerve, Meredith?"

"Are you calling me self-centered?"

"Meredith, you did nothing special for the Garcias. They helped when YOU needed it. You gave them jobs because they wouldn't accept money. You were alleviating your guilt. Nothing more. Luci was excellent with Ian. You saw a way of not dealing with the boy's incessant crying. Everything you did for them was to make YOU feel better about the decisions YOU made. You helped Fernando with his business to keep Luci indebted to you. You knew she'd be grateful – that she'd keep your secrets."

Meredith stared into Brian's grey eyes and saw sadness lurking in the corners.

"The thing is... Luci would have kept your secrets regardless. That's who she is. She's real. No hidden agenda. She genuinely loves us. All of us. It shames me to think about how we treated her tonight. Ian is probably crying his eyes out for his 'abuelita'.

At the mention of her son's name, Meredith began sobbing loudly.

Brian wasn't moved. "The loan you gave Fernando to start his business was just that "a loan". He paid back every penny plus six percent interest. You didn't do anything for him a bank wouldn't have done, so get off your high horse, Meredith."

She was stunned. Her sobs ceased. In all the years of their marriage, Brian had never addressed her so bluntly. For the first time in her life, she was at a loss for words. But Brian wasn't. "Was it worth it, Meredith?"

"I said I was sorry. I didn't mean to yell, accuse, or slap the precious Lucinda. I'm upset. My only son is gone! Then I learn that he was more comfortable with a housekeeper than his own mother."

"You see, Luci was more than a housekeeper to everyone but you. Fernando must have sensed your true feelings for his wife. I guess that's why he lit into you the way he did." He chuckled bitterly. "He's usually a man of few words."

Becoming defensive, Meredith yelled, "Ian's death is partly your fault, Brian."

"What? My fault?" Brian asked, surprised. "How, Meredith?"

"Lucinda said Ian called her about 2:00 or 3:00. I heard a "noise" close to 4:00. What if the noise was Ian falling or choking himself? YOU told me I was being silly... there was no way I could hear him on our side of the house. I wish to God I hadn't listened to you. I should have checked on him anyway. I may have been able to save his life."

Brian rubbed his tired eyes. "Meredith, we had no way of knowing..."

She ran to Brian and pounded on his chest. Tears exploding. "**I** knew. **I knew**. I let you stop me from following my gut. I let you make me feel like I was insane. I let you make me feel guilty."

She slid in a heap to the ground. Brian stared at his wife without offering comfort.

"Why didn't you check on him anyway, Meredith? I didn't chain you to the bed. **I** made you feel guilty? About what, Meredith? I simply asked a question. **You** chose not to check on him based on YOUR feelings. Guilty, huh?"

Meredith's tears ceased. She caught the edge in Brian's voice. Her heart starting racing. It was difficult to breathe.

At Meredith's silence, Brian asked warily, "Where do we go from here, Meredith?"

Brian rarely called her Meredith, yet throughout their entire exchange, not once had he used Mer. She was getting jittery.

"I don't know.... what you mean." Meredith replied, trying to steady her nerves. But her heart was beating so loud she knew Brian heard it in the quiet room.

"I'll make it easy for you," Brian said, studying his wife. "How long have you been having the affair with Detective Lawrence?"

DAY 3

Use every stumbling block as a stepping stone.

~30~
THE AIRPORT

After nearly twenty-four hours of destruction, the storm - named Iesha, because only a woman scorned could cause so much havoc and destruction- slammed into the sea.

The Charlotte Airport was no longer on lockdown. It was a mass of utter chaos. Passengers and airport personnel were ornery. Passengers slept on uncomfortable chairs or the hard cold floor with makeshift pillows and covers. Airport personnel pulled all-nighters to man the counters.

The scene the day after Storm Iesha was total mayhem.

Kevin eyeballed Kane and Kara huddled together on one seat. They seemed uncomfortable but were sleeping – thank goodness. He had a tough time getting them to fall asleep the previous night. Kara whined, and Kane cried. It was awful. Kevin finally won, or maybe emotional exhaustion did them in. Whatever the reason, he was grateful for the peace.

Kevin barely slept, afraid to take his eyes from his beautiful children. He didn't want to wake to find one or both missing. Although, after their performance, he doubted anyone would steal them.

He checked the time – 4:30 a.m. He glanced at Janice, who sat with a wide-eyed, vacant expression in her dark eyes. She hadn't slept either.

He knelt before her. "How are you?"

"Peachy," she replied sarcastically. Sighing, she added, "This job, my life, just wasn't meant to be."

"What are you talking about?" Kevin asked, exasperated. He didn't like the defeated tone in her voice. *Where was that feisty woman who just yesterday, was ready to kick butt and ask questions later? Yesterday? No, it wasn't yesterday. They cancelled Flight 3236 two days ago, right?* Kevin wasn't sure. He couldn't remember which day he first met the feisty Janice Monroe, but in any case, the woman before him wasn't her.

Janice said, "Checkout the circumstances – first, Flight 3236 is cancelled, the 7:30 evening flight is overbooked, then Storm Iesha hits. How many omens must God send before I get the message?"

Mockingly, Kevin said slowly, "I see. This is about you. A lot of other people were scheduled for Flight 3236, including my children and me, but God chose to mess with you. Thousands of people were affected by Storm Iesha - losing power, lives, having accidents, and who knows what else, but that happened because God has it in for Janice Monroe. He is punishing the rest of us - making us suffer because of His vendetta against you. Man, you must have really ticked Him off!"

Janice felt foolish. What made her think she was the center of God's universe? If she was, maybe she'd be in a better situation. She smiled sheepishly. "Ah... Um... well, when you put it like that... um, I guess I'm being a wee bit presumptuous. Thank you, Mr. Hinderblocker, for putting me in my place."

"It was my pleasure, Ms. Monroe. I'll gladly do it again."

She hit Kevin in the chest. The feisty Janice was trying to make a comeback.

"Ow!" He screamed playfully, clenching his chest.

"Oh please," she snickered. After a moment, she sighed. "But really... what am I going to do? I'll lose everything." She started hyperventilating. "Oh... my... God.

"Breath slowly, Janice. It'll be all right," Kevin instructed soothingly.

She continued as if he hadn't spoken, "I...can't... believe... how.... much... I... oh, God...." Janice broke down in tears, unable to coherently voice her thoughts.

"Shush!! It's okay. Take each knock as a boost. God doesn't give us more than we can handle."

She used to believe that. She wouldn't be able to survive this setback. If she got to New York, would the job still be available? Should she continue? Maybe she should cut her losses and go home. Nate Hill would not wait indefinitely. He was too important. But what if he waited for her? He stated his intention to start a division in Charlotte. She might be throwing away the chance of a lifetime if she didn't see the journey to the end.

Kevin's words resounded in her mind, 'take each knock as a boost'. He was right. She couldn't let these 'knocks' push her down. She had to use them to lift herself up.

"Dear God, show me the way? What should I do?" She silently prayed, looking to the heavens for guidance.

Not receiving an immediate answer, she glanced at Kevin. Her breathing was returning to normal. He was glad. He had to think of a way to maintain that tranquility.

"Janice, please watch my children while I see what arrangements I can make for our trips."

"Sure," she replied half-heartedly.

Kevin walked over to the long line of passengers. He stood patiently waiting for his turn, hoping... no... praying for a miracle.

Jade watched Kami in amazement. *How can she sleep so peacefully with all this commotion in an uncomfortable chair, in her con-*

dition? Jade wondered enviously.

"She must be tired," Jade concluded, barely having slept. She was too wound up. Her mind wouldn't turn off. She sat listening to the hypnotic buzz of the generator, hoping it would lull her to sleep. It didn't. She checked the time on her cell phone – 4:45. She studied the long lines at the information counter, then at Kami sleeping soundlessly. Should she wake her? *No!* She determined. She'd check things out then report to Kami her options.

Kami shouldn't stand in the long line anyway, she rationalized.

She chose a line where she could keep a protective watch over her new friend.

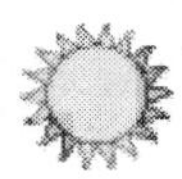

Kami awoke, stretched, and surveyed her surroundings. She thoroughly enjoyed talking with Jade the previous evening. They had many similarities. She sensed she didn't have to use caution with Jade. Her aura comforted Kami. She foresaw a lasting friendship ensuing between them. Though surprised, she welcomed it.

She couldn't wait for Debra and Dante to meet her.

Once again, she glanced around, this time searching for one person in particular. When their eyes met, they smiled.

"What do you mean you must honor the passengers with tickets for today's flight first?" Kevin exploded. Gone was the composed man who stood before the counter two days earlier. "I've been at this airport since Wednesday. It is now Friday. I have two children who were looking forward to going to New York, and you're telling me you can't get us on a flight until eight o'clock tonight. TONIGHT! Brother, do you know what time it is?"

"I sure do! I've been on duty for twenty-two hours, 42 minutes and twenty, no twenty-one, twenty-two..."

"All right. All right. I get it," Kevin said, surrendering. "My children and I have been here almost as long. The only difference is we're not working."

"Lucky you," the agent commented.

"Nor are we getting paid – over-time... for OUR inconvenience." Kevin pointed out.

Duly reprimanded, Armead changed his attitude. "Mr. Hinderblocker, I apologize. The early flights are full. There aren't any other flights, with available seats, leaving out today. This is the best I can do. The airline has added flights, and even those are full. There are air restrictions. We don't want air crashes."

Kevin really needed to get to Puerto Rico by tomorrow to catch the ship. He wanted – no, needed - to sprinkle his wife's ashes across the Atlantic Ocean.

He thought for a moment. New York was a bonus. It would have been wonderful, maybe even therapeutic for them to spend time with Yvette, but their ultimate goal was Puerto Rico.

"Do you have anything going to Puerto Rico?" Kevin asked, crossing his fingers.

Armead's fingers flew over the keyboard. He checked the computer screen. "You're in luck. There's a connecting flight leaving at 11:30 from Miami."

Kevin was ecstatic. "Great! Are there three available seats?"

"Yes, sir."

"I'll take them."

Armead grinned. "No problem, sir. Your flight from Charlotte will leave at 8:55 a.m. arriving in Miami at 10:55. That'll give you extra time in case there's a problem."

"Bite your tongue, Armead. We want NO more problems." Kevin chided.

Armead laughed good naturally, "I hear you, sir." Moments later he said, "You're all set. Your flight leaves Charlotte for

Miami at 8:55 a.m., connecting in Miami to San Juan at 11:30 a.m., arriving in San Juan, Puerto Rico at 1:35 p.m. Here are your tickets and boarding passes. Good luck, sir."

He had to call Yvette with the sad news they wouldn't be joining her in New York.

"Thank you, Armead. Eh, may I ask a question?"

"Shoot."

"My friend really must get to New York. It's an emergency. Are you sure there's nothing available until eight o'clock tonight? Stand by? Anything! Please!"

Armead studied Kevin, then his computer screen. Because of the problems in the last two days, things were haywire. Kevin seemed like a nice person. He wanted to help him, especially after getting snippy with him. He did something against airline policy.

"I see your friend is booked on a 12:00 flight leaving Charlotte to JFK in first class. You'll have to verify the name we have on file, sir." For the benefit of anyone watching, Armead added, "for security reasons."

Kevin wanted to jump over the counter and hug the ticket agent. Hell, he wanted to kiss him. He didn't know what the agent was doing, but it didn't matter as long as he wasn't jeopardizing his job.

"First name Janice – J A N I C E, last name Monroe – M O N R O E."

"Yes, that is correct," Armead said typing in the name, finding Janice's previous tickets, and transferring the information to the new one. He then printed the first-class ticket and handed it to Kevin. Kevin reached into the pocket of his jeans, pulled out a fifty-dollar bill, and inconspicuously, slipped it to Armead.

"That is quite unnecessary, sir," Armead said, quickly pocketing the money. "Pleasing the customer is what we are here to do."

Kevin bit back a laugh. He thanked Armead again and went to share the glorious news with Janice.

Kami stood in the line next to Jade. Ordinarily, she would have gone to the back of the line to wait her turn, but these weren't ordinary circumstances, and she was tired of being a rule follower. She wanted to see Dante. She would not let the twenty-five or so people ahead of her, had she gone to the back of the line, get the seat meant for her. Not this time. The despicable man from the airplane came to mind. *I should have pretended I would hook up with him just to get his seat.* Kami thought with a foul taste in her mouth. *Had I done so, I'd be in New York with my Dante right now.*

Kami was an honest person. Deceit was not part of her nature.

"Next," the ticket agent, Dana, called. Both Jade and Kami approached the counter.

"How may I assist you today?" Dana asked politely, suppressing a yawn.

Kami spoke first. "I had a 10 a.m. flight yesterday to Kennedy Airport. Since that flight was cancelled, I want to know what my current options are."

Dana said, "I can help with that. May I have your full name, please?"

"It's Kami Phillips with two l's."

A few keystrokes later, Dana found Kami's reservation. Innocently, she read the words on her screen. "I see you were originally booked on a 12: 00 flight but missed it." Kami rolled her eyes. "Then booked on Flight 3236, but it was cancelled because the pilot was sick. Hmm... they couldn't find a replacement."

Kami glanced at Jade with a raised eyebrow. Jade was about to comment, but Kami silenced her with a quick shake of her head. Jade kept quiet.

"Wow, then booked on a 7:30 p.m. flight. That was switched to a 10:00 a.m. flight then cancelled because of inclement weather. How awful. I guess you want the earliest flight we have going into JFK?"

"You've guessed right," Kami said humorously. "Ma'am, I need to get to New York like two days ago."

The three women laughed.

"Hmm... let's see," Dana said studying the screen with intensity. "You're in luck. There's an available seat on our 12:00 flight this afternoon. You'll arrive in New York at 1:45 p.m."

"I'll take it," Kami said. "Hopefully, it's not too late."

Dana looked at her quizzically. Jade understood perfectly.

With the new ticket in hand, Kami went to a quiet corner to call Dante and wait for Jade.

The call went to voice mail. She left a message. "*Hey lover, you're probably sound asleep. It's 5:30 in the a.m. Anyway, the first flight I can catch is at 12:00 – sound familiar? Yep, I'm right back where I started two days ago. My battery is low, so shutting off my phone. I'll be in New York by 1:45 and in your arms by 1:46. I love you, Dante, with my whole heart. We'll see you soon.*"

Kami hung up, grinning from one side of her face to the other. She purposely threw in the "we" part. She knew Dante would wonder who she was bringing. She couldn't wait to tell him.

Dana looked at the screen, waiting for Jade's itinerary to display. "Hmmm... you weren't as busy as your friend. You were also booked on cancelled Flight 3236 then the 9:45 non-stop flight to San Juan yesterday. I have bad news. That flight is completely booked. This airline's policy is to honor the passengers with current tickets first then everyone else."

"But that's not fair," Jade protested. "I should have reached my destination YESTERDAY. Technically, two days ago. Why am I inconvenienced because of some stupid airline policy?"

"The airline has to protect the safety of its passengers and crew members. They couldn't fly in bad weather. It was necessary to cancel that flight." Jade noticed Dana didn't acknowledge cancelled Flight 3236. "But we do have another flight going to San Juan later this morning. The bad news is it's connecting in Miami."

Jade wanted to choke the attendant. *Why didn't she just say that from the start instead of raising my blood pressure to stroke levels?*

Jade asked, "What time is that flight?"

"It leaves here at 8:55. The connecting flight from Miami to San Juan is 11:30 a.m. You'll have plenty of time to catch your connecting flight. Shall I book it?"

"Please!"

Five minutes later, she had her new tickets and was questioning Kami. "What was that about?"

"What?" Kami asked, focused on the prospect of seeing her husband.

"Why didn't you want me saying anything to Dana when she said Flight 3236 was cancelled because the pilot was sick?"

"Oh that," Kami said dismissively. "I heard a different story and didn't want her to alert someone higher, possibly changing what's on the record."

"Why? Are you planning to sue the airline?" Jade joked.

"You never know," Kami answered dubiously.

Flabbergasted, Jade said, "Come on. Who are you kidding? Someone like us could never win against a huge airline like WorldLine Airways. Besides, they've done nothing wrong. If they cancelled the flight because they didn't have enough coverage, and not for the maintenance problem like I was told, who would blame them? You can't fly a plane without a pilot, and you can't just let anyone fly a plane. Safety comes first, wouldn't you agree?"

"Of course! But... what if those **weren't** the reasons Flight 3236 was cancelled?"

"What are you talking about?" Jade asked. "What other reason could there be?"

"Think about this," Kami said dramatically. "Someone told you the plane was cancelled because of 'maintenance problems', right?" Jade nodded. "Dana said it was because of "a sick pilot", right?" Again, she nodded. "What if they cancelled the flight because they didn't have enough passengers to fill the seats?"

Jade was outraged. "Nah, that wouldn't happen. That's insane. What makes you think that?"

"When I checked in the other day, the agent made a strange comment." Jade waited patiently for Kami to get to the point.

Kami took up the same stance, Jackson Snow, the ticket agent, had the day she checked in for Flight 3236. "Honey, this flight is more than half empty." She whispered conspiratorially, the way he had. "I'm surprised they didn't cancel it. They do that sometimes you know, but you didn't hear that from me."

Kami remembered his words verbatim.

Jade stared at her, not wanting to believe what she'd heard. She prayed, for the airline's sake, that her friend was mistaken. If something happened, and she didn't make it to Puerto Rico, she would take her chances and sue WorldLine Airways.

~31~

MEREDITH WINTHROP

Meredith had not left her seat on the Queen Anne chair since Brian dropped the bomb the night before. Her head was pressed against the back of it. Her eyes stared at the sunlight streaming through the parlor windows. She was baffled and numb. She couldn't figure out how Brian found out about her affair with Detective Lawrence. She brought a prepaid cell phone so they could communicate without getting caught. Once a month, she disposed of it, and purchased a new one. She had a secret pocket made into all her pants, skirts, shorts, and dresses. She was very careful. Lucinda? No! In her heart, she knew Lucinda would never betray her. She must have slipped up.

She and Brian argued. Well, not really. Brian didn't argue. He had "discussions". Everything was always so orderly, so planned, and scheduled – so boring.

Since becoming a sought after orthopedic surgeon, Brian felt he had to uphold a certain image... even in the privacy of their home. She shared her need for excitement on several occasions, but he didn't get it.

She missed the spontaneity they shared during their brief dating stage. She wanted back the young doctor who cleared his schedule to hop on a plane to Milan, Italy, Paris, or wherever her modeling assignments took her. She was once one of America's top ten fashion models.

She craved the incredible lovemaking, unbridled passion, anywhere, anytime, wild sexual sessions she and Brian shared. She thought she could handle the role of the good, dutiful little wife. She tried really hard to perfect that role. She loved her husband and wanted to keep him happy.

But she was a passionate woman. She enjoyed sex – plain and simple. Not just the act but the feeling of it, the closeness of her body connecting with another human being. For more than half their marriage, she suppressed her needs to make Brian happy. She dealt with her drama-free, perfect life, and marriage for twenty-three years until...

Detective Daniel Ross Lawrence waltzed into her life at a fundraiser dinner she helped organize. She noticed the detective right away. He sat alone at a table set for eight, looking like he'd rather be anywhere else. He had boyish good looks, a full head of jet black hair with natural light brown highlights sprinkled throughout. His nose was aristocratic straight. A dimple in his left cheek, a cleft in his chin, a thin mustache above tiny lips, and a muscular body, screaming for release from the formal three-piece suit he wore. He appeared out of place among the elite crowd.

The detective reminded Meredith of her first love, Dylan Bates. They had similar looks and physiques.

Meredith was a seventeen-year-old college freshman. Dylan was twenty-three when they met at a local cafe. He was working part-time as a busboy while attending culinary school in pursuit of his dream of becoming a master chef. They dated six months before making love. Dylan was skeptical at Meredith's protest that she was a virgin. She was so skilled sexually it didn't seem possible. She wasn't a virgin in the literal sense. She explained she ***felt*** *like a virgin. She'd had intercourse with boys. She'd never* ***made love*** *to a man. Everything with Dylan was like the first time.*

There were no secrets between them. She told him what her brothers and mother did to her. She felt free. He was the only person she'd shared her past with. He didn't judge. He was furious. He prom-

ised to always protect her.

Deeply in love, they planned to marry. They'd been dating a little over a year when they went to her home to ask her parents' permission.

Bartholomew eagerly gave his blessings for the marriage. Dylan was the only man Meredith brought home whom he felt was worthy of his only daughter. Sara gushed about how happy she was for them, what a perfect couple they were, and she couldn't wait for Dylan to become her son-in-law. The pretense made her sick. Everyone, except Bartholomew, knew she was lying about everything except them being the perfect couple. Dylan and Meredith caught the jealousy in her eyes whenever she observed the two of them together.

Sara hated Dylan. She hated how loving and attentive he was towards Meredith. She hated how Bartholomew accepted and actually liked "the boy". She hated how Dylan looked at her... like he knew the things she'd done to Meredith. Most of all, she hated the threats he issued to Lollan and Norman about what he would do to them if they ever touched Meredith again.

She'd overheard the conversation while lurking outside of the library door, one afternoon. The men were waiting for Bartholomew. They were spending the day fishing together.

Meredith, dear, have you not learned anything? *Sara tsk silently to herself.* Family secrets are kept in the family. You are responsible, Meredith, for what I must do to protect our family name. *Sighing, she left the hallway.*

A few days later, her sons ran scared to Sara with a made-up story of threats Dylan made to them. They were unaware she knew the truth of their molestation. They were worried Dylan would tell Bart of their sins. They also feared their father would add him to the will after he became a part of the family, diminishing their part of their inheritance. Sara told them not to worry. She would take care of everything, as she always did. She assured them Dylan would never make it down the aisle.

Meredith had never been happier. She and Dylan shared everything. When she became pregnant, she told no one but him. They planned to share the news with their family and friends at their wed-

ding reception.

One night, a few weeks before their wedding, Meredith received a knock at her dorm door. It was campus police with the news that Dylan was dead. It was a mugging gone wrong. In her gut, she knew her mother was responsible. Her father tried comforting her. She finished up her college semester, hugged her father goodbye (had she known it was the last time she'd see him alive, she would have hugged him tighter and held on longer), and went to study abroad for a year. She chose Ireland.

She lived with Dylan's family while attending school and growing fatter. When her daughter was born, she signed her over to Dylan's parents. She didn't want her daughter to hate her like she hated her mother. Also, it was too difficult to look at the child who was the spitting image of Dylan. Meredith's heart ached each time she saw her baby.

The year ended. It was time to return home. Meredith had been home once since leaving for Ireland to attend her father's funeral. She returned home alone. No baby in her stomach or in her arms. Her child was 7 months old. She made Dylan's family promise to never tell her daughter of her existence. She sent a large sum of money to a lawyer, twice a year, to help with her daughter's care. Dylan's family thanked her for the most precious gift she could have given them – a piece of their son. They promised to keep her identity a secret.

Meredith didn't even know her child's name.

Impulsively, Meredith approached Daniel and asked him to dance. He stood about six feet tall. He accepted, enjoying what he saw except the two-carat solitaire diamond displayed boldly on her left hand above a band of ten ½ inch cut diamonds circling the beautiful wedding band.

Meredith wore a chic black cocktail dress that stopped two inches above her knees. Her long legs had the detective salivating, imagining them wrapped around his waist, an image that would become fruitful by month's end.

The couple waltzed beautifully around the dance floor, causing the other guests to pause. They gathered to watch Meredith and Dan-

iel dance. The two moved flawlessly together. They danced as if they were lifelong partners. They ended the dance to applause, taking modest bows, laughing all the way back to Daniel's table. For Meredith, it was a magical night. She hadn't felt that alive in ages. For Daniel, it was an end to a boring evening.

Brian was working late - again. He always worked, and Ian was very independent. Besides, Ian had Lucinda, who did everything for him. Sometimes, Meredith felt like she was taking up space in her own home. She was lonely and bored. She threw herself into her charity work.

Meeting Daniel Lawrence was the fresh air she desired. Neither wanted the night to end. Daniel drove to the event with the guest speaker. He politely explained why he wasn't leaving with her. He and Meredith left together in her Mercedes E350 Coupe. They drove to the Hilton *where they listened to a live band perform. The couple drank, talked, and danced into the early hours. Daniel was eight years her junior, but they complimented each other well.*

They agreed to meet again before the week ended. Within the month, they were sleeping together. At first, Meredith felt enormous guilt, but it was eliminated quickly. Daniel was a skilled lover. The sex was gratifying. Maybe because it was forbidden or new, but whatever the reason, she couldn't get enough. She tingled with excitement.

She demanded sex with the lights on so she could see everything his well-sculpted body did to hers. She never tired of looking at or feeling his body. Detective Daniel Ross Lawrence became her addiction. He was her drug of choice. He had sexual skills that would make E.L. James *take notes.*

Although Meredith once complained of Brian's late-night hours, she began welcoming them. She also approved of all of Ian's sleepovers or left it up to Lucinda to use her judgment. She found every reason to meet her lover.

After their "discussion", Brian packed a few things, stating he would return for the rest over the next few days. Working things out was not an option. He was adamant about giving her a divorce. Meredith didn't know if she wanted one. In Brian's world, it didn't matter. He grew up with a cheating father. He would not stay with a cheating wife.

It was too much for Meredith to deal with. Her world was crumbling fast. First the unexpected death of her only son and now the loss of her husband, all within a twenty-four-hour period.

It had taken her seven years to find real love again. Now it was gone... this time by her actions.

Amazingly, she still had tears left to shed.

~32~
THE AIRPORT

At 8:15a.m., Kevin found himself in another line. This time it was welcomed. He and his children were boarding the 8:55 flight to Miami. The children couldn't stop talking – neither of them. Finally, they were getting on a plane to somewhere. Destination didn't matter. They were leaving the dreadful airport. They couldn't contain their excitement. It was contagious.

The other passengers were just as giddy as Kara and Kane. Most of them also spent the night at the airport.

Jade was also smiling as she boarded the plane a few feet behind the Hinderblocker Family. Even Rosario, who sent a very nasty text the night before, blasting her for purposely trying to ruin her wedding, couldn't destroy her happiness. She knew she wasn't responsible for the events of the previous days. Instead of responding, she texted her oldest sister, Viviana, her new flight information.

At exactly 8:55 the boarded passengers heard the best words ever: *"Crew take your seats, buckle your seatbelts, and prepare for takeoff."*

As the plane ascended into the air, the passengers, led by Kara, clapped joyously.

Janice checked the time – 9:30. She had two and a half hours before her plane departed. She walked to the gift shop, purchased a crossword puzzle, and a *Janet Evanovich* novel. Returning to the waiting area, she easily found a seat.

Opening the novel, she mentally tried to prepare for the wait by reading the off-the-wall antics of *Stephanie Plum.* She couldn't concentrate. She missed Kevin. She felt protected in his presence. He was a good person. She was happy to have spent the last couple of days with him.

How he managed to get her a ticket on the flight to New York, she didn't know. And a first-class seat at that. She was eternally grateful to him. She prayed all of his efforts weren't for naught.

She tried unsuccessfully to contact Nate Hill at the office of *Bess House of Designs.* The calls wouldn't go through. The phone lines hadn't been completely restored after the storm. Then her cell phone died. Her charger was in her checked luggage. She wasn't sure if she should continue to New York without confirmation that Nate Hill would see her.

Recalling their last phone conversation she grinned. "If you don't foresee making it in today, tell me so we can make other arrangements." That's what the infamous Nate Hill said to her. The clincher was when he said, "My gut tells me you're perfect."

I have a first-class ticket, his gut says I'm perfect - that could only mean the job is mine.

He'll wait.

Janice felt confident for the first time in forty-eight hours.

Kami felt as if she and Jade had known each other a lifetime. When Jade departed, she waved her off with tears pouring down her face. It was the hormones. Although they clicked, she didn't know Jade well enough to cry a river over her departure.

She called Dante several times, but kept receiving the "all circuits are busy" message. She was irritated. She needed to speak with her husband. She didn't know if he was still in New York or had been deployed. She knew nothing.

She went into the nearest restroom, coolly opened an empty stall, walked inside, closed the door behind her, and screamed... banging her foot against the walls of the stall. When her fit ended, she counted to ten then casually walked out. As she emerged, a couple of women peeked in her direction before fleeing from the restroom. She glanced at her reflection in the mirror. Her ponytail was askew, makeup smeared, and the crazed look in her eyes sent her into hysterics.

A young woman and her child were at the sink next to her. The little girl peered at her erupting into tears. Her mother quickly grabbed her hand and pulled her from the restroom. She cast Kami an evil glare before exiting. Kami laughed harder. Her laughter turned into loud sobs. She couldn't help it. She had a ticket for a flight, but no idea what was waiting on the other end. She leaned her head against the nearest wall. The coolness was relaxing.

Get a grip, Kam. You scared a little girl.

She washed her face, brushed her teeth, reapplied her eyeliner, and lip gloss. She took out her brush and fixed her hair. She was quite pleased with the mirror image gazing back at her.

She gave her flat belly a gentle caress. "Just like that Mama, I'll always shelter you," Kami promised her unborn child.

She took a final glance at her reflection. "Much better." She smiled.

She walked out of the ladies' room in search of food.

An hour later, the passengers to Miami were no longer smiling.

Forty-five minutes into the flight, the plane started jerking, sputtering, and coughing. The pilot and crew were reassuring everyone all was well. Fifteen minutes after such assurance, black smoke emerged from the back of the plane.

Kevin, seated by the window, signaled a flight attendant. When she arrived, he pointed discreetly to the smoke. She nodded, stating everything was under control before hurrying off.

Jade, also by the window, wasn't concerned with the shaking aircraft, contributing it to turbulence. Panic seized her once she noticed the black smoke billowing from underneath the plane. As much as she loved Oscar, she prayed she wouldn't reunite with him because of a plane crash. She shook as much as the plane.

The shuddering plane began a slow descent towards the ground but was picking up speed along the way.

"Daddy, we're scared," Kara said, trembling. She grabbed Kevin's arm tightly.

Kevin was on edge.

"This is your captain speaking," a voice announced over the intercom system. "We are making an emergency landing in Jacksonville, Florida. The plane is experiencing maintenance problems. Please fasten your seat belts. Crew, take your places... now."

The passengers were too stunned to utter a sound. Kara and Kane whimpered quietly. Kevin wrapped them in his arms to console them. Their dream trip was turning into a nightmare.

~33~

BRIAN WINTHROP

Brian was angry on many levels. He was angry with Ian for taking the coward's way out. He didn't understand why his son couldn't wait a week. One more week. He had gone so long with the headaches another week shouldn't have made a difference. But it did.

Another week was like a year to Ian. His pain was worsening by the day – by the hour. The surgery wasn't guaranteed to be successful, even with the odds in their favor. Ian knew the risk. Brian understood all of that... but still... it was difficult for him to accept.

"Why didn't you talk to me, Ian?" He yelled to the heavens. "Why didn't you tell me what you were feeling? When did I fail you as a father?"

As angry as he was with Ian, he was furious with Meredith. He loved her but knew he would never trust her again. The tears were flowing just as rapidly as the memories.

Clearing his schedule, Brian went home early one night to surprise his family. The house was empty. He thought Meredith and Ian had gone out together until he saw a note from Lucinda telling Meredith that Ian was sleeping at his friend Tyler's house. Wondering where Meredith was and why Lucinda was informing her of the sleepover rather than asking permission made him suspicious.

He left the house. Not sure why, but something wasn't right. He parked his car a few spaces away under a large oak tree with low branches that extended into the street. He could see anyone pulling into or out of his driveway and garage. In the darkness, it was difficult to notice his dark, late model sedan.

He sat in the car, reading a medical journal with a penlight, feeling silly. As Meredith's car sped by him and into the garage, he extinguished the light, slid down behind the wheel of the car, and glanced at the time on the dashboard – 11:38. He usually returned home around midnight. He stayed where he was until 12:00, started his car, drove around the block then pulled into the garage beside Meredith's Mercedes.

Entering the house, the first thing he noticed was the note from Lucinda was gone. When he opened the bedroom door, darkness encrusted him. The scent of gardenia was piquant. Meredith had showered.

He turned on the nightstand light. She was buried deep under the covers. Sitting beside her, he kissed her cheek. "Did you have a rough day?"

Meredith stretched, struggling to open her eyes. Feigning a yawn, she said, "Hey there. When did you get in?"

A puzzled Brian played along. "I just came in. Busy day at work. What did you do today?"

She sat up. The covers dropped, revealing a lacey see-through nightgown. Brian instantly felt his manhood growing. He reached out and touched his wife's nipple through her gown.

At fifty-one years old, Meredith was sexy. She was a beautiful woman with violet eyes that focused on you intensely during conversations. Age had not been cruel to Meredith Winthrop.

"Brian, I'm exhausted," she said, removing his hand, yawning again. "I need sleep. We can make love tomorrow night."

"But sweetheart… I want you now. I promise to be quick," he begged, wanting his sexy wife… forgetting he was on a fishing expedition.

That's the problem, *she thought unkindly.*

"I want you too, darling, but I'm tired. I promise it'll be worth the wait."

Dejected, Brian asked, "Where's Ian?"

"Um... he wanted to stay the night with Tyler. I told him it was all right."

*"**You** told him he could stay at Tyler's?" Brian clarified.*

"Yes. He finished his homework before he left. Is there a problem?"

"No. So... you've had the house all to yourself. What did you do?" Brian asked, hook back in the water.

"Absolutely nothing. It's so boring when you're not here," Meredith stated. "I watched television for a while. Boredom sent me to bed early. I'm exhausted. I guess that's why I didn't hear you come in."

"Is that so?" Brian's antennas went up. Why is she lying?

The next day, as promised, when he entered his home at his usual time, Meredith was ready and waiting for him. She made love to him like never before, which was saying a lot. They'd had some wild lovemaking sessions in their past. Her behavior raised Brian's suspicions higher.

Hoping to discover why his wife had lied, he left work early, parked in his designated "watch" spot then entered the house at his usual time.

The first few nights, everything appeared normal. Brian began doubting his suspicions. Meredith was home whenever he returned.

On day four, he told himself, it would be the last time he spied on his wife. There had to be a reasonable explanation for her behavior. He would ask her. He trusted her. She would answer him honestly. Decision made, relief slipped in.

Then Meredith did the same thing she had done four nights earlier. She came in the house a little before he was due home, took a shower, and pretended to sleep so soundly she didn't move when he kissed her.

Suspicion was back in full force. He went back to "watching" his wife. Several more late nights of Meredith's odd behavior prompted him to hire a private investigator. He needed to know what she was doing. Asking seemed futile. She lied once. What made him think she wouldn't lie again?

The investigator found nothing for several months. Relief flooded Brian's body. Just before he closed the investigation Meredith goofed.

The investigator captured a video of her and her lover in what appeared to be a heated argument outside of a hotel room. The door to the room was slightly ajar. A shirtless Detective Lawrence was just inside the door, displaying chiseled abs and a muscled chest, giving Brian another reason to dislike the younger man.

In the video, Detective Lawrence appeared to be pleading for something. When Meredith started to stalk off, he grabbed her, turned her around, and pressed her body against his, kissing her first on the neck then passionately on the mouth. He ended the kiss with a handful of her ass in the palms of his large hands. Meredith turned an unknowingly lust-filled face towards the camera before being led back into the room – the door slammed behind them.

She emerged forty-five minutes later, as classy as ever, not a hair out of place or a wrinkle in her clothes. She went to her car and drove off. The investigator also had photo time-stamped of Lawrence exiting forty minutes following Meredith.

After the initial photographs, the investigator gathered plenty of evidence proving Meredith was indeed having an affair with Detective Daniel Lawrence.

When Brian saw the evidence, he was crushed. He could barely breathe. He felt like someone had placed a fifty-pound boulder on his chest. First, he was stunned then in denial. He couldn't digest what he saw clearly with his eyes. The picture of her lust-filled face was captured in his memory. She looked beautiful. Another man had caused that look. Brian couldn't handle that.

He never imagined Meredith cheating on him. She was always the perfect wife. How could she have an affair? He knew the answer.

His mind drifted back to their first meeting at the *Rooftop Restaurant* in the *Peninsula Hotel.* Meredith was a very sexual, physical person. She never shared what her brothers or mother had done to her but she admitted to having various sex partners throughout her life - especially during her career as a fashion model. Sex, money, power, drugs, and men were plentiful, and she partook of everything but the drugs. She was a free spirit. She would strut her stuff along the nude beaches in Brazil, Paris, and Germany. She enjoyed sex and wasn't ashamed to admit it. Brian loved her confidence. He loved everything about her. Being a reserved soul, he fed off her self-assurance and bloomed with her.

In the early years of their relationship, they made love anywhere their hearts desired – airplane restrooms, backs of limos, beaches, restaurant bathrooms, the kitchen table, hospital examining rooms, and elevators. There wasn't a place or country they hadn't christened.

Once Meredith retired from modeling, they didn't travel as much but their sex life was still plentiful. Sometimes, they made love three times a day, other times three times a week.

As Brian's prestige rose, he felt he should tone down their sexual prowess. He couldn't risk someone walking in on them. He had an image to uphold. Their lovemaking was restricted to their home - everywhere in their home. When Ian was born and Lucinda was hired, they were banned to their room. Meredith rarely protested. She became a doctor's wife – no... a prestigious doctor's wife. She claimed she understood. But did she really?

When Brian confronted her about the affair, the night of Ian's death, her eyes gleamed with guilt, not remorse. That was enough to send him packing his clothes and driving around in the pouring rain, searching for a place to rest for the night. Had Meredith showed the least sign of sorrow, Brian convinced himself he would have tried to work things out with the woman he loved, the mother of their deceased child.

Deep inside, he knew he could never forgive her, no matter how much he loved her. She became what he despised – his father - the cheat; the man whom he held no respect for; the man who spent his mother's hard-earned money on prostitutes and booze; the man who beat them at will; the man who left them for another woman; the man who the neighborhood knew as the "Wuss".

~34~

As hard as Brian tried to prevent it, a childhood memory forced itself into his head, bringing shame into his being.

One sunny afternoon, Brian Sr. took Junior with him to the corner liquor store. Junior waited outside, pretending to watch a group of children, around his age, play football. In reality, he was listening to two men sitting on crates near the store watching his father.

"Hey, Jim, that's the pansy we told you about the other night at Sam's."

"I don't remember. What pansy?" the man inquired, taking a swig from something in a brown paper bag then passing it to his friend.

"The one whose wife works as a receptionist, while he dallies all day spending her hard-earned dough on prostitutes and liquor."

"That's him, huh? Don't look like nothin wrong with him," the man said, taking a swig and returning the bag.

"He has three children. Fancy that. What kind of man lets his woman take care of him AND his kids?"

"A wuss!! I tell ya. That's who."

Brian Jr. heard enough. He forcibly pulled opened the liquor store door, banging it against the wall, startling the people inside and out.

"Did my door do something to you, boy?" Big Al, the liquor store owner, asked.

With humiliation filled eyes, Brian Jr. turned on his heels, letting the door slam closed behind him. He stormed up the street with the men's lewd remarks following his receding back.

"Hey boy, tell your Mama that if she wants a real man, my name is Louie Porter. I'm in the book."

"Your Mama sure is hot. I'd let her take care of me too – if I wasn't a real man," the man named Jim cackled.

Brian Jr. moved faster, not stopping until he reached the confines of the bedroom he shared with his siblings. The men's voices echoed in his head.

Several minutes later, Brian Sr. found young Brian pacing back and forth. Brian Sr. yelled at him for the disrespect he showed in slamming Big Al's glass door, stating the damage he could have caused had the glass shattered.

Filled with anger, embarrassment, and resentment, Brian Jr. mistakenly yelled right back at his father using the men's words. "And what would you have done about it, huh Pa? Nothing, that's what! You ain't a real man. You ain't got no money to pay for nothin. You know why? Because you ain't got no job. Because you ain't nothin but a Wuss."

Without thinking, Brian Sr. smacked Junior hard across his boyish face. Shocked, Brian Sr. stared at his hands as though they belonged to someone else. He'd never struck another person in all of his years of living. He turned and walked from the room.

It was the first time his father had ever struck him. Unfortunately, it wouldn't be the last. Brian Jr. vowed never to become a 'Wuss', whatever that meant, like his dad.

Brian wiped the tears from his eyes, recalling his troubled childhood.

He now knew the definition of a "Wuss" and worked very hard not to become one. He was determined never to be like "that man", may his soul rot in hell. Meredith should not have become like him either. She should not have gone outside of their marriage. She should have talked to him.

Sadly, he became a man watching his mother work, sometimes two jobs, to support three children, and a cheating bum. She made sacrifices.

Brian wanted so much to "rescue" her from the poverty in which she lived. That was the primary reason he chose his profession. He knew it paid enough to enable him to take care of her. But he was too late. She died from pneumonia while he was in medical school... a regret that stayed at the base of his being.

When he fell in love with Meredith, he worked very hard to give her the life she was accustomed to. It was his way of compensating for failing his mother. He refused to wear the badge of gold-digger, pansy, or wuss. It would have been easy to be as worthless as his father. Meredith was very wealthy. He didn't know that when they met. Had he known, he may not have pursued her.

Wealthy women intimidated him... especially Meredith. She had everything – beauty, a job she loved, confidence he admired, and more money than she could spend in a lifetime. He felt inferior to her. That's why he worked long hours. Any money spent on their household or their family came from the money he earned. He would never live off a woman.

It took many nights and conversations, before he relented to using her money to fund the upstart of his practice. He treated it as a loan, which only he, Meredith, and the Garcias knew about... oh, and the lawyers who drew up the paperwork. He paid Meredith every cent, including 4% interest. Meredith did not approve of the transaction. As she explained, they were partners in every way – love, marriage, family, and business. Brian didn't see it that way. To accept "free" money from her was to become his useless father.

To earn Meredith's respect, he threw everything into his growing practice. His family was the trade-off.

Brian moved into a hotel. He would live there until he found a place of his own – a house, condo, or townhouse. Over the next couple of days, he returned to the home he once shared with his family to pack up all of his belongings. He placed them in a storage unit.

Brian was divorcing Meredith. Nothing was keeping him

there. She could have anything she wanted except any part of his practice. He would buy her shares, if necessary. He planned to request one hundred percent of his business during the divorce proceedings.

Although the practice was built during their marriage, she invested in its start-up, helped it flourish... he had a paid-in full promissory note proving the business belonged to him. It was his sweat and hard work that made it successful. It was his sweat and hard work that cost him his family.

A memory hit him so hard he heard his own breath.

"Pop, why are you always working?" Ian asked innocently out of the blue one day. They were enjoying ice cream after hitting a few rounds at a batting range.

"What do you mean, son?" Brian asked.

"I mean..." Ian said with exaggeration in his voice, "just what I asked. Why do you work so much? Do you not want to be around me and Mommy?"

Brian was flabbergasted. He put down his spoon. "Son, why would you say that?"

"Forget it, Pop. You keep asking me questions instead of answering mine."

Brian thought for a few minutes. Before that moment he hadn't realized he worked "so much". He saw the scowl on Ian's face. He didn't like it.

"I didn't realize I worked all the time. I work when I'm needed. I've only missed one of your baseball games and two of your soccer meets. I try to be there for you when you need me."

Ian didn't reply right away. He seemed to have lost interest in his ice cream and the conversation. He swirled the melted ice cream around in his cup.

"What's really on your mind, Bud?"

Ian didn't dare tell his father his suspicions.

"You try to be there for me but what about Mommy? She needs you too, you know?"

Brian was stunned.

"What are talking about, Ian? Did your mother say something?"

Ian laughed. "Oh Pop, you are so clueless. Mommy wouldn't **say** *anything to me. She's too...uh...too... I don't know the word. Why don't you take her out sometimes? Come home and eat dinner with us sometimes, bring her flowers, watch television with her. Show her some attention."*

"I work hard for us."

"Nando also works hard, Pop, but he's always home for dinner. Do you think it's because their children are grown? If I wasn't around, would you come home early and eat dinner with Mommy?"

"Ian is that what's bugging you? You want us to eat dinner together as a family?"

Ian let out a frustrated breath. "No, Pop. Are you hearing me? Would it have been better if I was never born?"

"Don't you ever say anything like that again," Brian said harshly. At the crestfallen look on Ian's face, he softened his tone. "Ian, you are our miracle baby. We tried so hard to have a child. There were always complications... until you, son. You were a fighter. You're the only one that survived. God brought you into our lives. You are a gift... a blessing. I/we love you, son."

"I'm not questioning your love for me." The conversation was not going where Ian was steering it. "I'm questioning your love for Mommy."

Brian laughed awkwardly. "Ian, your mother knows I love her.

He stared at his father with a skeptical look. "Does she, Pop? How? You're always working. Try being her husband."

"What do you know about being a husband?" Brian joked.

Ian smiled. "I watch Luci and Nando. I see how much they love each other. They have a great relationship. Luci can't wait to spend time with Nando. When I get married, I'm going to have a relationship like theirs. I will not work all the time. I will spend a lot of time with my wife... spoiling her. I'd want her to know she is special to me. I wouldn't want her to ever get tired of me. I wouldn't want her to think of divorcing me."

"Did your mother say she was tired and wanted a divorce?"

Ian shook his head. "Why would a mother tell her twelve-year-old son that personal stuff? She didn't say anything. I **see** *how bored and restless she is when she doesn't think anyone is watching her."*

After careful consideration Brian said, "You wanted to know why I work all the time. Well, your grandfather was a lazy bum. He lived off of your grandmother and didn't care for us. I made a promise I wouldn't be like him. ***I*** *want to support us."*

"But don't you see what you're doing, Pop? You're trying so hard not to be like your father, that you've become him. Instead of living life with your wife and child, you're working so hard, we're living without you."

Brian was dumbfounded. It took the observation of his twelve-year-old son to point out the obvious. His father paid more attention to prostitutes than his children. How was Brian different? He paid more attention to his patients and practice than his family. In trying not to become his father, he became a version of him. He didn't like the man his son revealed.

Keeping his tears at bay, he said, "You're absolutely right. I'm going to do better. Thank you, son."

Brian didn't know those words were easier to say than practice. He had turned into a workaholic.

Ian smiled, glad that one of his points got across.

They were both silent for a few minutes.

Suddenly, Ian said, "Pop, Mommy spends a lot of time doing charity work. She's ALWAYS so happy when she returns home... especially from her evening "work". Maybe, YOU should help her."

"Why did you put work in quotes?

Ian laughed. "Pop, you're so.... regular. Don't change!"

He couldn't stop grinning. He slurped up his ice cream, looked at his father, and shrugged. He'd tried.

"Are you going to drink your ice cream, Pop?"

They laughed together.

That evening, Brian told Meredith his conversation with Ian. She laughed it off. "I can't tell you how a twelve-year-old boy thinks. That's your department."

Note to self, *Meredith thought as she and Brian laughed.* Be very careful around Ian.

Realization hit Brian like a car crash. *Oh, my God! Ian knew Meredith was having an affair. He tried to warn me.*

Brian shook his head in disbelief. He lifted his eyes towards the heavens.

Oh, Ian!

~35~

THE JACKSONVILLE AIRPORT

The plane crashed down onto the runway, trembling, coughing, and shaking to a stop, seconds away from smashing into the large plate glass window of the terminal. The passengers disembarked on wobbly legs, many falling to their knees in silent thank you prayers, some making the sign of the cross, and others thankful they were alive to tell their tale. The crew promised it wouldn't take long – an hour tops - before a new plane was ready to continue their journey to Miami. They assured the passengers with connecting flights that arrangements were being made to get them to their final destinations as scheduled.

"Daddy, I don't want to go back on that plane. I'm scared," Kane said.

Kevin kneeled before his son, pulling him into a bear hug. He rustled his hair.

"Son, I get it. We will not get on THAT plane, but we will have to get on another one."

The fear in Kane's eyes seized Kevin's heart. He whispered in Kane's ear. "Can daddy tell you a secret?"

He nodded.

"I'm afraid too, but we are far from home. We have to get on a plane to either go home or to Puerto Rico. We've come this far. Let's see our journey through. Your Mama can rest in peace once we sprinkle her ashes along the Atlantic as planned."

Kane considered his father's words for half a second. Then he eagerly agreed and moved from his arms.

Kevin stood up. He glanced at Kara, who hadn't spoken a word. The blood was slowly returning to her pale face.

"What's on your mind, little lady?" he asked, hesitant to hear the answer.

Kara shrugged, mumbling something incomprehensible. She didn't trust her voice to speak without trembling. She was scared but wanted to appear brave not only for herself but for Kane. She wanted to go home and put this nightmare behind her, but she didn't want to disappoint her father. She had disappointed him for the past year. She wouldn't do it again.

"Kara, what are you thinking?" Kevin prodded.

She shrugged, eyes blinking rapidly.

"Do you want to go home?"

Like you can't even imagine. Again she shrugged.

"Sweetheart, talk to me."

Kara said nothing – she couldn't without a waterfall starting.

"Do you want to go to Puerto Rico?"

She shrugged again.

Kane went to Kara's side, taking her hand. "Daddy, she's fine. She'll go to Puerto Rico. She wants to please Mama and you."

Kara's smile was shaky. She nodded. She was very proud of her little brother. She squeezed his hand affectionately. If he was brave enough to go to Puerto Rico then so was she.

Kevin hugged his children. He was the happiest man on the planet, despite his recent setbacks.

☹☹☹☹☹☹

Jade felt like the unluckiest person in the world. The five year curse skipped through her mind. *Are you the reason these things keep happening to me? What about the bald-headed man with the two children?*

He'd caught her attention for several reasons. First, he was tall and good looking; second, he was very attentive towards his children, and finally, there was always a woman around him. Her heart skipped another beat. *What is wrong with you?* She asked her double-crossing heart.

I wonder why his wife didn't join him. She knew he was married. She'd glimpsed a wedding band on his left finger.

Who the heck cares? She chided herself. *Oscar would always be the only man for me.* Although, her beating heart belied her thoughts.

Kami Phillips words regarding the five-year curse jumped in her head. "*But Jade, all those awful things that happened in the past directly affected you. The plane getting cancelled affected a bunch of people – including me.*" Kami was right. This was just bad luck not her curse. The bald guy was caught up in it too.

There you go thinking about him again. What is wrong with you? She didn't know. It was strange… her feelings… for a stranger.

She forced her thoughts to return to Kami. She enjoyed spending time with her. *She understood exactly how I felt… feel about Oscar… the ONLY man for me.* She was losing it.

She checked her cell phone for the time – 10:45. Kami wasn't due to board her plane for another hour or so. She pulled up her contacts, found the number her new friend gave her before they departed, and hit the call button.

"Hello," Kami answered.

"Hey, Kami. It's Jade Morales. How are you?"

"You must have ESP. I was just thinking about you. I wish you were here so we could continue our conversation. I had a great time talking with you. I called Dante. I can't reach him. I am worried sick. I don't know if I should go to New York or change my flight reservation and go home. Oh, Jade, I don't know what to do."

Jade chuckled. "I guess I did ask how you were."

Kami laughed with her. She instantly felt better. Jade had a sereneness about her that was contagious.

"Don't ask the question if you don't want the answer," they said in unison. They broke out into hysterics.

Kami recovered first. "My grandma used to say that all the time."

"My mima too," Jade said, remembering one of her mother's many quotes. "Why haven't you spoken to Dante?"

"Each time I call, I get a recorded message that all circuits are busy. It's driving me nuts, Jade."

"I bet it is. Just think, if all circuits are busy, then his CO can't get through either, so he's probably still at the hotel. Girl, you better go meet your man. Have a terrific evening and don't come up for air until he has to leave."

Kami felt relief. Jade was so different from anyone she'd ever met. She seemed innocent yet worldly. She was a breath of fresh air. Kami couldn't really explain it. It was endearing.

"You're right. I didn't think about that. Are you in Miami waiting for the flight to Puerto Rico?"

"I wish." Jade sneered. "There were maintenance problems. The plane had to make an emergency landing in Jacksonville."

"Are you kidding?" Kami asked incredulously.

"I kid you not. We're waiting for a new plane. They claim our connecting flights will wait and we should be good to go within an hour. It's been thirty-five minutes so far. I had nothing to do, so I decided to check on el prego."

"I guess I should feel flattered," Kami joked, enjoying the words "el prego".

They spoke for another twenty minutes until Jade heard the Miami boarding call.

"Good luck," Kami said.

"Thank you. I'll call tomorrow. You and Dante should be up for air by then."

"Only because he's leaving tonight," Kami retorted.

Jade concluded the call with some more jokes then boarded the plane to Miami for the second time that day.

Unfortunately, Jade will never make that call.

THE CHARLOTTE AIRPORT

"This is the last boarding call for Flight 2022 to JFK International Airport in New York. Last boarding call," a flight attendant announced over the airport intercom system.

Janice rummaged through her oversized handbag until she found the crossword puzzle booklet she'd purchased earlier from the airport gift shop. Finding a pen, she placed both on her lap then buckled her first-class seatbelt. Opening the book to the first puzzle, she settled in the over-sized, comfortable seat with a smirk she couldn't wipe off.

☹☹☹☹☹☹

Back in coach, Kami located her aisle seat without a problem. She was relieved her row companions were a mother with her four-year-old excited son who sat gazing jubilantly out of the window.

Before the announcement to turn off 'all electronic devices' was made, she tried Dante a final time. She wanted to alert him of her new flight plans. This time the call went directly to voice mail. She left a message: *We're on the plane. Will be in your arms soon.*

She disconnected the call. She was in a panic. *Why isn't he answering his phone? Why hasn't he called me?* She checked her phone – no missed calls, texts, or voice messages. Trying not to think the worse, she engaged the mother seated next to her in conversation. They talked the entire flight.

THE MIAMI AIRPORT

"Sir, your plane did not make it in time for the connecting flight," scoffed the airline agent.

"But your airline screwed up, not us. We missed the last flight to Puerto Rico, and you're saying there's nothing you can do but issue new tickets for tomorrow's flight. Is that correct?"

"You got it. We will not charge you for the new ticket..."

"You're damn right, you won't," Kevin interrupted. "The pilot or someone from **your** airline..."

"It is **not my** airline," the representative cut in.

"... promised everyone would make their connecting flights. Well, we didn't. WorldLine Airway's staff lied, yet you're not willing to put us – this woman, my children, and I – into a hotel until morning. It's 1:45 p.m. What are we supposed to do for almost twenty-four hours?"

Jade hadn't brought her credit or debit cards for fear they might get lost or stolen. She'd brought enough money and Travelers Cheques for her expenses in Puerto Rico. She had nothing extra. She hadn't expected to get stranded at an airport - twice.

She attached herself to Kevin once they learned they missed the connecting flight to Puerto Rico hoping he could talk the airline staff into paying for a room (*uh-huh, sure. Oh shut up,* Jade told her brain). It wasn't working. She didn't know what else to do. *Guess I'm spending another night in the airport,* she thought miserably.

The agent rubbed his tired eyes, explaining for the second time the events that occurred earlier that day. "We paged you both several times and held the plane for thirty minutes awaiting your arrival. Please understand, the passengers were antsy. We couldn't hold the plane indefinitely."

"We understand that. Now understand this. We're not from

Florida. We cannot hop in our cars, drive home, and wait until tomorrow. We know no one. All I'm asking is for WorldLine Airways to put us in a hotel for one night. One night. It doesn't have to be a hotel. A motel, an Inn, anything will do. We've already slept in an airport. I must tell you – it's getting old. I have small children and this woman is traveling alone."

He looked at Jade for confirmation. She nodded.

"There must be something you can do."

"Sir," the agent replied, exasperated. "I do not have the authority to approve hotel accommodations. I will issue new tickets to Puerto Rico for tomorrow's flight. I'll even upgrade them to first-class and include comp tickets to anywhere we fly within the United States, the Virgin Islands, and Puerto Rico. Do you want that?"

"We'll take the first-class tickets for tomorrow's flight. You can keep your comp tickets. I'm never flying on this crappy airline again."

Jade nodded, although she really wanted the comp ticket. She could then fly to Puerto Rico to see her family on the airline's dime, but she felt compelled to stick with the man speaking on her behalf.

"Let's see if I understand what you're saying," Kevin continued. "You will give us complimentary tickets – four of them, but you cannot give us two rooms in a hotel?"

"That is correct, sir. I can, however, give you lunch and dinner vouchers.

"At least we won't starve," Kevin said sarcastically.

The agent sighed loudly. "Look, sir, it's been a long day. I was one of the unfortunate workers stuck here overnight. I am tired. I will not continue going in circles with you. I do not have the authority to approve hotel accommodations, and the managers have left for the day or are on their break. I have no idea when they're returning, but as soon as I'm done with you, I'm leaving. Here are your tickets and boarding passes for tomorrow's flight to Puerto Rico and your food vouchers. Please review your tickets carefully. If everything is in order, have a pleasant flight."

The agent began packing his things.

What the f…? Kevin was speechless.

Jade took the items. In reviewing the tickets, she learned the bald-headed man was Kevin. He was traveling with his two children, Kara and Kane Hinderblocker.

What an odd name, she thought, tucking her things in her handbag and holding his in her hand.

Kevin wasn't quite done with the agent. "Are you saying you have no way of contacting anyone for approval?"

"Yep!"

"This is crazy," Kevin shouted. "I have small children. What am I supposed to do? Sleep in the airport - AGAIN?"

"Do what you must, sir."

Kevin was outraged. He glanced at his children. They were staring at him. He had to get his temper under control.

"What's your name and the names of your supervisors?" Kevin demanded.

In a snooty voice, the agent replied, "I'm not giving you that information."

"You better check yourself, Mister. WorldLine Airways, your employer has inconvenienced me, but you have the attitude." Kevin hesitated long enough to read the man's name tag revealed when he threw his tie back in a huff. "Mr. Raj Patel."

The airline employee forgot he conveniently covered his required name badge after the first irate customer of the day threatened to report him to his superiors. He had only been on the job a few weeks and wasn't accustomed to wearing it or dealing with irate customers. The airline was so short-staffed he was alone at the counter. As he stated, most employees from the night shift spent the night when the hurricane or whatever they were calling it hit the East Coast.

Kevin wrote down Raj Patel's name, gave him the finger, and left the counter. He noticed Jade hadn't uttered a word. He turned slowly towards her getting a grip on his emotions.

"Let me introduce myself. We seem to be tied at the hip."

She blushed.

"My name is Kevin Hinderblocker. These are my children – Kara and Kane."

The children stared at the pretty lady. They didn't know what was happening. They finally got on a plane - twice but weren't in New York or Puerto Rico. Listening to the conversation between the clerk and their father, they were sleeping at the airport again. After this nightmarish trip was over, they never, ever, wanted to fly again.

Jade handed Kevin his items. "It's nice to meet you. My name is Jade Morales. I recognized you from the Charlotte Airport a few days ago."

"You were there?"

Jade was disappointed he hadn't noticed her. To make herself feel better, she reasoned, *he probably didn't see me because of all those women hanging around him.*

"Yes, I was going to New York. The flight was cancelled," she answered.

"Flight 3236?"

She nodded.

Kevin sighed. "We were scheduled on that flight, too. What are you going to do?"

"I guess I'm staying here."

"All day?"

"I guess.... I hadn't thought about it. I must call my sister to tell her I won't be on the plane landing in San Juan. That'll go over well... not."

Kevin chuckled. "Listen, why don't you join my children and me for lunch?"

Why are you hesitating? You know you want to. Jade wished she could hogtie her thoughts.

"It's free. It only costs a cancelled flight, a night in an airport, maintenance trouble, and a missed flight. What do you say?"

She grinned.

Jade, Princesita, it's time to let me go. Live Princesita, live!!! She looked around, wiping the chills from her arm. She heard Oscar's voice as clearly as if he'd whispered in her ear. *Nah! Es im-*

posible. Oscar is not reaching out from beyond. Even if he were, why wait five years?

Because it's time. You weren't supposed to die with me. Live Princesita, live."

Jade grew pale. This was way too creepy.

"Are you okay?" Kevin asked, reaching for a swaying Jade.

"Huh? I'm fine. Please excuse me." She steadied herself before scurrying away.

"Are you going to lunch with us?" Kevin called after her.

Jade chuckled nervously. "Sure, why not?"

That-a-girl. Open your heart. You're going to be all right. Goodbye Princesita.

Suddenly, Jade felt empty. It wasn't a bad feeling.

"Remember… I have two phone calls to make. It'll only take a few minutes." She reminded him.

"Two? You said one," Kevin yelled in a teasing tone. "Do you need to tell someone you're with me in case you go missing?"

"Uh-huh! I don't know anything about you, Mr. Hinderblocker. You could be a murderer." She said with a southern drawl before disappearing from sight.

Kevin laughed.

Kara groaned. *Another woman attaching herself to my daddy. What's up with that? Go find your own daddy!* She wanted to scream.

Seeing the displeasure flash across his sister's face, Kane leaned over and whispered, "You will always be daddy's number one girl."

Kara smiled and squeezed Kane's hand. He was an all right kid for a little brother.

Jade went into the bathroom to wash her face. She studied it in the mirror. The sadness that lived in her blue eyes for five years was dimmer.

Leaving the bathroom, she found a quiet corner. She called Rosario. After listening to a mouthful of expletives, she hung up. Rosario really knew how to make her blood boil. She took a few minutes to compose herself before dialing Kami's number.

It went straight to voicemail. She checked the time and smiled – 2:15. She didn't leave a message. *She must be with Dante.*

She was happy for her friend. Smiling, she walked back to Kevin and his children.

"Ready when you are," she said.

Kevin noticed the Jade that returned seemed different from the one who left them.

She seems lighter... happier. Her beautiful blue eyes are brighter, he thought to himself.

"I gather your phone calls went well," he said.

"Argh, don't want to think or talk about it. Lead the way."

"Your wish is my command, princess. Let's go."

Jade stared at Kevin with a weird expression. "Wha... what did you say?"

"What?"

"Wha...Wha..." She cleared her throat over the lump forming there. "What did you call me?"

"Huh?"

Kara whispered in her dad's ear.

He smiled. "Princess. Why?"

Jade dropped onto a nearby chair. "Why?"

"Why? I don't know. It fits. I didn't mean to offend you."

"Ah... no... you..." Jade steadied her shaking hands. Of all the names, why did he choose Oscar's pet name for her? She needed to get a grip. *Relax! He has a daughter. He probably calls her princess. It means nothing. Let Oscar go. You've mourned for five years. Don't close your mind or heart to love any more. This man is married, but there is someone out there waiting for you."* Jade shook her head. Her thoughts... the "voice" was right. It was time for her to live... to move on. *Besides, Pápa calls me princess all the time. No big deal, right*?

"Are you okay?" Kevin asked.

"I am just fine." The smile on Jade's face took Kevin's breath away. She was beautiful.

"Shall we?" He asked.

The four of them went in search of a place to dine.

Smiling, Oscar watched Jade leave with the Hinderblocker family. Finally, after five years, he could rest in peace. Jade was on her way to finding happiness again.

~36~
NEW YORK CITY

JANICE MONROE

"Hello, I'm Janice Monroe. I have... well, had a 10:00 appointment with Mr. Nate Hill..." Janice paused... embarrassed. "... yesterday..." She rushed on. "But when I spoke with him **yesterday**, he knew I couldn't get a flight.... he said..."

His personal assistant, Candice Cartwright, interrupted her. "Ms. Monroe, Mr. Hill **was** expecting you, but..." She looked at Janice apologetically, "...you just missed him. He had to leave town unexpectedly. His sister, Jewels, lives in Paris. She fell down a flight of steps and broke her hip. She's no spring chicken." Catching herself, she put her hands over her mouth and coughed. "I'm sorry. Mr. Hill doesn't tolerate talk like that."

She continued briskly, "Miss Jewels was rushed to the hospital. She's having emergency surgery. Mr. Hill wanted to be with her when she emerged. He had planned to go overseas after his interview with you so once he's done with his sister, he will continue to London to conduct his business affairs. Unfortunately, he is not returning to the states for several months. He called you many times, but the calls went straight to voicemail."

"My cell phone died, and my charger was in my suitcase," Janice explained, half-heartedly. Her disappointment was clear.

Softly Candice said, "Ms. Monroe, Mr. Hill wanted to speak

with you. He felt confident you were the right fit for his newest expenditure. He didn't want you traveling all this way for nothing. He asked me to take your picture if you made it. Do you mind?"

"Why, may I ask?" She asked politely. Inside she was screaming, *what the hell for? I didn't get the damn job because your boss is so frigging anal. Why does he need to see what his personnel looks like before hiring them? So what if they're well qualified! They have to LOOK good. Preposterous! I guess a super qualified, ugly person wouldn't get hired. That's discriminatory. If I had the money, I'd sue him.*

"Mr. Hill prefers to have pictures of all potential employees."

Janice perked up at the words *potential employees*. Wait! She still had a shot at the job? She prayed very hard.

"Why didn't he ask **me** for a picture?" She asked. "I would have given him one."

"So many people send digitally enhanced photos, photos from their teenage years, or of their friends. *Photoshop* has made it difficult to discern the real from the fake person. Since you're here, in person, he'll know it's a legitimate picture," the assistant explained.

"Would you mind if I freshen up before you take my picture? I came straight from the airport. My luggage is downstairs in the lobby. The security guard is watching it for me. He's a sweetheart."

"That's Earl. He is a great guy," Candice responded fondly. "Follow the white arrows to the end of the hall then turn left. It's the third door on your right. I'll have the camera ready when you return."

"Thank you, Ms. Cartwright," Janice said, bouncing to the bathroom to redo her hair and makeup.

Several minutes later, she returned, all smiles with the words "potential employees" dancing through her head.

"You look very pretty, Ms. Monroe. Please stand right there and look into the camera. I'll snap the picture on the count of three. Ready? 1 2 3." Snap. She inspected the digital display. "Ah, that's nice. I'll take one more... if you don't mind."

"That's fine," Janice said, still smiling, "*potential employees*".

"On the count of three – 1, 2, 3. Smile!" Janice did just that. "Thank you very much. You take beautiful pictures, Ms. Monroe."

"Thank you," Janice said, beaming. "When should I expect to hear from Mr. Hill?"

Candice looked at her quizzically. "Excuse me?"

"About the job? When will he contact me?"

"When/if another qualifying position becomes available."

Janice was stunned. "You mean... I didn't get the job?"

"I'm sorry. Did I not say that?"

No bitch, you didn't!

"Mr. Hill asked his personnel director to hire a recent FIT graduate. She doesn't have a lot of experience... just internships. She's beautiful, young, and very energetic. She lives in the City, so it's convenient for her to do the six-month training. She has family in Charlotte. She was planning on returning eventually. She misses them, especially her nieces and nephew. Her sister died about a year ago from cancer. Her mother isn't handling it well. This job is perfect for her."

No, no, no! It's perfect for me, Janice ranted inside her head.

"While waiting on you, Mr. Hill had time to reconsider other candidates that applied. Trust me when I tell you there were a lot! Although that particular young woman interviewed for an entry-level position, he spotted uniqueness and talent in her. He's taking a chance hiring her. Her salary is almost half of what he offered you. He liked her openness and honesty. Maybe once the boutiques are opened, she'll hire you to work for her, or maybe something else will become available. We have your beautiful picture. Mr. Hill will feel comfortable conducting a telephone interview if there is a next time. Good luck, Ms. Monroe. I'm sorry you made this trip for nothing."

Janice was in shock. *A recent graduate? Someone without experience? Why Lord are You testing me? You know how much I need this job. Did that assistant say something about me working in the boutique... like a salesperson?*

Janice found herself outside on the sidewalk with her luggage in hand. She didn't remember getting on the elevator, let alone collecting her belongings, and walking out of the doors of *Bess House of Designs*. She hoped she thanked the nice Earl for watching her bags.

She walked to the nearest subway to take a train to *Penn Station,* to catch the *Long Island Railroad* to *Hempstead.* She was going to her friend, Mecca's house to figure out her next step. She needed money. She had none. She had depleted her bank account paying for the trips to Texas and New York. The only money she had left was in her pocket. $83.32! She didn't have enough for a plane ticket to return home to Charlotte.

KAMI PHILLIPS

Kami was so over-joyed she skipped out of the cab into the hotel lobby, right up to the counter. She couldn't wait to see Dante. Her smile was wider than the Grand Canyon.

"May I help you?" The clerk asked, appraising the beautiful woman with the perfect teeth.

"You sure can. My husband is staying here. The reservation is under Dante and Kami Phillips."

Of course, she's married. All the good-looking ones are. The clerk thought, searching for her reservation. "Ah yes. I see your husband checked in a few days ago. May I see your ID please?"

Kami presented her driver's license.

"Thank you. Here's your key - room 632. Take the elevator around that corner to the sixth floor then follow the signs. Let us know if we may be of service during your stay. Have a pleasant one."

It took all of Kami's reserve not to grab the proffered key and run to the room. She took the key, thanked the clerk, and skipped around the corner to the elevators.

If I ever get marry, I hope my wife is that eager to see me, the clerk thought, watching the gorgeous woman skip to the elevators.

As soon as she pressed the button, the doors opened. She happily skipped inside and pressed the 6th floor button. The elevator stopped on the second, fourth, and fifth floors letting in the ghosts of the hotel because no human beings entered.

"I'm coming, Dante," she yelled in the empty elevator as the doors closed on the fifth floor.

Finally, the sixth floor! Kami squeezed out of the small space before the doors fully opened and ran to room 632. Her hands shook so badly the key fell several times when she tried sliding it through the slot in the door. *Why am I so nervous? I've waited for this moment for three days!* She took a deep breath and tried once more. Jackpot! She heard the click. She pushed the door open, dropping her suitcase and handbag just inside the room.

"Dante, I've made it," she yelled, running through the suite, not taking in the fine decor. "I'm ready to ring those bells. Dante, where are you?"

Where was he? It's not like he knew when I was coming. She rationalized. *I'll take a shower and relax a bit before he gets back.* She went into the medium-sized bathroom, decorated in burgundy and grey. An envelope with her name scribbled across the front was taped to the rectangular mirror.

Ripping it down, she ran to the bed, sat down, tore it opened, and removed the single sheet of paper.

Hey lovely lady, I'm glad you finally made it. It took you long enough to get here. ☺ I had to take the bells off and put on some clothes. It got a little chilly.

A ghost of a smile danced across her lips.

I'm sorry. I had to leave.

A tear traveled slowly down her cheek. *No Dante.* Kami protested sadly.

Storm Iesha messed up a lot of neighborhoods. There are

floods everywhere. People are stranded and homeless. I'm on my way to Newark, New Jersey, to assist some people trapped in a flooded basement. Hopefully, I'll finish early and can get back to you before I ship out tonight. Keep your phone near. Answer any strange number you see because it may be me. I don't have my phone. It's a long story. I'll tell you when I see you. I love you, my pretty one.

Forever yours, Dante

All is not lost. There's a chance he'll come back today. I'll shower, order room service, put on my negligee, and wait for my lover to join me.

~37~
THE MIAMI AIRPORT

Jade, Kevin, and the children spent the day together. After lunch, they went sight-seeing. They left the airport by taxi service. They went on the Miami City tour, enjoyed the forty-five-minute tour through the *Vizcaya Museum & Gardens,* and ended their tour at the *Monkey Jungle.*

Kevin bought plenty of souvenirs to remind them of their trip. Against Jade's protest, he paid for everything. Although she didn't want to admit it, she was grateful. Her funds were limited.

The children had a blast. It was the most fun they'd had in over a year. They enjoyed "Miss Jade's" company. She was silly. She teased, chased, and talked with them. It was the most comfortable they'd felt with anyone in a long time.

Jade also enjoyed herself. She hadn't felt joy since Oscar's death. She was relaxed. She didn't want the day to end.

They returned to the airport to use their dinner vouchers. After dinner, Kevin announced, "Time to check into a hotel. Why don't you share a cab with us? I'll pay for it."

"That's very nice of you, but honestly, I'm fine." She was too embarrassed to admit she hadn't brought a credit card with her.

"Come on, I won't bite. I promise."

I'd let you bite me anywhere you want. JADE! She scolded herself. *Ladies, don't act in such a manner.* She blushed. *Sure they do. They're just discreet about it.* She was going crazy inside her head.

"I'm sorry. I didn't mean to offend you," Kevin said.

Just shoot me now!!

"Uh no I was... um... it's just...," Taking a deep breath, she admitted, "Here's the truth... I can't afford a hotel room."

Never one to leave a damsel in distress, especially a pretty one, Kevin said, "Don't worry about the money. I'll pay."

Jade surveyed the handsome man whom she spent the day with. *He's probably about 5 years older than me, seems nice. He's already spent quite a bit of money on me. What do I have to lose? Once we get to Puerto Rico, I'll probably never see him again. Probably, huh? Cállate!* She ordered her brain.

"Kevin, honestly, I'm fine."

He held up two fingers. "No strings attached. Scouts honor."

Skepticism boogied all over her face. "Were you even a boy scout?"

He laughed. "Come on. Are you afraid of me?" At her silence, he added, "Really? My children are with me. What can I do? Aren't you tired of sleeping on hard airport chairs?"

She hated to admit she was.

"Listen, you've spent a lot of money today."

"I'm not complaining. Besides, I plan on giving the bill to the airline for reimbursement. So technically, I won't be paying for the rooms." He gave her a charming smile.

"What if the airline doesn't reimburse you? Then you're out double the money."

"How will you know? I won't send you the bill. I don't even know where you live."

Another good point. How would she know? He seemed honest. After spending the day with him, she felt she could trust him. Maybe that's how he lured his victims. Make them think they're safe. Get them in a hotel room alone and wham... go for the kill.

Ted Bundy was a charming, handsome, seemingly honest man as well.... we won't recap that story.

It was fine when they were in public and the children were around, but Kevin would know which room she was in. He could convince the hotel clerk they were together, get a key, and... no, she couldn't chance it.

"I appreciate everything you've done for me today, but I simply cannot accept anything more."

In a final attempt to persuade her, Kevin said, "We can get separate rooms on separate floors in separate hotels. I'll give you money to make your own arrangements."

As tempting as it was, she couldn't do it. She'd feel cheap... like she owed him something. Besides, she didn't have a credit or debit card. She couldn't secure a room.

Oscar help. What should I do? She called desperately. She felt nothing. If Oscar were around, he would protect her, but there was no sign of him. *I knew it was my imagination. The dead don't talk to you.* She was disappointed. She really believed Oscar had finally reached out to her from beyond the grave. Supongo que aún estoy sola. She had to make her own decision.

"I'm sorry. I can't. I don't feel comfortable accepting anything else from you. You've done so much already. I'll see you tomorrow. If you'll excuse me, I see a chair with my name on it. I must grab it before someone takes it," she joked, walking away from the family.

Turning before she reached the chair, she shouted, "Mr. Hinderblocker, thank you for a lovely afternoon." That southern drawl was back.

Kevin grinned, shaking his head, watching her continue on her way. *Humph, what a body.* He glanced around the almost deserted airport. He couldn't live with himself if anything happened to her. There was something so innocent and special radiating from her.

He peeked at his children, swallowed air, and asked, "How about another adventure?"

They groaned in response.

Undaunted, Kevin said, "Let's sleep here tonight?"

Kane smiled his answer.

Kara rolled her eyes thinking, *another airport? No, thank you! Been there, done that, don't want to do it again.*

"Full disclosure guys... Miss Jade is sleeping here. I don't want to leave her by herself.....sooo.... what do you say?"

Kara considered her father's request. She wanted to spend the night in a comfortable hotel room, not the dumb airport again. She contemplated Miss Jade for a few seconds. She was sitting on one chair with her legs straddled across another. She didn't want to leave her all alone. She liked her. She was fun. She kind of reminded her of her Mama.

"Okay, Daddy. We'll stay with Miss Jade so she won't be afraid."

"That's my girl," Kevin said, picking Kara up, swinging her around, and then giving her a big hug before setting her on the ground again.

Kane chuckled, watching the two people he loved most in the world interacting with each other. *Finally*, he thought. *It's been so long since we've had fun together.* He smiled upwards, winked, and mimed a silent thank you. He knew his mother was with them. He talked to her often.

The threesome walked over to Jade.

Kevin said, "Mind if we join you?"

"Don't be silly. Go to the hotel. You have children to think about."

"We want to have another adventure. Right, kids?" No one responded. "They're worn out from our excursions today." Kevin explained their lack of enthusiasm. "We had a family discussion. Everyone's in agreement. If one stays, we all stay. We're a package deal now. Right?"

This time the children earnestly agreed.

Jade moved her stuff to let the Hinderblocker family join her.

After talking and laughing about their day together, Jade turned a serious expression on Kevin. "There's something I've been dying to ask," she said. "Feel free to tell me to mind my own business. I won't get offended... well... maybe a little, but I'll get over it.... one day."

He chuckled. "Fire away."

"Why isn't your wife on this family trip with you?"

Kevin was puzzled. "My wife?"

"Yes, why didn't she get on the plane with you?"

"My wife?"

"Your wife," Jade drawled deliberately. She knew he was too good to be true. He seemed like a decent man, not a cheat. *Figures*, she muttered to herself. *Good thing I didn't go to the hotel with this creep. Wine 'em and dine 'em. I guess he thought he was going to get lucky tonight.* Jade got an attitude. She wanted nothing more to do with Kevin "The Slick" Hinderblocker. *And I thought Papá was bad. At least he never did his dirt in front of us. Flirting with me in front of his children. What a class A asshole.*

"My wife was on the plane."

Jade huffed and rolled her eyes. "So what did you do with her? Leave her in Jacksonville?" Attitude was dripping all over her.

What's her problem? He wondered.

Kane and Kara were staring at her oddly.

"Why are they looking at me like that? What's wrong with you guys?" Jade was getting angry.

"Jade, we don't know what you're talking about or why you're getting upset. My wife is dead."

"Dead?" Jade echoed, instantly feeling remorseful. The color drained from her face. "Dead?" She said again. "I'm sorry." She meant it. She tried processing what she heard. She glanced at the children. There were tears in their eyes. She felt horrible. Curiosity got a hold of her tongue. "Then... who was the woman sitting with you and the children at the airport - both days, or was it three?"

"Scoping me out, were you?" Kevin teased to lighten the mood. Jade turned scarlet. She wished she could take back her question, or at least her observation.

"I uh... I... um... wasn't checking you..."

"I'm teasing. I think you're talking about Janice Monroe. Was she a beautiful, petite, Black woman?"

I wouldn't call her beautiful or petite. Not with those hips, she thought enviously.

"She was attractive," she acknowledged, hesitantly.

"She's not my wife," Kevin said. "I met her at the airport. We sort of hit it off."

So I noticed... for three days!!! Jade thought bitterly. *Get a grip. Tone it down.*

"Why did you think we were married?"

"She kissed you. You're wearing a wedding band. It equaled marriage."

Kevin couldn't stop grinning. He wouldn't embarrass her again about keeping tabs on him. He found it endearing.

He held up his left ring finger. "I don't feel comfortable taking it off. My wife, Kimberly, died about a year ago. We're taking a cruise from Puerto Rico to sprinkle her ashes across the Atlantic Ocean. One of her dreams was to celebrate our fifteenth wedding anniversary in Puerto Rico."

"Oh! That's why you said she was on the plane." She felt like a moron. "I'm sorry about my suspicion. It's so hard to trust people."

"I get it. I guess it did look bad."

Sadness immersed her. "Will you tell me about her... your wife?" Jade asked softly.

Kara and Kane moved closer. They didn't want to miss a thing. Jade listened to Kevin reminiscing about Kimberly. He told some hilarious stories. His voice grew melancholy, recalling their battle with cancer. She could tell he loved his wife very much. She glanced at the children. They were weeping. Her heart ached for their loss and for hers. She and Oscar never made it down the aisle, but they shared five glorious years together. She took Kara and Kane in her arms. She held them while they cried.

Her eyes glistened.

Kevin noticed. "I didn't mean to upset you. I get carried away when I speak about Kim."

"No worries," Jade hastened to reassure him. "Hearing you speak so lovingly about your wife brought back memories of my fiancé, Oscar."

Kevin stared pointedly at the wedding band worn on her right ring finger above her engagement ring. "Is that from Oscar?"

The children's cries ceased. They moved from her arms.

Jade nodded slowly. "This is the ring he would have given me if our wedding took place."

Kevin's face was full of open curiosity. Jade didn't notice. She was pulling something from beneath her shirt.

Showing it to Kevin, she said, "This is the ring I was going to give him at our wedding. It's too big for my finger. I keep it on this necklace, with his cross close to my heart. This necklace and cross belonged to him. It was on his bod...."

Jade stopped, refusing to cry. "Like you, I can't part with them. This is all I have left of him... and my memories."

At Jade's silence, Kevin urged softly, "Your turn... spill."

"I'd like that. Yesterday was the first time I've really spoken about him and his..."

It still hurt to say the words – even after so much time had passed.

"Take your time," Kevin encouraged, eager to hear about the man who held her heart.

She blinked quickly to keep the tears from falling. "It's a long story."

"We ain't got nothing but time."

"True! Oscar Livingston was the handsomest man on this earth – correction in the universe. He was so kind. We met at Concord Mills. It's actually a wild story." Jade smiled at the memory. "I lost my car...."

Jade told them her entire five-year history with Oscar. When she finished, emotions were all over the spectrum. A bond was formed between Jade, Kevin, Kara, and Kane.

"Whew, I need to go to the bathroom," Jade declared.

"May I go with you, Miss Jade?" Kane asked.

Jade looked at Kevin for permission.

Kevin noted the near-empty airport. "Sure, but make sure you wait for Miss Jade outside of the restroom, okay little man?"

"Yes, sir," Kane replied.

"Uh un, this little guy is coming inside with me. You got a problem with that?"

"No," Kane said, blushing.

"I'm jealous," Kevin said, half kidding.

Jade smiled.

"Daddy and I will make sure no one takes your stuff, Miss Jade," Kara said with an air of importance.

"Thank you, Miss Kara. Little man and I will be right back."

Kane took Jade's hand. They walked off together, hands swinging.

"I like Miss Jade, Daddy," Kara announced.

"You do, huh?" Kevin grinned, staring after the two of them.

"Yes, I do," Kara stated firmly. "She's so nice, and brave, and pretty – just like Mama."

Kevin didn't trust his voice to speak. He was experiencing emotions he didn't think he would ever feel again. He didn't understand it.

He noticed Kane and Jade rush from the restroom. He looked at them questioningly.

"We have to find a different one," she yelled. "This one's closed."

"Okay," Kevin yelled back. "Be careful!"

Thirty minutes later, Kara said, "It sure is taking them a long time."

Kevin was thinking the same thing but refused to accept his concerns.

"They sure are. Ten more minutes, then we go look for them."

"Okay, Daddy," Kara said, consulting the time on her Princess Tiana watch.

Eleven minutes later, they hadn't returned. Kevin was extremely worried.

"Daddy, I gave them an extra minute. They're not back. I'm scared."

"I'm sure they're fine," Kevin said, not believing his own words. "They probably got lost or are browsing the gift shop windows."

"Yeah, okay," Kara responded doubtfully.

A security guard came into view. Kevin called him over.

"Excuse me, sir, but my son, Kane, and a female friend, Jade, went to the restroom over forty minutes ago. Will you please try to locate them?" Kevin asked. "I'd rather not leave the area in case they return."

"Understandable. Give me their descriptions," he requested.

Kevin took out Kane's passport and showed it to the guard.

"Got it," he said, writing down the information he needed. "And the woman?"

"Her name is Jade Morales. She's of Hispanic descent about 5' 7", fair complexion, curly dark hair, and slanted blue eyes. She's in her late twenties, early thirties. She's wearing a red tank top, a blue denim skort, and gold open-toe sandals with a heel about an inch and a half high. She has large gold hoop earrings, a thin gold bracelet, and a gold necklace with a cross and wedding band on it. They went in that direction." Kevin pointed in the direction they'd walked.

"That's a thorough description, sir, thank you."

Kevin surprised himself. He didn't realize he'd noticed that much about Miss Jade Morales.

"We'll see what we can find," the security guard said, walking away, pulling out his Walkie Talkie and spewing out instructions.

Kevin got up from the chair. He paced back and forth. He was licking his lips unconsciously – something he did whenever he was nervous. He knew he should have gotten a hotel room. *Who in their right mind voluntarily stays in a Miami airport? You hear horror stories about the drug cartel in this city, on the regular. I must have been out of my mind.*

".... or blinded by a blue-eyed beauty," a voice whispered in his ear. The voice sounded a lot like Kimberly's, his deceased wife. The hairs on his arms stood up. He stopped pacing. Glancing around, he shook his head to clear it. He felt Kimberly's presence beside him.

Kara whimpered silently in her chair. Something was terribly wrong.

Twenty minutes later, a different security guard approached

him. “Mr. Hinderblocker?”

“Yes! Did you find them?” Kevin asked anxiously.

“Sir, we found a woman fitting the description of...” He checked his notes, “a Jade Morales. She’s in awful shape, but the boy... he’s still missing.”

You were right Kim, Kevin thought. *I put my children at risk trying to protect Jade*. His 6’4” frame sagged slightly. “What do...?”

“Don’t worry, I’ll protect him,” The voice whispered. The presence Kevin felt was gone.

“Sir, from what Miss Morales could tell us before losing consciousness - we believe.... your son... may have been.... kidnapped.”

~38~

MIRIAM BAINBRIDGE

Miriam received a frantic telephone call from Mr. Coppenhauge stating no one had seen or spoken to Erich in several days. He wanted to know if he had contacted her. He had not. She ended her "girls" vacation in South Beach to rush back to Charlotte. Her friends opted to accompany her instead of completing their Florida vacation.

That worked for Miriam. She couldn't have gotten through the drive back without them. She was near hysterics. Her cousin, Carol, drove most of the way back. Her other friends tried consoling her. The closer they got to Charlotte, the more unhinged she became. Her friend, Ingrid, read scriptures to calm her. It didn't work. She didn't know where Erich was. She hadn't heard from him either, believing it was because he was in New York recuperating from the surgery. Knowing that wasn't the case was driving her insane. She was beyond worried.

Ten hours later, she was calmer. She could drive but her mind kept screaming, "Where is he?" She dropped each friend off then drove directly to Erich's home in Lake Norman. Her car was not there.

She went back to her home. Her car wasn't there either. Her roommates hadn't heard or seen him. She was at a loss. She had no idea where he was with her car, nor did she know where to look. Erich was a loner but close to his family. They didn't know where he was. His dad turned to her for answers.

What was even more worrisome was Erich loved his Hummer... for him to go without it for as long as he had frightened her. She tried not to fear the worst, but a person just didn't disappear into thin air.

Really? What about your mother? *Miriam pushed the awful thought from her brain without addressing it. It was not a topic up for discussion or thought.*

Another thought popped in her head – also unpleasant. Maybe Erich has been in a car accident. It made sense – he's missing, my car's missing, and the weather had been bad. Erich would do anything to save Erika's life, including risking his own. Storm Iesha would not have stopped him.

What didn't make sense was why his parents wouldn't know he was in an accident. He should have had his license on him.

An even worst thought hit her, what if Erich's mother knows he's in a hospital and won't tell anyone, especially me? Nah, she's not that evil... is she?

Miriam knew his mother could do something that underhanded. Does she hate me that much?

Desperate, she called his parents' home, hoping they had heard from him. A couple of days had passed. Surely, they knew something. She prayed Mrs. Coppenhauge wouldn't answer. As the phone continued to ring, she grew wearier and wearier. Please answer Mr. Coppenhauge. Please.

Mrs. Coppenhauge answered. Miriam considered hanging up, but that wouldn't get her the results she was after.

She cleared her throat. "Hello Mrs. Coppenhauge, this is Miriam. How..."

"I know who it is," Mrs. Coppenhauge snapped. "What do ***you*** *want?"*

Miriam inhaled and exhaled as slowly as she could. She kept reminding herself that the woman... no, the rude woman on the other end of the phone was Erich's mother. She had to play it cool.

Miriam cleared her throat again. "Have you heard from your son?"

"Which one? I have two."

Witch, you know damn well which son I'm talking about. *Miriam wanted to scream but said, "Do you know where* ***Erich*** *is? Mr. Coppenhauge said he's missing."*

*"Figures, **he** called you. I have no idea where **my** son is. If I knew, I wouldn't tell the likes of you. Hopefully, he's somewhere coming to his senses. Maybe with another woman... one more suitable for him. You're no good for him. The sooner he realizes that the better off we'll all be."*

Mrs. Coppenhauge disconnected the call.

YOU WRENCH! Miriam shrieked at the dead phone in her hand. She wanted to throw it, but breaking her phone would only hurt her. She was so tempted to call the witch back and tell her what she really thought of her but knew that would hurt the man she loved, who for some unexplainable reason idolized that woman.

She placed her cellphone on her bed. If he called, she wouldn't miss it. Why hasn't he reached out to me? Why is he abandoning me?

He knew her story.

Miriam Bainbridge was the third of four children born to Todd and Naomi Bainbridge in Lancaster, South Carolina. Naomi met handsome, college basketball star, Todd Bainbridge. The very first time they had sex (she believed in calling it what it was) she got pregnant. She told Todd, hoping he would give her money to eliminate "the problem". He didn't. He was a good guy. He said, "We'll get married". Naomi was 17, Todd was 20. She expected his parents to protest. They offered their blessings. Her parents were no better. They were thrilled. They didn't want an unwed, pregnant daughter disgracing them in front of their snub-nose friends. Todd was the type of man every parent wanted their daughter to marry – handsome, caring, intelligent, hard-working, and responsible. No one cared that she did not want to get married or have children.

Todd gave up college and the chance at becoming a pro-athlete to become a father. He worked at the South Carolina Textile Plant. Naomi was a stay-at-home mom. Todd, Jr. (called TJ) was born six months after the wedding ceremony. The next three years produced Nedra, Miriam, and Tommy. They lived on a dysfunctional farm in a small three-bedroom house with a dog and two cats. They owned an older model Chevy SUV and a second-hand pickup truck Todd used for work.

Naomi was beautiful. Her one dream was of becoming a model. She possessed the face and body. She often sat and stared at her face in her bedroom mirror, searching for any imperfections that might have appeared while she slept. She was obsessed with the fashion world: purchasing and reading every fashion magazine available, following all the top runway models, and searching on the internet for anything remotely related to fashion. After Tommy was born, she had her tubes tied, unbeknownst to Todd. She went on a rigid diet and exercise marathon. She regained her drop-dead figure. However, in her eyes, her facial looks were slowly fading. What happened to her dream?

At twenty-one, with four children, Naomi was feeling stressed and depressed. Changing diapers, crying babies, getting up at all hours of the night was not the dream she had for herself.

Todd was in the house burping Tommy when Naomi insisted on taking out the garbage. She placed the trash in the can and continued walking down the driveway and up the road. She flagged a passing car. Miriam was two years old.

When Naomi failed to return, Todd was filled with dread. Something awful must have happened to her. He, their fathers, and the neighbors searched for her. After 24 hours, they filed a missing person's report. Each time the telephone rang, he'd cringe, knowing that would be the call notifying him that his wife's body was found. At month's end, Todd's VISA bill showed an Amtrak ticket purchased from the Columbia, South Carolina railroad station to Penn Station in New York, bought the day after Naomi's disappearance. After interviewing the railroad clerk, the police determined Naomi purchased the ticket. The VISA card was never used again. The search was terminated.

Todd was more hurt than angry. He would not have stood in her way if she wanted to leave. He wanted the best for his children. Knowing Naomi was safe and hopefully happy, he moved on with his life.

Unable to care for four children ranging in age from one to four and hold a full-time job, Todd and the children moved in with his par-

ents. The older Bainbridge's were delighted to have their grandchildren with them. However, Mrs. Bainbridge was forty-eight and not ready to retire. She hired a live-in nanny, Cleo Richards, to help.

Cleo Richards was 26 years old and single. Because of a birth defect, she couldn't produce children. She loved her job. She rose each morning at 6 a.m. and put in a full day with the Bainbridge clan.

One year after Naomi left Lancaster, Todd received divorce papers for his signature postmarked: New York, New York. Attached was a note that read:

> Todd,
>
> I have filed for divorce. I am setting you free to get on with your life. I want nothing from you. Please note, I have given up all parental rights. I never wanted to be a mother. All I ever wanted was to go to New York and become a model. Well, I am halfway there. I discovered I am still young enough to model. I want to live the life I have so often dreamed of. Being married and tied to four babies, constantly demanding my attention was draining the life from me. I couldn't do it any longer. I had to leave. I tried to tell you. You wouldn't listen. I am where I want to be and doing what I want to do. It's difficult. The competition is mammoth but I will make it. What's most important is I am happy. I wear beautiful clothes, live in an elegantly designed apartment, and make a lot of money.
>
> Todd, I never loved you nor did I want to get married. I only wanted to date you because you were a basketball star and fine as hell. We made an attractive couple. I am not asking for forgiveness, for I have done nothing wrong. As for the children, you can tell them whatever you wish. Just NEVER tell them I loved them, for if I did, I never could

have walked away so easily.

Goodbye,
Naomi

He signed the papers.

By then Cleo had fallen in love with the Bainbridge children. She treated them as if they were her own. She and Todd began spending a lot of time together. Eventually, they fell in love. One year after his divorce was finalized, Todd Bainbridge proposed to Cleo. They married. As a wedding gift, Todd's parents paid down on a modest four-bedroom home located a short distance from their home. Cleo adopted the four Bainbridge children. They called her 'Mommy'. Todd decided to wait until they were older to tell them about bio-mom. In the meantime, he did nothing to rob them of the motherly love Cleo so freely gave them. She was the only mother they knew.

One night, while the family was enjoying a movie, TJ unexpectedly asked, "Daddy, where is our other Mommy?"

His siblings turned towards him. They stared at TJ as if he had grown antennas. TJ stared at Todd expectantly. He was four years old when Naomi left. He was the only one who remembered her.

Memories often flashed through his mind of the other Mommy asking him to do things - like hold his sister's or brother's bottle of milk while they drank, or bring her something. She was always looking at herself in the mirror and muttering words he couldn't understand. He wondered what happened to her.

His siblings too were waiting for their father's answer. Cleo was their Mommy. What was TJ talking about?

Todd and Cleo exchanged looks. Cleo nodded, got up, and left the room.

Todd muted the TV. There was instant quiet. Todd gathered his children around him and said, "TJ is correct. Once upon a time, there was another Mommy – your birth mother. Her name is Naomi. We met in high school. She had a dream of becoming a famous model. I fell in love with her and talked her into marrying me and becoming a Mommy instead. She still had her dream. Being married with chil-

dren was not part of it. We got a divorce so Naomi could follow her dream and I could give you another Mommy."

Then Todd did the unthinkable – he lied to his children. "Your mother loved each of you and it really broke her heart to leave. But she had to choose. She knew I would dedicate myself to taking care of you, which is what I am doing. Both Cleo and I love you very much."

Todd then produced a photo album that contained pictures of him and Naomi when they first married, an album he had hidden away. The children gasped when they saw her picture. She was gorgeous. Miriam noticed she and Tommy had inherited Naomi's eyes. TJ asked if he could keep the album. Later that night, when Todd went to tuck TJ in his bed, he found him asleep with it lying opened next to him – an attractive Naomi smiling.

The children did not discuss Naomi's existence among themselves, but her discovery affected each of them. They loved Cleo. She was their Mommy and had been for six years. But somewhere there was another mother who left them because she was selfish and only thought of herself and her dreams, which did not include them. Their father said she "loved" them. How could she? She left when they were babies and in eight years, had never tried to contact them. TJ vowed to one day go to New York to find her. He needed answers.

Tommy was affected the most by the Naomi revelation. The guilt ate at him. He took responsibility for her leaving. She hung around for four years then left the year he was born. He became rebellious and disrespectful. He spent a lot of time in the streets with shady acquaintances. At sixteen, he was shot and killed in a gang-related incident. Miriam was crushed. She blamed Naomi.

That same year, Nedra enlisted in the U.S. Army.

On her 18th birthday, Miriam graduated with honors from high school. Bags packed, she went to New York to attend John Jay College *majoring in Legal Studies. She wasn't sure if she wanted to become a lawyer, but after attending her brother's funeral, anything associated with the law would suffice.* John Jay *did not have housing. She moved in with her brother TJ, who was living with relatives in the Bronx.*

TJ was also a student at John Jay. *He was in the process of attain-*

ing a degree in Criminology. He wanted to become a New York City Police Officer. He would graduate with his BA a couple of weeks after his 21st birthday – the age required to apply.

True to his word, one week after graduating from high school, he moved to New York to look for his biological mother. Eventually, he located her. She was using her maiden name. He introduced himself. Her refusal to acknowledge him was like a knife jammed into his gut. It was exactly what he needed. He packed away her photo album, accepted her denial, and moved on with his life.

Nedra had no inclination to meet her birth mother. She had a mother who reciprocated her love. She was fine.

The one and only time Miriam mentioned Naomi was while she was looking at a fashion magazine. She very casually said, "Erich, here's my birth mother."

The picture was of a tall, stunning, fair-skinned, African American woman, modeling some designer's evening gown that accentuated every curve of her body. Erich looked up from the photograph to a darker version of the same face and green eyes staring at him. He was speechless. He thought Cleo was her birth mother. Miriam looked at Erich with vacant eyes and smiled a smile that did not reach those eyes. He saw a deep hurt lodged in them.

Later, Erich asked Miriam if she wanted to talk about the 'picture'. Miriam replied, "We already have." She never mentioned her birth mother again.

She shared with him a lot of personal information about growing up in South Carolina with her siblings, TJ, a NYC homicide detective, her sister, Nedra, a Lieutenant in the U.S. Army, and her younger brother. Her eyes misted whenever she spoke of Tommy.

~39~

"Erich, where are you?" Miriam asked the heavens. Her eyes fell on the recent picture placed on a corner table in her room. She walked over and picked it up. Tears formed in her eyes. She and Erich had dinner with her parents at a jazz restaurant in Charlotte. The atmosphere, the music, the food, and the company were pleasant. They had a great time. Erich asked their Server to take their picture. He wanted to "capture" the evening. He had his arm wrapped around her mother. She was in her father's embrace. Their smiles were relaxed.

Erich and her family got along great. TJ was the most resistant at first in accepting their relationship. He didn't understand why she would sell out "the brothers".

"I just don't get it, Sis? Why are you dating a white guy?"

"TJ, his name is Erich. He's really cool. You'll see."

"No, I won't, because I'm not meeting the cat."

"Because he's white?"

"Can you think of a better reason? Call me when this "thing" is over."

"I don't believe you. When did you become prejudice?"

"When did you become a sellout?"

That stung. "Just because the man I'm dating is white doesn't make me a sellout, big brother."

"Then what does it make you, little sister?"

"A woman giving a very nice man a chance."

"What's wrong with Black men? Your daddy, the man you love, is a good Black man. I'm a good Black man. I can get you a decent Black

man, Sis. Just because you have green eyes doesn't mean you have to date a white boy or be a turncoat."

"Wow!" Miriam said, "I can't believe you! My eyes have nothing to do with my dating preference. I've dated Black men. My former fiancé was Black. You do recall him, right? The jerk that got a woman pregnant while he and I were engaged."

"He was... is an ass. You're not giving up on the brothers because of that asshole, right?"

"I'm not giving up on anyone, TJ. Just meet him, please. If you don't like him, I'll stop dating him."

TJ stared at his sister in awe. "My opinion means that much to you."

Miriam hugged her brother. "I know you'll like him."

"Fine, I'll give the white dude a chance."

"His name is Erich, TJ. Erich Coppenhauge. He's..."

"Oh God... he's Jewish too? Oh, Sis, what are you doing? He must be rich."

"TJ STOP! Don't judge him before you meet him. Please! Have an open mind."

A few nights later, the six of them went out to dinner - TJ and his wife Angelina, Erich and Miriam and her parents. TJ acted stubborn at first, but Erich was unperturbed. He chipped away at TJ's block with his charm. At the end of the evening, TJ said to Erich, "You know, you're pretty cool for a white guy."

Everyone laughed.

TJ pulled Miriam aside. "Were you really going to leave him if I didn't approve, little sister?"

Miriam winked at her brother. "I knew it'd be a mute-point. Erich is the best thing that has ever happened to me. I knew you'd see how happy he made me."

TJ hugged Miriam. "I meant what I said. I like him. I do see how happy he makes you. But if he hurts you I'm going to make him pay."

Miriam laughed. "I love you, TJ."

"I love you too. Maybe I should get a white chick."

"Angelina will cut you!"

"You ain't lying. That Puerto Rican temper is something I'm not

messing with."

They rejoined their family, laughing.

Erich and TJ became friends. Whenever Erich was in New York, he visited with TJ and Angelina.

When they returned to Erich's place, he pulled Miriam to him. "How'd I do? Did I pass?"

"With flying colors, baby. Flying colors."

"All right!"

They laughed at her choice of words. Erich picked a squealing Miriam up, swung her around, and carried her up to his bedroom where they made mad passionate love for the next few hours.

Erich was nowhere. Miriam was beyond worried. If he could he would have contacted her. She knew it in her heart. There could only be two reasons she wouldn't hear from him. He was either in the hospital or de... she wouldn't let her thoughts finish. With tears streaming down her face, she picked up the phone and called the one person who was available 24/7.

The phone stopped ringing. "Miriam, what's wrong, sweetheart?"

"Erich's missing. His mother may know something, but she's not telling me anything. I don't know what to do, Mommy."

Cleo slipped out of bed, so as not to wake a sleeping Todd, and to comfort their daughter.

☹☹☹☹☹☹

Richelle Coppenhauge would not embrace the reality that her precious son was engaged to a Black woman. Although, a professor of literature at *Long Island University* where she came in contact with people of various racial, social, and economic backgrounds, she did not recognize her own bigotry. She convinced herself that her feelings were out of fear of her son dating outside of his race and culture. The world was cruel. Jewish people were persecuted and Blacks were discriminated against. To throw the two races together was a formula for disaster.

Please Lord, don't let them have children. Then he's trapped with her for the rest of their child's life. She shook her head to remove the evil thoughts from them.

Why can't he be more like Erika and marry a nice Jewish, hard-working man... not a man but a nice, Jewish hardworking woman? Actually, she didn't have to work. Erich had plenty of money. She could stay home and give birth to beautiful Jewish children. She smiled at the thought. Erika and Lennie had given her two darling little boys. *Maybe Erich and his Jewish wife could give me a granddaughter.* She sighed, *that would be lovely... a little mini-me.*

I wouldn't even mind if Erich was like his brother, Junior, unmarried, a confirmed bachelor, always has the perfect JEWISH woman on his arm. Richelle didn't understand why he didn't settle down and marry one of those "perfect" women. When asked, Gerold Junior would say, "She wasn't the right one, Mother." She hoped he found the "right one" before she was too old to enjoy the fruits of his labor.

Richelle would be horrified if she knew the truth. Junior was gay. The women he brought home were from an escort service, the "perfect" cover-up. It was easier to hire a date. He was a good-looking man. He didn't want the entanglement of a woman falling in love with him or using her. He required the no-strings attachment a dating service afforded him.

He was in love with a successful, non-Jewish businessman named Tucker, who understood why Junior kept him hidden. It was a while before he came out to his family. They shared a two-bedroom apartment on the Upper East Side of Manhattan. The second bedroom was for guests unless Richelle was visiting. Then it was Junior's "bedroom". He kept his things in the guest room just for his mother's visits. Richelle was aware of Junior's "roommate". She couldn't comprehend why Junior needed one. He had plenty of money. He could afford his own place.

His siblings knew of Junior's sexual orientation. They didn't judge. They liked Tucker. He made their brother happy. That's all that mattered.

One night, after dinner, Erich, Miriam, Junior, and Tucker were enjoying a nightcap in front of the fire at Erich's home. They'd had a wonderful dinner. Before the couples retired to bed, Erich made a toast. "To Mother, may she one day come into the twenty-first century." Miriam and Tucker were reluctant to toasting "that woman". They shared that bond. They looked at each other, stifled a grin, and lifted their glasses.

Erich joked with Junior. "Will you hurry and bring Tucker home to meet Mother, dear brother? She has a problem with me dating Miriam, wait until she learns about your sexual preference." Erich snickered, imagining the scene. "I hope I'm around. I bet Miriam won't seem so bad after that." Junior grabbed Erich in a headlock and knuckled his head. They all laughed.

Richelle couldn't understand why her husband, Gerold, accepted Erich and Miriam's relationship. He seemed almost smitten with her – calling her whenever he could. On several occasions he mentioned that he wished he had Miriam's face in his Facebook album at work. Gerold was a plastic surgeon. Richelle caught him staring at Miriam. He seemed mesmerized by her.

That also infuriated Richelle and made her a little jealous... just a wee bit. *I guess some people may consider her pretty if you like that type.* Richelle admitted only to herself.

Miriam looked like an Egyptian Goddess. Her nose was straight, lips full and plump, emerald eyes, perfect teeth, and high cheekbones. Her hair was a mast of natural tight corkscrew shoulder-length curls. To accurately state the exact coloring was impossible. It was a mixture of browns with highlights of red and blonde, all natural, and beautiful. It looked great against her mahogany skin. Her stomach was flat. She had nice long shapely legs, an enviable bosom, and the right amount of 'junk in her trunk'. She was five feet five inches and one hundred thirty pounds. There was not an ounce of fat on her lean, muscular body.

So what! Richelle thought. *I still don't see what the fascination is. It will take a miracle for me to accept* ***that*** *woman into our family,* she vowed.

ONE MONTH LATER

Hope is like a flickering flame, one wrong move may result in darkness.

~40~

KAMI PHILLIPS

Kami was showered, hair still damp, and dressed in a grey and white short set. Apollo, her 145 pound Harlequin Great Dane, was at the foot of the bed resting his giant head on her legs. She sat on her bed, eating a bowl of cereal, listening to *Live with Kelly and Ryan*, while flipping through a photo album featuring her life with Dante. She felt closer to him when she could 'see' and 'talk' to him.

She'd spoken to him once since receiving his note at the hotel in New York.

"Hello," Kami asked apprehensively. Dante told her to answer any strange number that called. She usually didn't and he knew it.

"Hi pretty lady, it's me. I'm glad you answered."

"Hi, lover. I made it. I'm at the hotel waiting on you. Hold on a sec. I'm sending you a picture of what you're missing."

She took a quick selfie and pressed send.

"Make sure you delete it from the phone you're using. It's for your eyes only. You should get it in a few."

The phone dinged. "I think it just came through. Hold while I check." A few seconds later, Dante was back, voice tight. "I can't believe I'm missing that."

Kami was posing seductively on the bed, long hair flowing freely down her back, fully made-up, wearing a little red see-through negligee and 3" red pumps.

"Babe, you look gorgeous. I am the luckiest man in this world. Is that new?"

"Bought just for you. What happened to your phone? Whose phone are you using?"

"I picked up a prepaid phone when I left the hotel. My phone... well..." He hesitated. "I didn't want to miss any more of your calls, so I took it with me into the bathroom. Like an idiot, I placed it on the sink."

"You didn't," Kami groaned.

Dante chuckled. "I'm brushing my teeth and washing my face. Gotta look good for the missus, you know."

"Uh-huh," Kami said, knowing which way the conversation was flowing.

"You know clumsy me... when I went to grab the towel to dry my face, I knocked the phone into the running water."

"The klutz strikes again," Kami teased. He never heard the "we'll see you soon," message. "How did your officer get in touch with you?"

"Via the front desk. He left word telling me to report to Newark to assist in the flooding rescues."

"My hero," Kami said.

They fell silent. There was so much to say. Kami broke the silence. "Babe, do you really think we'll see each other tonight?"

"I'm going to try my best. Let me talk to the captain. I may show him this picture so he sees what's waiting for me. Only a heartless person would deny a thirsty man water. Boy, do I need a drink from your fountain."

Kami laughed. "Don't you DARE show that picture to ANYONE, Mister. It's for your eyes only."

Dante laughed with her. "And you know it, lovely lady. Seriously babe, no matter what happens, as long as there's air in my lungs, I will always find my way back to you."

"Nothing's going to happen to you!" Kami declared, fighting the tears threatening to fall. "Our love is so strong, it'll keep you safe."

"From your lips... gotta go, precious lady. I'll call you when I'm on way back to you. Don't change. Gotta see you up close and personal in that sexy outfit – what little there is of it."

"Oh hush, you." Kami blushed.

Dante grinned. "I'm sure my captain will give me permission if only for a few minutes."

"We'll be waiting, lover."

As she was hanging up, she heard Dante yelling, "We? We who? Who's with you, Kam?"

She hung up with a grin as large as the rock of Gibraltar.

She knew he would do his best to get to her now. She got up, put on a robe, settled back on the bed, and instantly fell asleep. She had sweet dreams of her reunion with Dante.

In New Jersey, the "we" comment was driving Dante nuts. Is Deb with her? Nah... that doesn't make sense. She wouldn't dress like that in front of Deb. We? *Then little tidbits flashed through his head...* Kami had something important to tell me. Every time she tried something happened... I wonder... hmm... could it be? Could Kam be pregnant?

Dante was determined to see his wife. He had to see her. He had to know for sure. He went in search of his CO. He would show him the picture if he had to. Her most prized parts were covered – barely – but they were covered.

The rescue mission took longer than anyone expected. Dante was sent directly to the airport to serve his time in Afghanistan, grabbing prepaid calling cards along the way. His CO never granted permission because Dante didn't get the chance to ask. He called Kami to let her know he was leaving and to confirm her pregnancy. She didn't answer. He called repeatedly. It just rang. He got on the plane with a heavy heart.

Kami awoke to five missed calls from her husband. She ran to the bathroom, releasing the delicious lunch delivered by room service into the toilet.

Somehow, during her conversation with Dante, she hit the silence ringer mode on her phone. That must have happened when I sent him the picture, *she thought, miserably. "Why are you doing this to me?" She yelled into the empty room.*

She played the one message Dante left, knowing what it was going to say, or so she thought.

Hey, pretty lady, I wish you had answered. I won't get a chance to see you. I'm shipping out now! Where are you? We REALLY need to talk. I think I know what you've been trying to tell me, but I want to hear it from you. Oh, Kam, I desperately need you. I love you and anyone else who may be coming along.

Kami's heart skipped a few beats. He knew! Dante knew! He just wanted confirmation. She cried very hard. Her tears told many stories – happiness, sadness, joy, and pain.

She prayed he would return to her safely.

Dante called Kami a few times since his arrival in Afghanistan. She missed every single call. Once he left the time he would try to call. She waited all day. The call never came.

Frustrated, she called Jade, but her cellphone wasn't accepting messages. Her voice mailbox was full. Kami was disappointed. Prior to the full mailbox announcement, she had left several messages. Jade hadn't returned any of them. Kami thought they had formed an alliance, a friendship at the Charlotte airport. She guessed one never knew another's true intention. It was her childhood friend, Michelle Green, all over again – promises to keep in touch – then nothing.

Debra was worse. After years of friendship, Kami thought she was the one person she could always depend on. Debra was so consumed with guilt for sending her to Charlotte that she kept her distance.

Kami felt alone. Once again she had no one – no Dante, no Debra, and no Jade – people whom she felt a deep connection with.

Not one to wallow in self-pity, she counted her blessings. Jessica! She called her. Jessica answered. She told her everything. Jessica was sympathetic and uplifting. She flew to Arizona to spend a few days with her. They had a great time. Jessica was there for her when she needed someone. They spoke regularly.

She also realized she had an entire family that loved her –

Dante's. She shared the wonderful news of their expectant birth but swore them to secrecy. She informed them she hadn't told the father-to-be. She explained that she believed Dante knew but needed to confirm. She wanted to hear the love in his voice once the news was revealed. She was determined to tell him the next time they spoke.

Mrs. Phillips, Dante's mom, was over the top with excitement. She sent her daughters to check on Kami and bring her a home cooked-meal. She wanted her daughter-in-law healthy and her first grandchild plump when he or she exited Kami's womb. Jessica and Dante's family filled the void left by those she thought loved her.

☹☹☹☹☹☹

As Kelly Ripa introduced the first guest, the doorbell sounded.

Getting up from her bed, Kami mumbled, *"Who on earth could it be?"*

Placing her bowl on the counter, she threw open the door to two military officers standing on her front porch.

They removed their hats.

"NO!!!" She screamed, stumbling backward until her back hit the ivory wall in her carpeted hallway. She slid to the plush floor, tears streaming from her face, staring at the men dressed in their officer's uniform.

One officer knelt before her, "Mrs. Phillips?"

When Kami didn't answer, the other officer said, "Mrs. Phillips, we're very so..."

"Don't say it," Kami screamed. "Please, don't say it." Her body shook with sorrow.

The officers glanced at one another. They had done this numerous times. They stood back and waited. They would wait as long as it took for her to regain her composure. The one thing they'd learned well in the military was patience.

Apollo walked out of the bedroom and down the steps to Kami. He licked her face, trying to catch as many tears as possible. She put her arms around him and cried into his black and white neck. *This wasn't supposed to happen. Dante should be home... rejoicing with me. He had a few more months before he was to be deployed. How could he be go...?*

Kami couldn't say it, couldn't think it. If she didn't say, think, or hear the words, maybe they wouldn't be true.

"Mrs. Phillips, is there someone we can call?" One officer asked, kneeling before her.

Kami stared at him blankly. W*hat*?

The other officer placed his hand under her arm to assist her up.

While she was being lifted, a sharp pain hit her in the gut. She screamed, bent over, and clutched her stomach. Apollo started whining.

"Oh... my... God... it.... hur... hurts.... so.... bad." Kami forced out.

"Mrs. Phillips, what's wrong? What hurts?" The officer didn't know if she was referring to her slightly protruding stomach or her heart. Although she hadn't officially heard the words, she knew why they were there.

The other officer gently asked again, "Is there someone we can call for you?"

"Oh, God, please help me. It hurts so.... bad. The pain.... Oh, God."

The officers were getting nervous. Apollo was hysterical - barking loudly, uncontrollably, turning in circles.

"My baby... please," Kami gasped.

"Baby?" An officer asked.

The other one shrugged. They'd reviewed Dante's paperwork before contacting Kami. There wasn't any mention of a pregnant wife. There were different protocols handled by different officers for expecting spouses.

When they finally got Kami off the floor, an officer noticed blood trickling down her leg.

Dear God!

He caught the eye of his partner. He nodded towards the small droplets of blood on the carpet.

"Mrs. Phillips, we're taking you to the hospital. It's quicker than waiting for an ambulance. Where is your purse?"

The officer was talking to an unconscious Kami.

~41~

MIRIAM BAINBRIDGE

Where was Erich?

Miriam sat at his kitchen counter. She slowly lowered her head onto her folded arms. She could feel the start of a headache. She was exhausted. She hadn't had more than a few hours of sleep. Her brain was worn out, worn down, and no longer functioning. Try as she may, she could not think of where Erich might be. Again, she searched the townhome from top to bottom… thinking… hoping she'd missed a clue in her previous searches. Still, she found nothing indicating Erich's whereabouts. The only change was her car was now parked in his garage. The accident theory was out.

Relief flooding her body, she inserted her key into the locked door, heart pounding with anticipation of seeing Erich. She pushed open the door from the garage. She ran from room to room calling his name. Silence. The house was empty. Where was he and why wasn't he returning her calls?

As far as anyone knew, Doctor Israel was the last person to speak with him. That was four weeks, two days, and three hours ago. Their conversation was cut short when apparently the signal from one of the cell phones was lost during the "storm from hell" - the storm that delayed Erich's flight to New York.

When Storm Iesha cleared, Erich was not on the next flight to New York or any flight thereafter. His parents checked with the airline.

Miriam checked with Erich's job only to discover he had resigned without an explanation. Erich was gone. Poof! Vanished into thin air.

Out loud, Miriam said, "How can someone just disappear?" Then, she heard a sound. Like a cat, she raised her head. Her ears went on alert. It was coming from upstairs. Like a bat out of hell, she ran up the steps, two at a time. At the top landing, she stopped and listened. The sound was coming from the master bedroom. She entered and opened the closet door. It grew louder. She identified the source. Reaching inside a blazer pocket, she removed Erich's cellphone, which remarkably was still charged. Looking at the caller ID, she answered.

"Hello."

"Hello? This is Gerold Coppenhauge." Uncertainty followed. "Is this Miriam?"

"Yes," she replied.

"Finally!" Mr. Coppenhauge said with a sigh of relief and excitement in his voice. He had been calling Erich's phone every day for four weeks. "Miriam, may I speak with him?"

She started crying, "I heard the ringing and found his phone. I'm at his place, but he isn't here. He's still missing."

Miriam heard the air being let out of Mr. Coppenhauge like the deflation of a balloon. "I was hoping Erich was there. I have no idea where he is. We checked with the police yesterday. There's still no news."

The day after Storm Iesha caused havoc along the eastern seacoast, the Charlotte Voice *ran a full-blown article of the destruction. On page three, below the fold, was a sidebar item that read:*

IESHA DESTROYS MAN'S SANITY - a prominent resident of Lake Norman appeared to have lost his sanity while waiting for a New York bound flight from the Charlotte airport. His flight was cancelled, as were all the flights along the eastern seacoast due to the horrific storm. The man was later taken to a CMC mental facility. His name has not been released to the media.

The police saw the article in the Voice, *interviewed the staff at the CMC mental facility, and learned that Erich Coppenhauge had indeed been a guest there for several days following the storm. He checked himself out, leaving a cold trail in his wake. The police shared the information with his family and fiancée.*

A missing person's report was filed with the Charlotte police department a week after Erich's disappearance. There was no record of him boarding an airline, bus, or train in Charlotte or the surrounding states. The private/charter flights were checked, as well as the area hospitals. An alert was placed on his bank accounts and credit cards. To date, no money had been withdrawn or purchases made.

"If I learn anything, Mr. Coppenhauge, I'll give you a call. Is this your cellphone number?" She asked, not wanting to deal with Mrs. Coppenhauge.

"Yes it is. Call me anytime," he said. "Miriam? Thanks!" He disconnected disappointed.

She looked at the cell phone in her hand like it was a missing piece to a puzzle. She scrolled through the call list. The last two outgoing calls in his phone log were his job's human resource department and Doctor Israel.

Miriam was comforted with the fact that he must have abandoned his phone recently. There was no way his battery lasted over four weeks.

At least one of her questions was answered. She now knew why Erich was not returning her calls. Where was he? He was a loner. The few friends he had hadn't heard from him.

Why isn't he contacting me? A memory slapped her in the face.

When she dropped Erich off at the airport, she recalled the words he said to her, "Remember... no matter what happens, I love you."

Hmmm, I remember having a weird feeling when he said that.

Did he know something? Was he planning to disappear? Had his brief stay in the mental facility affected him permanently?

~42~

KAMI PHILLIPS

Kami awoke in the hospital a few hours later. Debra and the Phillips family were present, all wearing solemn expressions.

A quick survey of the room revealed the absence of the military officers.

"They're gone," Mrs. Phillips stated flatly.

"What happened?" Kami asked, praying she was in a bad dream.

Avoiding eye contact, each wondered which of them would deliver the bad news.

One of the officers took the unconscious Kami to his car. The other quickly searched the house and found Kami's purse in a hall closet. He looked inside, found her emergency contact information, and dialed the second name on the list, Debra Collins – Dante's was the first. He explained the situation and told her which hospital they were taking Kami to. Debra promised to meet them there. En route, she phoned the Phillips' home and informed them of what transpired. They agreed to meet at the hospital.

By the time Debra reached the hospital, Kami was in the operating room. The officers reported on her condition and told her about Dante. They also let Debra know they had not confirmed Dante's casualty. Debra promised to tell her friend the devastating news, thanked them, and watched them leave.

The Phillips family came in shortly after the officers' departure. They found Debra weeping in a corner of the waiting room. Glancing furtively at each other, they feared the worst.

"Well, is anyone going to tell me?" Kami inquired weakly.

Debra walked to her friend's side and took her hand. She'd been telling the story all afternoon. Why take a break? The doctors said it was best for Kami to know while she was under observation, recovering from the procedure.

Debra's red brimmed eyes spoke volumes. She shook her head in an attempt to clear away the ugliness of the day. It didn't work.

She heard Dante's sisters whimpering in the background. Mr. Phillips excused himself, not wanting to hear the senseless words again. Duane, Dante's brother, had his arms firmly around his mother, giving her support.

"Um... well, your baby boy..."

Kami's intake of breath was the only sound she made. She studied a spot on the coral hospital wall.

"... didn't make it. He was so tiny, Kam. About 4 ounces. He couldn't survive."

He? A baby boy! Little Dante Jr. My precious son is gone! Tears threatened to spill again. She wouldn't allow them to fall until she'd heard everything.

"And Dante?" She said in a strange voice.

Debra could no longer control her own tears. She let them flow. At the mention of her youngest son's name, Mrs. Phillips, overcome with anguish and grief, was removed from the room by Duane. Dante's sisters Olivia, Meghan, and Sophia, tried hard to maintain control. They wanted to be strong for their sister-in-law.

"Well... it seems Dante didn't make...." Debra's voice quavered. "Eh... enemy fire hit the gas tank of his plane. It erupted into flames. Five soldiers were on the plane. There is no way anyone could have survived. Dante's body hasn't been recovered." Debra whispered the last part. "The National Guard is trying to identify the body parts of the men."

Dante's body not found? This caught Kami's attention. She removed her hand from Debra's. She tried sitting up.

"Lay still," Debra ordered, nudging her back down.

"No," Kami yelled, struggling against Debra's hold. "Let... me.... go! I have to find him. He's out there somewhere. I know it. I would have felt it in my soul if he was gone."

Dante's sisters quietly exited the room to join the rest of their family in the hallway. They were trying to remain calm, but watching the denial emoting from their sister-in-law triggered their own agony. The family entwined their arms in a circle, bowed their heads, and grieved.

Inside the hospital room, Kami was struggling with Debra.

"Let... me... go."

Nurse Shirley came in to check on her patient. "What on earth is going on in here?" She barked. "Young lady, get off that bed immediately. I will not have you upsetting my patient."

Debra did as she was told. Kami immediately shot up. The pain sent her back down. Her insides hurt. They burned. They were... empty.

Taking Nurse Shirley aside, Debra explained the situation. Nodding, she made a note on Kami's chart. She left the room, returning with a sedative. She inserted it into the IV.

"This will ease the pain, both emotional and physical," the nurse told her.

Kami wasn't listening. The words of her lover, uttered just over a month ago, echoed in her head... "Seriously, babe, no matter what happens, as long as there's air in my lungs, I will always find my way back to you."

She had to believe that. She had to... she had... she couldn't... She turned her head away from Debra and the nurse and cried into her pillow. Life was so unfair. In a blink of an eye, she'd lost the loves of her life – her beloved Dante and her seventeen-week old baby boy.

EIGHT MONTHS LATER

Every thought, every touch, every second...... matters.

(Author unknown)

~43~

For eight months, the patient remained in a coma. Everyone, including the doctors, urged the patient's family to let go. Everyone was in agreement that the patient was "gone"....everyone, except the patient's mother. She was determined to fight the fight her child could not – the fight for life.

The patient's mother took a leave of absence from her prestigious job to move into her child's residence, which she cleaned and readied for her child's return. Family members told her she was wasting her time. She knew differently, for she was a mother.

With a determination that only a mother could manage, she was by her child's side every day, talking, caressing, and moving her child's limbs - back and forth, up and down, so when her child finally emerged, her child would have full use of all limbs.

The mother urged the patient's friends to visit as though the patient was recovering from heart surgery... not in a comatose state. They did. They told jokes, stories, and kept the patient abreast of what was happening in the outside world.

The mother encouraged the family to sit with the patient as well. Although they felt it was useless, they took turns visiting a few times throughout the month to relieve the mother from her vigil by her child's bedside. The family knew she couldn't fight for her child without her strength... her rest. Deep down they were hoping she was right – that the patient was just sleeping, resting for the battle of a lifetime.

After eight months of the protection of the coma, the emergence began slowly. First, the smell of ammonia tickled the patient's senses. Then the voice of the patient's mother had the patient's mind spinning. The patient was confused and disoriented. Then the patient's nose started itching from the mother's tears. Finally, the realization that the patient was in a hospital hit so hard, that when the doctor went to examine the patient, the patient temporarily slipped back into the coma.

While the doctor was outside of the room informing the patient's mother that there wasn't a change in her child's condition, the patient emerged once more. This time there was tingling in the patient's fingers, then the hands, toes, feet, legs. Then the memories came. The patient didn't want to remember what happened. But the nightmare at the airport came flooding in any way. The patient wanted to dive back into the safety of the coma, race back into time... make a different choice. The patient wanted to fly into the arms of the patient's best friend, the patient's life partner... the patient's....

Tears exploded from closed eyes.

COMING SOON

Cancelled: The Trial

FROM ABRIDGE PUBLISHING

Never be afraid to try something new. Remember amateurs built the ark and professionals built the Titanic.

(Dave Barry)

PROLOGUE

As John, the Bailiff stepped into the large, airy courtroom, silence descended over the crowd.

"All rise. Court is now in session," he ordered. "The Honorable Sandra Tate presiding."

The court rose.

Judge Sandra Tate entered, her long black robe flowing around her ankles as she walked. The stress of the trial was clearly molded upon her tired face. The stillness in the courtroom was palpable. As she took her seat, she requested the court do the same.

"John, please bring in the jurors," she instructed.

Twelve jurors and two alternates filed in and took their respective seats. The seats they've occupied for over a month. They were nervously looking everywhere except at the defendants.

Not a good sign, thought the defense attorney, Roger Roper.

Judge Tate asked, "Has the jury reached a verdict?"

"We have Your Honor," replied Jim Bowman, the Foreman, standing up and passing a small folded sheet of paper to the bailiff, who without looking at it quickly handed it to the Judge.

Expressionless, Judge Tate stared at the paper in her hand - a paper that held one or two words – words that would change the lives of everyone, not just those in the courtroom – but all over the world. After what seemed like an eternity, she returned the verdict to the bailiff who handed it back to the foreman.

Addressing the jurors, she asked, "Are you all in agreement with this verdict?"

Confused, the spectators cast furtive glances around the courtroom, yet the quietness prevailed. No one dared to speak in fear it might delay the proceedings or worse - Judge Tate would clear the courtroom as she had during the trial proceedings.

"Yes, we are, Your Honor," the foreman replied.

It had all come down to twelve individuals deciding the fate of one of the largest airlines in the world.

Judge Tate let out a long, exhausted sigh. "Proceed."

Jim Bowman knew everyone was watching and waiting. Once the jury's decision was rendered, it would change the lives of everyone across the globe - from Presidents and Queens to victims of cancelled flights and airline CEO's to the FAA Regulators. This case had reached heights that even the plaintiffs hadn't imagined, drawing media attention from all over the world. The media cameras were quietly rolling to convey the long-awaited verdict.

The plaintiffs peeked at one another – grabbing the hands of the persons sitting beside them. Their voices had been heard. This was the moment they've been waiting, no fighting for. They stared at the man who would tell the world if WorldLine Airways, International Global Giant, was guilty of destroying their lives.

Jim Bowman slowly looked at the defendants, then the plaintiffs, then out into the packed courtroom. After fourteen long days of deliberations, he was not letting his fifteen minutes of fame pass without a little suspense.

He glanced at the Judge who nodded slightly.

In a loud, clear voice he addressed the court. "In the case of the Passengers of Flight 3236 versus WorldLine Airways, we the jury find the defendants ......"

Suddenly the courtroom doors flew open, interrupting Jim Bowman in mid-sentence. All eyes turned towards the cause of the disruption - all eyes but one because at that precise moment she felt her baby kick for the very first time.

ACKNOWLEDGEMENTS

Thanks, Heavenly Father, for all of my earthly blessings.

I am so blessed by the outpouring of love and support I received when I announced I published my first book. Thanks for purchasing, Cancelled: Flight 3236 and encouraging your friends and family to do the same or buying multiple copies to share with them. I am forever grateful!

Thanks for reposting & advertising Cancelled: Flight 3236 on social media, reading it, and reviewing it on Amazon and/or Goodreads. I can't express how much I appreciate you.

There are so many people to thank, if I named you all it would be a book all in itself. I hope you know who you are and how much I treasure you.

For this book - Part 2, I am going to keep my acknowledgements short.

To my editors - Julia A. Hill, Toni Stovall and Jane DeVries. **Julia,** co-author, editor, psychologist, and punching bag - thanks for sticking with me through everything. I love you; **Toni**, co-author, motivator, editor - thanks for believing and encouraging me to believe in myself. You are the reason I finally published my first novel. **Jane**, editor, cheerleader - thanks for your encouragements, enthusiasm, and for falling in love with the characters. Your positivity keeps me writing.

Stephanie McKay – thanks for allowing me to sample some of the lyrics from Jackson Avenue. It brings back memories of our days in the South Bronx, South, South Bronx. Keep singing my friend.

Kristy Beausoleil – thanks for the beautiful covers you designed. You are a very talented and patient professional with a heart of gold.
KayLan, Kyle, Krystopher, and Kyra, thanks for assisting me in so many ways I don't have enough room to list them all. Thanks for being proud of me. I love you all so much.

Colin, I always save you for last because besides our children, you are the best thing to ever happen to me! Thanks for loving and supporting imperfect me.

Much love to you all,
TD

Made in the USA
Columbia, SC
10 September 2021